The characters in *A Frontier Wife* are fictitious, but Carrie and Josh are vivid representations of the strong-willed people who helped settle the American frontier. Most of the characters are modeled after real people, and author Susan Hatton McCoy's vibrant depiction of Carrie was based on one of her real-life ancestors. McCoy comes from a small town near where New Salem once stood, and she has been able to capture frontier life and the settlers in rich and engrossing detail.

McCoy's roots go back to pre–Revolutionary War America, and that, together with her painstaking research, makes her story a sweeping epic of early America not to be missed.

D0036682

# A FRONTIER WIFE

## Susan Hatton McCoy

BALLANTINE BOOKS • NEW YORK

Library of Congress Catalog Card Number: 87-91881

ᴵSBN 0-345-34702-1

Manufactured in the United States of America

First Edition: August 1988

# Chapter 1

*May, 1830*

"Good-bye . . . good-bye . . ." I said quietly. Friends and family clustered around Josh and me, down by the river in Cincinnati.

"Good-bye, Carrie. God be with you."

The early morning mist lay thick and liquid over the Ohio River. Peach-colored streaks spread slowly through the dove-gray sky. Our long flatboat, with its little cabin in the center, sat waiting for us, its hard angles softened by the haze. The rich, moist river smell, the distant mournful call of a steamboat's horn, the hushed voices of the people gathered there— all weighed on me until my heart felt heavy as lead.

My stomach tightened as I kissed everybody one last time. I hadn't known the farewells would be so painful. When Josh talked of moving out to Illinois, he always made it sound like a grand adventure.

Going to Illinois was Josh's dream. My only dream had

been to marry Josh. And just the day before, my dream had come true.

I glanced at my new husband, hoping to share this wrenching moment with him, but he was smiling as he shook hands all around and said, "We'll come back and see you in few years. Just as soon as my gunsmithy gets a good start."

"Make sure you bring me some grandbabies when you come," his mother called out.

With a laugh Josh grabbed my hand and led me aboard our flatboat. The sun gilded the mist now, sparkling, shimmering. He untied the ropes and gave a mighty shove with the long oar. The topaz waters of the river slapped against the boat and pulled us out into the current. We were on our way.

"Good-bye! Good-bye!" I waved to the people on the shore. Papa. Dear, gentle Papa, lifting the corner of his wire-rimmed spectacles to wipe a tear from his bright blue eyes. My older sister standing beside her husband. Lydia, my stepmother. I would not miss her stern, exacting ways.

Josh's giant German father. His jolly mother and ten tall, blond brothers and sisters. Neighbors were there, too, and friends from childhood days. All waving, waving, waving us farewell.

I looked at them all, trying to engrave their faces on my memory. I knew I would not see them again for many years.

I waved again, and the weight inside me expanded until it filled my chest. As I watched, the figures on the shore slowly faded into the town's hazy silhouette. Modern, bustling Cincinnati. Streets ascended the hillsides to the highest point overlooking the river, where Josh and I had stood and talked of all our dreams.

Farewell to the city where I was born. Farewell, my home

and family. Farewell till God knows when. Tears made my last look a blur.

Josh wept no tears. He held the boat's rudder with a steady hand. Now he gently called to me as I stood looking back, long after everyone was out of sight. "Come sit by me, Carrie. I'll show you how to steer."

A few blinks cleared the tears from my eyes. "Just teach me, Josh. I'll help you any way I can."

"You'll have to steer when I use the oars, to push us away from other boats at docks or pull over to the bank at night. Think you can do that?"

The rudder handle looked enormous. I hesitated for an instant. "Sure I can," I said.

He placed my soft hand, so ignorant of heavy work, on the rough wooden handle. As his work-calloused hand covered mine and gently guided its movements, I felt a bond of partnership with this new husband of mine.

I looked up to his face and thought my heart would surely burst with love. He seemed so strong and fearless and full of life, so handsome, with his pale, sun-bleached hair and level gray eyes. I loved this man completely. Nothing mattered, after all, but that we two be together. For him I had left my comfortable, secure home to go out to the frontier. I would have gone with him to Tibet just as readily.

And so, I was now a married woman—Mrs. Joshua Strauman. I still could not believe it. Only yesterday I had stood, a bride of nineteen, beside my tall and handsome Josh. I guess I had always loved him, even as a young girl. Three years older than I, he had been a serious, hard-working lad, whose intelligence and quiet strength made all the other boys seem immature.

As we grew older, I spent countless hours with him, enraptured hours, listening to his dreams of a brighter future west on the frontier: Illinois, the land of rich fertile soil, pure air and water, far from the disease-filled Eastern cities.

"Why," he always said, "a family can live well there with just a little garden, and hunting and fishing for meat. The trees give you logs to build a house, fire for heat and cooking, raw material for furniture and tools and utensils. A couple can build a farm and make themselves a fortune. The land triples in value as it's cleared and cultivated. And there's always need for a skilled gunsmith." My pulse raced, my whole body tingled with excitement when he spoke of it.

Papa and my stepmother were not so optimistic. "It will be very difficult for you, my dear," Papa said. He was a professor at the Academy, and his voice rang with authority. "You are used to living in this big house, with a hired girl to do the heavy work. I don't think you realize the hardships you are facing."

Lydia pursed her lips and glared at me. "You could have married a professional man, like your sister did. But no, you want to marry a common gunsmith. You are a stubborn, headstrong girl."

She was right, of course. I *was* stubborn. But I could think of nothing but Josh. Every time I saw him, he talked of moving to Illinois, his enthusiasm bubbling over like a spring. And if he went without me, I knew I might never see him again.

From the age of fourteen, Josh had worked alongside his father, a master gunsmith, learning bit by bit the art of making fine Kentucky long rifles. His forebears had brought the craft from Germany to Pennsylvania, and his father carried it over the mountains to Ohio. Now Josh would take it to the new frontier.

He had saved money for this trip for years. Our boat groaned beneath the weight of the gun barrels he brought along. Beside them in the cabin lay the curly maple wood for gunstocks, the fittings, and his precious tools, all wrapped in oiled paper and old quilts.

One afternoon a month before our wedding, he had stopped by my house and said, "Carrie, come see the flatboat I'm building to take us down the river. When we get to Shawneetown, I'll swap it for a wagon, and we'll head for the best land we can find."

"What about a steamboat?" I asked, visualizing my stepmother's shock when I told her I would be traveling in a common flatboat.

"We have to save our money for more important things. I'll make us a fine boat, with a cabin and some long oars and a rudder piece. Then we'll sit back and let the water carry us along. Who could want a better wedding trip than that?" His smile drove away my lingering doubts.

On our wedding day brilliant sun shone through the arched stained-glass windows of our big brick church on the hillside, forming multicolored patterns on the friends and family gathered there.

"I do," I answered our minister faintly as I stood before him. I wore a white silk gown, with full leg-of-mutton sleeves and rows of ruffles around the wide skirt. With a tight corset emphasizing my slim waist and a scooped neckline revealing my fashionable curves, I felt in the height of style. Beneath a delicate lace veil, my long hair was parted in the middle and twisted up in back, with a soft mass of dark brown ringlets framing my flushed cheeks and deep blue eyes. My heart beat wildly, a sharp staccato in my chest, as I stood there beside him.

Josh looked so formal, unfamiliar in his new swallow-tailed coat and vest. Was he as nervous as I? "I do," he repeated.

With those words, I became a wife. And . . . do I dare write of it? That night I became a woman. In the dark and quiet I learned the joy of two in one flesh, the trust in loving that makes everything seem right. Lydia's veiled warnings about man's animal nature and a wife's grim duty all seemed meaningless. I loved Josh. Josh loved me.

As I sat now on the boat deck beside him, I wondered at the magic of this love, this force that had driven me to take up a strange new life, so different from anything I had ever known.

The river flowed serenely in wide curves through ancient forests. Sunlight and breeze played among the trees, creating a hundred hues of green. Birds sang out in celebration of the morning. I closed my eyes and listened to their song and to the swishing of the water as our boat cut through it.

A harsh panting sound broke through my thoughts. When I looked up, I saw a steamboat coming around the bend toward us.

"Careful, Josh! Here comes a steamer!" I shouted, just as its horn let forth a deafening blast. I stood and clenched my hands together nervously. The noise of the high-pressure engine, the shrill hiss of scalding steam, came ever closer, until I could see the violent agitation of the water in the boat's wake. Wide paddles drank the current of the river, gulping in great mouthfuls and letting it spill out again.

Our raft seemed small and vulnerable before this giant. But Josh turned the rudder and pulled over near the bank, and we passed Goliath unmolested.

The sun rose higher on the river, while the woods alongside seemed to offer inviting shade and mystic secrets. Hot and sweaty now, I crept through the low doorway to our tiny cabin and removed my stiff petticoats. The vanities of fashion would mean little in the months ahead, I realized.

In the dim light there, I surveyed our meager stock of worldly goods. Trunks and barrels and boxes lined three sides of the cabin. The pillow slips and linens I had embroidered for my hope chest were all packed away. We carried a lantern, food staples, pans and kettles, cooking utensils, bowls, and dishes. A feather bed and pillows, some books, a Bible. A new medical book—a gift from my sister. Our clothes, Josh's tools and gun supplies.

At night we would unroll the fluffy feather mattress to fill the clear space by the door. I hadn't realized how cramped we'd be. But I would be there alone with Josh and that was all that mattered.

Deep within my trunk of clothing, in my small blue-lacquered jewelry case, lay my most prized possession—a cameo. It was precious, my only link to the mother I had never known. She had died when I was just six months old.

At noon I opened the big wicker lunch basket Josh's mother had packed for us. "Oh, look!" I laughed. "There's enough here for all your brothers."

I won't have to cook tonight, I thought, looking dubiously at our cooking fire, a few logs burning in a large flat box of sand. At home I had learned to cook—quite well, I thought. But could I do it under these primitive conditions?

That first day we met two more steamboats, huge three-tiered vessels trimmed with lacy filigree. Their high-pitched horns shrieked at us in bursts of vapor, and each time I trembled as the waters churned and boiled around them, slapping hard against our fragile boat. The passengers on board seemed friendly, though, leaning over the side rails, waving and calling to us. I waved back, laughing and lighthearted.

We saw other boats, too: little fishing craft, keelboats, a great barge loaded with produce for some distant market, another settler's raft carrying a large family and all their belongings, complete with cattle, pigs, and chickens.

When evening came, Josh reached out and took my hand. "Come sit beside me, Carrie. Let's watch the sun go down before we stop for the night."

He set the rudder and pulled his stool beside mine along the front of the cabin. Resting our heads against the rough lumber, we sat, hands entwined, and watched the forest leaves dance in the fiery glow of sunset.

*Shush, shush, shush*, the river whispered. A dove's mournful coo broke through the stillness, as the rich, moist smell of river encircled us. Then the sun sank, leaving behind a trail of gold on the water.

In twilight Josh pulled to the bank and tied up for the night. We strolled along the shore gathering firewood. How good the firm and stable earth felt beneath my feet again.

Darkness fell. We sat on the deck beside the fire and talked of future plans. "When we get to Shawneetown," said Josh, "I'll ask about the best places to settle. I know the northern part of Illinois still has Indian troubles, but the southern half is fine. Good land, plenty of timber. We'll sell our boat, or trade it for a wagon, and we'll soon be on our way to our new home."

"I still can't believe all this." I paused and watched the moon's reflection ripple gently in the stillness.

Josh slipped an arm around my waist and drew me close to him. "I know," he murmured in my ear. "Just being married, being here alone with you, is a wonder."

A wonder. Yes, the passion that blazed between the two of us was wondrous. My blood stirred at the thought of it. But later that night I slept uneasily, lying on the feather mattress on the unyielding cabin floor. The trunks and barrels and boxes loomed about me in the dark, grotesque and strange smelling.

The forest, filled with birds and wildflowers by day, had changed to a forbidding jungle. A distant owl's whoo startled me. The river slapped harshly against our boat. From deep within the forest a wildcat's shriek cut through the blackness. Too frightened to be modest, I flung myself against Josh and spent the rest of the night in the haven of his arms.

As the days passed, we were lulled into the easy rhythm of life on our boat. We gazed upon the ever-changing vistas of the river and the lands along its banks. Deep forests alternated with farmland. Little towns surrounded by lofty hills perched beside the water. And all along the way we passed willow-covered islands, large and small.

A pleasing variety of trees filled the forests—oak, hickory, walnut, ash, dogwood, and others, covered by an entangled canopy of wild grapevines. Huge sycamores, some with trunks ten feet in diameter, grew near the banks, extending long pale branches out over the water. Eagles soared overhead, and wild turkeys scurried along the forest floors. Red cardinals, blue jays, and yellow finches moved like flying flowers through the trees.

Occasionally we passed thriving farms with large brick houses, even larger barns, and flocks of white sheep grazing up on the slopes. From the distance, the clang of cowbells echoed through the hills.

We got our drinking water fresh from the springs and clear

brooks that flowed into the river. For bathing and washing clothes, we dipped out buckets of river water.

"Let's stop here," Josh would say at evening, and pull over to the shore. Then he would catch some fish for supper, gather firewood, and shoot a squirrel or duck or rabbit for tomorrow's stew.

The fresh air and sunshine put a keen edge on our appetites. One evening, after Josh had cleaned the fish he caught, he sat and watched my nervous efforts to cook over the open fire. Kneeling to keep my long skirt away from the flames, I melted lard in my footed iron skillet and rolled the fish in cornmeal before frying them. In a smaller covered pan, I baked some little corn cakes. That night we had a treat— fresh green beans we had bought at one of the little river towns along the way.

"That sure smells good," Josh said, with a teasing smile. "Before I married you, I didn't think that such a pretty girl could be a master cook, too."

I laughed. "Oh, Josh, anything would taste good just now." Our other meals had been light, and we had put in a long day, navigating around snags and sandbars. After I turned the fish with my long-handled fork, I noticed a grassy clearing near the shore. "Look! Isn't that a patch of wild strawberries? Why don't you pick some while I finish supper?"

By the time our simple meal was ready, we were ravenous. No royal banquet ever tasted better.

Later that night we sat on the deck and listened to a chorus of cicadas. Hazy wisps of smoke curled from our fire, keeping the mosquitoes at bay. "I feel so different—like a child of nature," I said. "It's like we're living in our own world.

When you live by the angle of the sun, it's easy to forget that hours are called by numbers in the city."

He drew a long, deep breath. "I love it. I think I could stay on the river forever." He paused; his eyes slowly searched my face. "Are you happy, Carrie?"

"Can't you tell? Yes, Josh, I'm happy. Even this trip—I thought it would be tedious, but it's been an adventure! When we get to Shawneetown, I want to buy a journal and write down everything about our new life. When we're old, we can look back and remember these days."

"Good idea. We'll have a record for our children and grandchildren."

When he spoke of children, a warm glow crept through me. I wanted a whole flock of children. In my mind's eye I could see their shining little faces—boys and girls, growing like stair steps, surrounding me as I rocked contentedly, telling stories, singing songs with them.

I thought of Josh's lively mother, with her eleven sons and daughters. To me, her life seemed happy and complete, so unlike that of my icy, barren stepmother. I wanted to be like Josh's mother, strong and fearless.


We were floating along smoothly in the morning when I heard the familiar panting of a steamboat behind us. Josh began to steer us toward the bank. From my vantage point in front I could see a tree snag jutting far out into the river.

"Josh, look out!" I shouted.

Swiftly, he veered around the tree. I grabbed an oar with both hands and pushed us away from it.

A deafening horn blast split the air. We had misjudged the steamer's speed. It was right behind us now.

"Take the rudder!" Josh yelled as he rushed to seize the oar.

Again the giant horn shrieked. My heart raced madly. Openmouthed, I stared up at the huge white wall of the bow bearing down on us.

I screamed. "Josh! Josh! The pilot can't see us! Oh, God, we're going to be killed!"

Our boat was seconds from collision. If somehow I escaped from being crushed, then I would drown. I couldn't swim.

"Take the rudder! Steer to shore!" Josh seized the oar and gave a desperate shove against the towering side of the steamboat.

Our boat surged over toward the riverbank. We were saved—by inches.

A moment later we were tossed up in the thrashing, angry waters behind the paddle wheel. Waves boiled over the sides of our little craft. Spray stung my face and arms.

Josh pulled us over to the shore. I sank down on the stool and watched, trembling, as the big boat steamed away. Gradually the fury of the river spent itself.

My dress and shoes were soaked. My teeth chattered uncontrollably. I crossed my arms and hugged myself, trying to stop my shivering.

"Let's get your shoes off, so they'll dry," Josh said shakily. Head hung, avoiding my eyes, he eased my drenched shoes from my feet and sat them in the sun beside his own. "Looks like there's problems up front. The waves drowned the fire and knocked over the pot of stew. Guess I'll have to stop at the next town and borrow some fire."

Silently I surveyed the damage. After we had pushed out

from shore again, I set about cleaning up the mess. I added water to the stew left in the pot and decided to call it soup.

Josh and I were strangely quiet as the day passed. We spoke but avoided meeting eyes. Chores needed to be done, and we did them, tensely. Finally I burst out, "I can't swim, Josh. If we're ever overturned, I know I'll drown."

He smiled at me. The world seemed brighter then. "I'll teach you when we stop tonight. Your clothes would weigh you down, but you can learn enough to save yourself."

That evening we docked beside the mouth of a stream, where sandbars reached far out into the river. Blushing with modesty, I stripped down to my underclothes and followed Josh into the clear water. His powerful arms enveloped me, and he taught me to float and dog-paddle. I could do it. With Josh there beside me, I could do anything.

As we continued on our journey, other gigantic steamboats chugged by us, their colorful flags flapping in the breeze and clouds of black smoke billowing from the tall black chimneys. Fresh white paint glistened on the sides; fancy gingerbread trimmed all the decks.

When the steamers passed at night, bells clanging and steam hissing, I no longer feared them. From where we were tied up by the shore, they looked like floating palaces, their bright lights reflected on the water.

We floated on and on down the river's curves, enjoying the sunny days, enduring days of rain and wind and fog. In the evenings we pulled over to the shore and played in the shallow water, laughing, splashing each other, feeling cooled and wildly free after long hours in the sun.

And while the moonlight rippled on the dark water, we lay locked in each other's arms.

Each day, after Josh pored over his navigating book, his

eyes gleamed a little brighter. Each day he seemed a little more tense, watching, waiting. Then one bright midday he pointed ahead and shouted, "There it is! The Wabash River! Beyond that is Illinois."

I hurried to his side and raised my hand to shield my eyes. "I can see it! I can see Illinois!"

Illinois! We stood breathless, gazing on that promised land as our boat drifted past the point where the Wabash joined the Ohio.

To tell the truth, I thought Illinois looked about the same as Indiana. But, of course, I knew that it was special. All our years of dreaming were about to be fulfilled.

Oh, yes, we were so young, so full of dreams back then. Life beckoned to us with open arms, and we embraced her as eagerly as we embraced each other.

# Chapter 2

A few miles farther downstream we arrived at the river port of Shawneetown and found a spot to tie our flatboat along the teeming waterfront. Josh jumped ashore and knotted the rope to a weathered piling.

"Will you watch our things while I go hire a wagon?" he asked, then strode off into town, leaving me to wait and glance about me nervously.

As a well-brought-up young woman, I had never been alone down by the Cincinnati waterfront, and this place buzzed with activity like a swarm of bees. A confusing tangle of boats were tied along the bank: steamboats decorated fancy as wedding cakes, keelboats, crude rafts, and fishing boats. Rough-looking boatmen hurried about the docks, calling to each other raucously. One of them, a swarthy fellow with a long scar on his cheek, stared boldly at me when he passed. With a sudden twinge of fear, I scowled and looked away.

Finally Josh returned and began unloading all our things into a rented wagon. "I saw two decent-looking taverns," he said, beaming. "We'll stop at one and have a hot meal and a good night's sleep on dry land. Tomorrow we'll scout around for the best place to settle."

As we drove up from the river, bustling Shawneetown spread out before us—nearly a hundred houses, a few built of brick or frame, the rest of logs. Crowds of people milled along the streets. I noticed several stores and banks, a post office and land office, a printing shop. Ugly mud-colored stripes on the buildings told of past floods.

I searched the faces of the people drifting in and out of offices and stores and craftmen's shops. Could I find some understanding, some kinship in their eyes? They seemed to be a sea of rough, work-hardened folk, skin bronzed and creased from sun. Their clothes were shapeless home-spun garments in a dozen shades of home-dyed butternut-brown. I felt gowned like a princess in my blue calico housedress.

After leaving our belongings in the care of the livery stable, we crossed the street to the big two-story tavern building. "Fixin' to stay long?" the innkeeper asked, scribbling our names in his big leather-covered ledger.

"We plan to settle here in Illinois," Josh said proudly. "I'll have to talk to the land office about the best location. What's your opinion?"

The large-bellied man wiped his mouth on the back of his hand. "Well, son, I hate to toss cold water on a feller, but you're about ten years too late. All the decent land in southern Illinois has done been settled. What's left is swamp. Plumb full of ague and fever. I can't rightly recommend nothing hereabouts."

"Is that right?"

"Yep. You go on downriver toward Cairo and it's even

worse. Good land's scarce as crowin' hens. Mosquitoes and horseflies big enough to carry you away.''

I felt a tightening in my stomach as I glanced toward Josh. The muscles in his jaw worked slowly as he clenched and unclenched them. He said no more.

Then the innkeeper's wiry wife showed me to the women's quarters, telling me I had to share a bed with a widow woman who was traveling back East. Josh went upstairs with the man to a big open room filled with half a dozen beds.

A short time later, as we wordlessly drank some coffee in the public room, I sat lost in the whirlwind of my thoughts. What if we couldn't find a decent place to settle? Our raft could not make the trip back upriver. Travel overland was brutal, the roads rough and poorly marked. Steamship passage cost too much money. Would our dreams all die so quickly?

My spirits sank as I looked about me. The tavern was rough and crude and noisy. Dank odors from yesterday's supper and unwashed bodies hung in the air.

Josh set his cup down with a thud and turned to me. ''Let's walk down to the store. You wanted to buy some writing paper.''

Numbly I rose and followed him into the sunlight. We walked along the side of the street, stepping aside as passing horses and wagons kicked up puffs of dust. My thoughts foundered in a fog as brown and dirty as the dust that settled on my shoes.

''See how low this town sits,'' Josh said, sublimely unconcerned. ''They say it floods every spring.''

I turned to him, tears rising in my eyes. ''Josh, what

will we do now? If there's no good land left . . . if the place is full of sickness . . .''

"Now, don't get excited. Remember the maps we looked at? Illinois is a big state. There's all kinds of good land, just waiting out there for us. We'll go farther north, that's all."

"North! That's where the Indians are!"

He chuckled. "We won't go that far north. Don't worry, I can always make a living as a gunsmith. We won't give up, Carrie."

Chagrined, I turned to him, managing a faint smile. "Well . . . we've only been in Illinois a few hours. I guess it is a little soon to think of giving up."

We stepped into the crowded general store and looked at the tables and shelves which were piled high to the ceiling. Pungent smells of home-cured tobacco, tanned leather, linseed oil, and coffee beans from distant shores filled the air. Bolts of calico and gingham and one of shimmering blue silk drew my attention, while Josh inspected the rifles hanging on the back wall.

"Well, sir, I could fix you up with a mighty fine rifle," the storeowner drawled, as he sauntered over. "Yes, sir, these here was made by the finest smith in Kaintuck."

Josh grinned and shook his head. "No, thanks. I'm a gunsmith myself. I'm looking for a place to settle here in Illinois."

"You could stick around this town. Always room for a smithy. But if I was a mite younger, I'd head north, my boy. They're openin' up the prairies as fast as the oxes can pull plows. It beats all I ever seen."

"I've been hearing about Illinois land since I was a kid," Josh said.

The man shrugged his shoulders and shifted the piece of straw in his mouth. "When I come to these parts, near fifteen year ago, we all figgered that prairie grassland was plumb worthless. Just seemed logical. If ground won't grow trees, it shore ain't worth a hoot for nothing else. But some bright boy tried it, and now they're growin' corn that's nigh to fifteen foot high, I hear. Pumpkins a man can't git his arms around. Y' come to the right place, young feller." He slammed a knotty hand on Josh's shoulder.

"Just how far north do you figure a man needs to go?"

"Well . . . what I've been hearin' from folks passin' through from Kaintuck . . . I been hearin' a heap of talk 'bout Sangamon County."

"Sangamon County," Josh repeated slowly. "There's good land there, you say?"

The man chewed his straw and shifted it again. "Well, just make sure you git where there's good water. That's the trouble folks've had in these parts. Bad water, and horseflies as big as sparrows. And skeeters fat as hogs from suckin' all us poor folks' blood."

"That big?"

"Well, purty near it. And many's the body suffers with the ague and fever round here. Yep, I'd move on myself if my woman could make the trip. She's been poorly for a long spell."

After I bought a sturdy, cloth-covered journal, Josh and I strolled back to the tavern with a lighter step. The sun seemed to shine brighter; Josh whistled a happy little tune.

Later that evening, while I scribbled in my journal all the details of our river journey, Josh asked the tavern owner if he knew of someone who might buy our boat.

"Well, now, let me think," the man said slowly. "I know a feller with a still. Seems like he was talkin' 'bout taking some barrels down to New Orleans. Could be he'd take your boat off your hands."

"Tell me where he lives." Josh's fingers were tapping a drum roll on the table. "I'll hire a horse and ride out to talk to him tomorrow."

I wrote two letters, to tell our families we had arrived safely. Soon I found myself yawning, and bid Josh a reluctant good-night. I went into the women's room, quickly slipped into my gown, and crawled between cool linen sheets. The bed felt strange to me. I missed the gentle rocking of the river, the soft lapping of its water against our boat. I missed Josh, the clean man-smell of him, fresh from his swim.

The bed felt even stranger when my bed partner, a tiny birdlike widow, crept in and silently lay down beside me. Enveloped in a cloud of liniment, she quickly eased into a soft and rhythmic snoring. I thought of Josh in the room overhead, sharing his bed with a stranger, too, and I prayed for luck in selling our boat . . . and for a short stay in Shawneetown.

My prayer was answered, for the next morning we found a buyer—the farmer with the still. With the cash he gave us, we went back to town and bought a used wagon with a sturdy canvas cover.

The third day, Josh counted out some hoarded dollars for a stout pair of oxen. "We'll load the wagon this afternoon and take off first thing tomorrow," he told me, his voice rasping with excitement.

I fidgeted, shifting my little purse back and forth between my hands. "It won't be long now, will it, Josh?"

"Oh, it's quite a ways—another long trip," he said, as he ran his hand along the ox's smooth mahogany back. "But every mile will bring us that much closer to our new home."

Sharing the anticipation that gleamed in his eyes, I smiled. "It sounds so sweet when you say it. Home."

The next morning Josh harnessed the oxen to our wagon, which sagged under the weight of trunks and boxes and his gun barrels and tools. Then we climbed up on the high seat, and he grabbed the reins.

"Gee! Haw, now!" he called. The oxen slowly plodded out of town and down the long, dusty trail.

By midmorning we had passed from rolling hilly country into immense green spreads of tall grass, higher than my head, broken only by distant groves of trees on scattered knobs and bordering the stream banks.

The few small towns and scattered settlers' cabins did little to relieve my haunting sense of isolation as we crossed the prairie. Out as far as I could see, the horizon lay around me in a perfect, uninterrupted circle.

The sun climbed higher and heat rose from the grass in shimmering, dizzying waves. "We don't have much drinking water left," I said. "We'd better find a spring or stream to fill the jug."

"We'll stop at a farmhouse before sundown and beg some water. We might even trade for some eggs and vegetables."

"What do we have to trade?"

"I brought some special bullet molds my dad and I made up. Any man could use one of those."

As the shadows began to lengthen, we pulled off the rutted track and down a narrow lane toward a small, isolated log house beside a stream, nearly hidden among giant poplar trees. Three hound dogs and five children of assorted sizes came bounding down the lane when they caught sight of us.

"Howdy! Howdy! Who are you?"

"Josh Strauman's my name, and this is my wife Carrie. We're traveling up to Sangamon County. Are your mama and daddy around?"

The oldest, a skinny boy of ten or so, nodded toward a distant field. "Pa's still out with Junior workin' the corn. They'll be in shortly. Ma's inside fixin' up supper. I'll go fetch her."

The others ran ahead, but one young girl remained beside our wagon, looking up at me. "You're purty," she said, then flushed and lowered her eyes.

"I was just thinking the same thing about you," I told her, smiling. "You're the sweetest little girl I've seen in a long time."

She gazed up at me again, her huge eyes the palest shade of green against her sun-tanned face.

A feeble twist of smoke curled from the chimney of the weathered log cabin. A flock of dusty chickens scratched briskly in the weeds around the dooryard. When we drew closer to the house, a woman stepped outside the door and stood, looking us over closely. I looked her over, too. She was a gaunt, hollow-cheeked woman, with eyes shadowed in sadness. I was shocked: I suppose I expected all Illinois women to be robust and joyful.

The woman nodded her head slightly and asked, "Been travelin' far?"

"We've come downriver from Ohio, and now we're headed up to Sangamon County." Josh jumped down from the wagon seat. "We'd like to beg a little water for our jug and some for the oxen. That sun gives a man a mighty thirst."

She touched her hair with a gnarled and work-worn hand. "Lord knows we ain't got much, but water we got. Good water, too. That's more than lots of folks can say in these parts."

As Josh left with the oldest boy to get water from their spring, the woman turned toward me. "Ohio," she said with a wistful sigh. "I used to know some folks from Ohio. They packed up and moved on, though. Seems like folks is always movin' on."

"You don't have any close neighbors here, do you?"

Her eyes followed mine out to the windswept prairie. "Nope. I'm right glad you folks stopped by. Does me good to talk to womenfolk now 'n' then." She brushed at a stained spot on her apron. "Jest step inside. I'll fix us a cup o' coffee while I finish up supper."

"Oh, we don't want to be any bother. We'll just get some water and be on our way."

"It's 'most sundown, girl," she scolded. "No need to be goin' farther tonight. I'll jest set out two more plates. Lord knows someday one of mine might be out on the road and need some warm vittles."

Just then a man trudged slowly around the side of the long, low barn, a heavy hoe on his shoulder. He was spare and weary looking, his back bent over like a question mark. "Evenin'," he muttered, as Josh walked up with a wooden pail of water.

"Evening, sir." Josh reached out to shake the farmer's stained and knobby hand. "Nice place you have here. And a fine family growing up to help you work it."

"Work aplenty for us all, I reckon," the man said. "Junior's still out in the field . . . finishing up his row. Where might you be headin'?"

"Sangamon County. All the way from Ohio, and still a ways to go, I guess."

His wife stepped over to the man. "I asked these folks to set down with us to supper, Jimmy."

"Why, shore, and welcome," he said. "Ma's garden is givin' us fresh greens these days, to serve up with the ham and hominy."

Matilda, the little green-eyed girl, spoke up. "Bobby Joe and me and Cinda, we picked half a pail of wild strawberries this mornin'. Guess we knowed we was havin' company for supper!"

A short while later we all crowded around the table. Matilda sat beside me and shyly touched the fabric of my dress. "I never seen a dress like that," she said. "The buttons is so purty, too . . . all shiny. Is that the clothes they wear in Ohio?"

I smiled and tweaked her turned-up nose. "In Cincinnati they have whole stores just filled with bolts of cloth—every color of the rainbow."

"They do?"

"Some day when you're older, you'll have to find some cloth and make a dress to match your eyes. A soft green velvet, maybe."

Matilda looked at me wonderingly, then turned to her mother. "Can I, Mama? Do you think some day I can?"

"Poor chance of that, babe, what with money scarce as hens' teeth," the woman replied, patting the child's shoulder absently. "Velvet, yet! This lady's got a heap to learn 'bout settler life."

I took a deep gulp of coffee and changed the subject.

The farmer barraged us with questions. He craved news of Ohio, of the river, of Shawneetown, of the world outside his isolated farm. His wife just craved conversation with another woman. Any topic was welcome.

And I was filled with curiosity about their life, so different from the one I had always known. As I helped the woman with the dishes, I looked down at my hands and arms, so pink and plump and soft beside her bony, leathered ones. She seemed elderly to me, with her lined face and missing teeth. And then she mentioned she was twenty-nine.

Twenty-nine. I felt an icy chill. Would I look like that in ten more years? I shuddered and stood silent for a long while, listening to Josh's never-ending talk of Illinois and its bright future. My head began to ache.

The evening passed, and finally the younger children climbed the ladder to the loft. I gazed into the crackling fire, trying to supress a yawn.

"You folks is welcome to use our bed," the woman said. "We'll spread us a pallet on the floor."

"Oh, no, we couldn't take your bed from you." I shook my head emphatically. The crowded sleeping quarters and lack of privacy in Shawneetown had been trial enough.

Josh stood up and stretched. "We sure appreciate your kindness, ma'am, but we have our wagon fixed up with a featherbed and all the comforts of home."

The farmer slapped him on the back. "I don't know 'bout that, but I reckon I can recollect what it's like to be newly hitched." He guffawed as Josh's face turned as pink as mine.

"We'll see you'uns for breakfast in the mornin'," the woman called as we went out into the darkness.

The canvas of our wagon shone like molten silver in the moonlight. We climbed inside, undressed quickly, and lay down together, listening to the hushed night sounds around us. Gentle breezes rustled the leaves; crickets shrilled a serenade.

"I can't wait to get there," Josh said softly.

I hesitated and gulped a deep breath. "Sometimes I'm a little bit afraid."

"Afraid? What do you mean? You're not having a change of heart, are you?"

"Oh, Josh, I want whatever you want. You know that. It's just that everything is new to me. Sometimes I wonder if I'm strong enough and brave enough for all of this."

A long silence hung between us. Then he reached out and embraced me. "Well, strength is something I have plenty of—enough for both of us. Courage, too, I hope. Just stay by me, my pretty Carrie. The whole world is ours."

And there in the warmth of his arms I remembered why I had left my home and family.


As the days passed, we saw fewer farms and fewer trees, until it seemed our wagon was a ship sailing through an endless sea of grass. Gazing out across the prairie, I watched the breeze ripple through the grass, like waves across the water. I sat mesmerized, caught up in the illusion, as the oxen's hooves counted off the tedious miles.

Sometimes the discordant squeak and squeal of the wooden axles, the jingle of our hanging pots and pans, and the steady plop-plop of the animals' hooves, all faded from my mind as I sat on the wagon seat beside Josh and planned in smallest detail how I would arrange and decorate our house. And we would have a cradle of smooth polished wood, padded soft inside, a cozy nest for a sweet-smelling babe.

Maybe even now . . . My heartbeat quickened. I felt an ache, a longing to hold a baby in my arms. Josh and I would be Papa and Mama. We would hold our grandchildren, too, someday. The road we would travel would be much longer than this narrow path before us, cutting through the sea of prairie grass.

One evening after we had stopped beside a tree-lined stream, Josh lifted his gun from inside the wagon. "I'll fix a fire and then go see if I can find us some quail or prairie chicken for supper."

"And I'll put on the coffeepot and mix up corn bread. It should be all ready by the time you get back."

I was dipping water into our big jug when I noticed some raspberry bushes downstream. What a nice surprise for Josh, I thought. After setting the coffee on the fire to boil, I strolled off with a wooden bowl to gather some.

Suddenly, the singing birds in the trees overhead shrieked out a loud alarm.

"Don't be afraid of me. I won't hurt you, little birds," I murmured, and began to hum a merry tune.

The golden glow of evening lay on all the trees and bushes and on the carpet of wildflowers underfoot. "I'll pick some flowers, too. We'll have a banquet here tonight," I told myself, as I turned from the berries to pluck a bouquet.

Then I saw the cause of the birds' shrill cries. A snake!

A big black ugly thing that stared at me before it slithered off into the grass.

I screamed and dropped my bowl of berries. Grabbing up the bowl, I bolted for the wagon.

I leapt up to the seat and burst into tears. Long-forgotten tales of rattler bites, of agonies of death from their poison, echoed in my mind. If I hadn't seen the snake, if he had bitten me, Josh might have come back to find me moaning and swollen, breathing my last breath.

The image of the snake kept haunting me. Its eyes had looked so sly and knowing. An iron band seemed to tighten around my chest. My breath came in shallow painful gasps.

When Josh returned, I was still sitting on the wagon seat, trembling. The coffee was boiling on the fire; the corn bread long forgotten.

"What's wrong?" he asked. "You look like you've seen a ghost."

"A snake! Down by those berry bushes."

"Was it a prairie rattler?"

"I don't know. It was big and ugly."

"You should learn to tell the difference. Most snakes are harmless. You can kill them with the ax, you know. Just one good blow and that's the end of it."

His lack of concern surprised me, and I slowly searched his face. "The ax?"

"Sure. It's not too heavy. Here, lift it once and see."

My quivering fingers clutched the ax he gave me, lifted it above my head, and brought it down to earth with all my strength. Beneath its fine-honed blade, in my imagination, lay two neatly separated halves of one black snake.

Josh chuckled. "Careful, now. Don't dull it. That ax is going to come in handy in a lot of ways."

"Maybe if I ever killed a snake I wouldn't be so afraid of them. But I'd rather start with a small one. That snake I saw was big!"

He put his arm around me. "Don't worry, Carrie," he said. "You'll get used to these things. Snakes are just pests we have to fight against, like the horseflies and mosquitoes. And the wolves."

"Oh, yes. The wolves." Last night I had heard one howling in the distance. My skin had tingled with goose bumps at the eerie sound.

The lengthening shadows of evening seemed ominous to me. "I'll hurry and clean these quail," Josh said. "Then, while you cook them, I'll go pick some berries for us."

Still breathing in shallow pants, I stirred the dying fire and quickly mixed the cornmeal with water and a little salt. As I patted it between my hands to form a small flat loaf, I threw frequent glances at the ax resting against the wagon wheel.

Just let that snake dare come back here, I thought. I'll show him a thing or two.


Each day we continued northward toward Sangamon County, fording streams, stopping at night beside a creek or settler's cabin. The prairie was full of brilliant and fragrant wildflowers now, waltzing in the wind that blew across that endless flatland. Bees hummed as they worked among the luscious blossoms: giant golden sunflowers, wild indigo, yellow mustard, red clover, purple nettle, pink and crimson phlox, bluebells, wild roses, and buttercups.

As we slowly made our way along the narrow dirt road, a tunnel through the tall grass, I sometimes felt confused. The prairie looked as boundless and uncharted as the sky. "Are you sure you know the way?" I asked Josh.

He grinned. "Don't worry, I won't get us lost. I check with everyone we meet. That last fellow on horseback said he's going to a new town that's building up fast—New Salem. He said it has a grist- and saw-mill, and a ferry across the Sangamon River. With all these new people settling up that way, it's bound to be a big city soon."

"I'd like to be near a city. These prairie farms seem so isolated."

"Well, with my gun shop, I'll need to be near people . . . but I want some land to farm, too. Between the two of them, we should be sitting pretty in five years or so."

"Five years will go by fast."

"Sure. Just think, we've already been married almost a month." He looked into my eyes and murmured softly, "We might already have our family started."

A tender web of feeling spun between us, a precious closeness.

Mile after tedious mile the oxen pulled our wagon northward. Some days the heat was so intense we took refuge in a shady grove and waited to travel on by night. Then, freed from the sun and the torment of the big green flies, the oxen seemed more content to plod up the path, that narrow thread of silver in the moonlight.

On our final night we were shaken from our sleep by a sudden storm. Lightning and roars of thunder split the skies. Chilling dampness crept inside our wagon, and powerful winds tore at the billowing canvas walls. I peeked outside. Tree branches whirled in a crazy dance.

Wide-eyed, we lay and listened to the wind and thunder, the steady pelting of the rain. I felt a captive of the storm, small and vulnerable. All my anxieties seemed magnified. "Josh, will you really be looking for a farm when we get to New Salem?" I asked softly.

"I plan to. Why?"

A thickening rose up in my throat. I swallowed hard. "I'm afraid I don't know much about farming. We had that little garden behind our house, but that's as close as I've come."

"Well, I'm really a city boy myself. All I know I learned working a few summers on Uncle Rudy's farm. But there's good value in land, especially in a place that's growing fast."

"There's value in city property, too. Papa said those lots in downtown Cincinnati are worth a fortune now."

Josh lay silent for a long while. He turned away from me and watched the rain lash at the prairie. "Are you telling me you don't want to live on a farm?"

"It's not that," I said, reaching out to touch his arm. "But it will be such a change for both of us. Such hard, backbreaking work for you."

"I'm young and strong. I'm not afraid of work."

"I know you're not, but you're a gunsmith. That's your craft, not farming. You'll probably keep busy all the time with that."

"It's slow work, that's the truth." He looked into my eyes and said in a husky voice, "I know you're used to city life, Carrie. You're used to having a nice home and dressing up and all."

With a low chuckle I buried my face in the hollow of his neck, feeling the warmth and strength of him against me. "Don't you know by now I don't care beans for city life and fancy clothes? I only want to be where you are, Josh. It's just . . . Well, it's nice to have neighbors nearby, don't you think?"

The storm had finally blown over, leaving behind its echo in the steady dripping from the trees. Josh sat up and took a deep breath. "If New Salem is growing as fast as everybody says, they'll probably need a full-time gunsmith. Let's just wait. We'll look the situation over and then decide."

The next afternoon we reached New Salem. At last. With a final burst of strength, the oxen tugged us up a thickly wooded hill and out into a clearing. The fading sun threw long shadows across a big log house beside the road, shading the painted sign above the door: NEW SALEM INN.

Josh halted the oxen and hopped down from the wagon. "We made it, Carrie!" he cried, with an exultant laugh. "Come on! Let's look this place over before we go inside."

I climbed down less spiritedly. My muscles ached with stiffness from the long trip. But we were there. At last we were really there.

Reaching out to take my hand, Josh led me through the high grass alongside the road. A heavy pounding grew louder as we walked toward a distant cabin.

"What's that?" I asked. The noise seemed foreign to this idyllic wooded spot.

"The mills, I guess. Look through the trees here. See all the horses and wagons tied up on the hillside?"

At the edge of the high bluff, we pulled aside some lacy leaves to view the wide vista below us. Bordered by trees, the Sangamon River snaked across the broad, fertile prairie, then tumbled noisily over the dam beside the mill. Three young boys were swimming near the dam, laughing, splashing water on two more who stood fishing from the bank.

The staccato sounds of a horse galloping up the hill broke through the pounding of the mill. A rider carrying a rooster under his arm flew past us in a cloud of dust and pulled his horse to a skidding halt beside a log cabin down the road. "Hey, Jack! I brought 'im!" he yelled, as he ran into the building. "Now jest let's see whose is the feistiest!"

Men's voices guffawed. "We'll have us a cock fight to beat all!" someone yelled.

Josh frowned. "Let's walk down the other way."

"It sounds like here's where all the action is in this town," I teased.

"Didn't your stepmother teach you a saloon is no place for a lady?" he asked me, grinning.

The road was dry; dust rose in waves around our feet as we strolled along. Ahead of us, we saw only a general store and a few cabins, their logs looking raw and newly cut. Puzzled, I turned to Josh. "I thought they said this was a booming city."

"We're on the frontier now, Carrie," he said. "It'll be a big city in a few years. That's what everybody says. The mills draw from forty miles around here. There's that saloon, and the tavern for meals and lodging. The store. It's just a matter of time before this place grows up. Oh, it won't be as big as Cincinnati for a while, but New Salem is a town with a future."

His clear gray eyes gleamed; his whole face seemed to

light up as he gave my hand a squeeze. "And we're getting in on the beginning of it. That's how those men in Cincinnati made their fortunes and built all those fine homes. I tell you, Carrie, one day we'll have us a fine home, too. One that will do you proud."

# Chapter 3

A big, genial-looking man stepped out to meet us on the wide porch of the two-story inn, and greeted us in a soft and easy Southern drawl. "Welcome to New Salem, folks! Been travelin' long?"

Josh shook the man's outstretched hand. "Down the Ohio and up from Shawneetown. My name's Josh Strauman, and this is my wife, Carrie. We hope to settle in these parts."

"Now, I'd say that's a real smart idea."

"I'd like to find out more about your town here. I heard a lot of mention of it on the road."

"Well, you're talking to the right fellow. I'm Jim Rutledge and I laid out this town last year. Me and my nephew."

"It's such a pretty spot here," I said, listening to the faint melodious bubbling of the milldam. It was eight feet high and could be heard throughout the town.

"We sure like it. We built the mills down by the river first, and they've been so busy, it seemed a likely place to make a town. There's no towns to speak of north of us, so folks will do all their trading here in New Salem. We've already got a general store and a cooper shop. We've even got our own post office now.''

He smiled and pointed to the door expansively.

"Step inside, folks. You're going to stay overnight with us, aren't you?''

"We'll probably stay a few days and look things over," Josh said. He turned to me, excitement gleaming in his eyes. "Well, Carrie, shall we go in?''

Waves of heat and savory smells enveloped us as we stepped into the large main room of the inn. Big iron pots and kettles gurgled over the flames in the stone fireplace at the side. Two women worked around the cooking fire, while in the corner a little girl rocked a baby's cradle.

Jugs and crocks and platters overlapped each other on the mantel, and beneath it dangled a mix of cooking tools. Shining dishes, delicately patterned blue and white, lined the open shelves of a heavy walnut china cupboard. Along the sides sat stools, baskets, wooden boxes. The room seemed overflowing with furniture and utensils and people.

Mr. Rutledge led us to the fireplace. "I'd like you to meet my wife, Mary Ann, and Jane, my oldest girl. Those two in the corner are my youngest kids. My others are around here somewhere.''

The older woman smiled at us with a gracious dignity. The younger, a sweet-faced girl about my age, nodded, spoke, then turned back to her task of stirring a huge kettle of beans.

Just then a small slender young woman in green calico came through the back door, and I looked up to meet her periwinkle-blue eyes sparkling beneath a straw sunbonnet. She was lovely and spoke in a soft, melodious voice as she laid two heavy crocks on the table. "Here's the butter and cream from the root cellar, Mama.'' Then her eyes, teeming with curiosity, turned to Josh and me.

Jim Rutledge nodded his head at her. ''This is my girl, Ann. She's seventeen. You're not much more than that yourself, are you, Mrs. Strauman?''

Well! I stiffened my spine and frowned, trying to look the dignified matron. ''I'm nineteen, sir. I'm from Cincinnati.'' That should impress him.

''Are you now? Big city folks, eh? Well, you may find things a mite different out here.''

Ann pulled off her bonnet and shook back heavy auburn hair. Her skin was pale and flawless, striking against the vivid hues of her hair and eyes. Those eyes shone with interest now as she smiled at me. ''Cincinnati! I've always wanted to visit a big city like that. You'll have to tell me all about it.''

''Ann, you'd best start setting the tables now,'' her harried mother interrupted. ''The ham and beans are ready, and the corn bread's almost done.''

The girl quickly laid out an astounding number of plates on the two big tables in the room. When all the people finally congregated for supper, I learned that there were nine Rutledge children, stair-steps from young men and women down to baby Sally. Harried, work-worn Mrs. Rutledge and the children ate at one table, while Mr. Rutledge sat at the other with his guests: the mail carrier, a doctor, two drovers, Josh, and me.

''I've seen some of the world myself,'' Jim Rutledge told us. ''I was born in South Carolina and lived in Georgia and Tennessee. Came to Illinois seventeen years ago, before it was even a state. I've watched it open up and grow. Guess I'll be here till I die.''

Josh laid a thick slab of butter on a square of corn bread. "Tell me, do you think a gunsmith could make a living here?"

"Sure could! Are you a gunsmith?"

"Yes, I've worked it from a boy alongside my dad. Now I'm all set to strike out on my own. I brought along my tools and supplies."

"Folks around here would sure be proud to have you settle in New Salem. I'll sell you a lot, and you can have a cabin up in no time."

"How much are the lots?"

"A hundred-fifteen foot frontage will run you ten dollars."

Josh glanced over at me, his face solemn and intense. "I'd really like to get a farm, but maybe I should save up some more money. A dollar and a quarter an acre isn't a bad price for land, but with a minimum of eighty acres . . . They want cash, too . . . Maybe I will start out in town and get myself a farm in a year or two."

Mr. Rutledge sipped his coffee, nodding in agreement. "If you don't need those oxen yourself, you could sell them for a pretty price. It takes six or seven yoke to plow up the prairie the first time. You won't believe how tough these roots are."

The next morning we strolled around the town again, stopping at the bustling general store. Sam Hill, one of the owners, stood solemnly before the loaded shelves, looking like a Yankee ship captain at his helm. His hooded eyes surveyed us impassively before he finally granted us a smile and welcomed us to New Salem.

A jumble of people crowded on the porch outside the store. Their voices mingled as they discussed the latest news, and we soon found ourselves the objects of their undisguised curiosity.

"Where do you'uns hail from?"

"Plannin' to settle down in these parts?"

"Did I hear tell you're a gunsmith?" one lanky man in faded homespun asked Josh. "Can you rerifle my old flintlock?"

"Sure thing. Just as soon as I get my tools unpacked."

The man spat tobacco juice out into the yard and grinned. "A feller's gotta have a good gun, don't he? Yes, sir, you'll be mighty welcome here in Sangamon."

Josh and I sauntered down the main street, studying all the lots for sale. They were large and wooded; huge oak and maple and walnut trees extended branches overhead. But most lots had a grassy clearing in the front with space for house and garden.

When we reached the edge of town, we stopped. The air was cool and sweet, and just above our heads a robin chirped. Josh looked around him, pondering. "We might buy two lots and put one of them in garden. That way we could break into this farming business gradually. When the town has grown, we could sell them both for a good price and move out to the country."

"That's fine with me." I gazed at the lacy patterns on the grass, where sunlight filtered through the leaves, and suddenly I could see it all—our finished home, our children playing in the yard. A lump rose in my throat as I said, "This would be a lovely spot to build."

Back at the inn Josh negotiated with Mr. Rutledge for the two lots at the western edge of town. It was all happening so fast. "How long will it take to build a house?" I asked eagerly.

Mr. Rutledge grinned at me. "Don't you worry about that. There's plenty of men around here to pitch in and help. We'll have us a house-raising party, and in two or three days, you'll be all moved in."

"Do you think they'll want to help us?" Josh asked, with a slight frown. "We're strangers here, you know."

"If you move to this town, you're not strangers anymore. You're neighbors. And you'll get plenty of chance to pay back when somebody else needs help. That's how we do it here."

Two days later a whole crew of strapping men assembled on our site. Their hearty laughs and jests rang out loudly in the crisp morning air. Jim Rutledge was there, and other men from town and from the farms nearby. They all seemed to be old friends.

I stood off to the side and watched while the men divided into four parties and walked back to the woods behind our lots. I could see them pointing, carefully selecting straight trees, one foot in diameter. Then knotted muscle fell in behind axes. Bright blades ate into the trees, fibers split and ripped, and trees roared through the air, crashing down to earth.

One group of men cut down the trees; another cut them to the proper lengths. A third group chained the logs to an ox team and dragged them to the sawmill by the river, where honed blades cut them evenly on two sides. Off to the side, another group sliced off shingles for the roof.

Sounds clamored all around me—axes chopping, trees thundering down, chains clanking, male voices shouting "gee" and "haw" to the oxen. Excited, I paced back and forth, watching, listening, wishing I dared to join in and help.

At noon some women brought big pots of stew and pans of corn bread. One of them, a slender, dark-haired woman with huge blue eyes, came over to my side. "Why don't you come with me, honey?" she asked. "It's too hot to stay out here all day."

I shook my head. "I want to watch them build my house. It's exciting."

"They'll be all day just gettin' the logs ready and in place. They won't raise it till tomorrow." She placed a coaxing hand on my shoulder. "Come to my house. It's just outside town. I'll show you the new quilt pattern I'm workin' on."

Reluctantly, I left the noisy pageant and started down the road with the woman. Blinding glare struck me like a blow as we left the shady grove. My eyes narrowed to a squint, and beads of sweat popped out on my brow.

"I'm Sarah Graham," the woman said, stepping along firmly. "My husband's helping back there. He's the one with bright red hair. He teaches school here in the winter. And there—that's our house up the road."

Shielding my eyes against the piercing sun, I looked out across the prairie to a large brick house nestled in a grove of trees. "What a pretty house, Sarah! It's as big as Rutledge's inn. Have you lived here long?"

She smiled as she gazed toward her home. "We came up from Kentucky four years ago. First we lived in a little cabin while Mentor made all those bricks for the big house. We have forty acres here we farm, and Mentor teaches at the school and makes bricks to sell, too." She sighed. "You know, there's just never any end to all the work."

When we finally reached the farm, Sarah showed me her

garden, with its green rows of vegetables all neatly laid and hoed. Inside the house her fresh-scrubbed kitchen and the patterned dishes in the china cupboard gave a pleasing sense of home.

I passed the afternoon sewing with Sarah and playing with her two little daughters. Their mother had made them rag dolls, stitched with yarn hair and smiling faces, which they pulled around the room in a tiny wooden wagon.

The littlest, pink-cheeked Minerva, climbed on my lap and snuggled in contentedly. "Sarah, you're so lucky to have these precious little girls," I said, running my hand over the child's silky hair.

Sarah's eyes rested fondly on her daughter. "Kids and corn. Those are the best crops in these parts."

The shadows were lengthening in late afternoon when I walked back to town and stopped by our lot. Bulky stacks of logs, all cut to proper size, lay ready for raising the next day. The men sat on the logs now, passing around a jug of whiskey and telling stories. Bursts of boisterous laughter punctuated their talk.

Josh joined me, and together we walked back to the inn. "These are my kind of men," he said, his voice filled with enthusiasm. "They see a job that needs doing and they do it. No questions asked. Yes, pretty Carrie, I think we're really going to like this town."

At early morning the next day, all the men were back at work. I watched as they laid stones for the foundation and then began to set the logs. Shouts and laughs and loud instructions sounded in the dew-damp air. An axman at each corner notched the logs for a close fit, while the other men heaved the heavy timbers into place. In just a few hours all the walls were standing, finished.

Then the men, straining and grunting, lifted up the gable end pieces with long forked poles. Finally they laid the wooden shingles for the roof.

"Hey, Carrie, look!" Josh called exuberantly. "We've got ourselves a house!"

I paced around the lot, picking up odd scraps of wood, surveying my new home from every angle. A warm feeling glowed inside me. In the maple branches overhead a tiny wren sat on her nest and chirped contentedly. I understood exactly how she felt.

By late afternoon the puncheon floor was laid. Some men brought clay up from the creek and began to chink the cracks between the logs.

"Party time tonight! We'll have us a big housewarming!" an eager-faced young fellow called out.

"Did you tell Old Joe to get his fiddle tuned up?" another asked.

I longed to unload our wagon and move into our new home. Instead, I stood beside the doorway after supper and greeted the work crew as they returned with their wives and children. And a good supply of whiskey. People packed inside the empty little cabin and milled about the yard. Outdoors, the children ran and chased each other, playing tag among the trees.

Then Old Joe took up a post in the corner. He was a jolly-looking man with a gray beard and a thatch of gray hair falling across his forehead. When he began to play his fiddle, all the people picked up the lively rhythm with their clapping. Shouts and laughter, sounds of merrymaking, and the clean smell of new wood filled the crowded room. Soft breezes drifted through the unchinked walls and teased the flames of tallow candles nailed to holders all along the sides.

The men and women danced four-hand reels and jigs, as Old Joe bowed "Money Musk" and "Turkey in the Straw" and "Skip to My Lou"—all the old favorites. Laughing, feeling wildly carefree, Josh and I joined in the dance.

I glanced across the room and noticed several young men vying for a dance with Ann Rutledge. Smiling vivaciously, she gave them all their turn, her shimmering auburn hair flying out behind her as she twirled about the floor.

All the hours of grueling work seemed forgotten; the people danced far into the night on the new boards. Along the sides, little children stood with eyes glazed from fatigue, but they would not give up the festivities.

"Carrie, did you meet my husband, Mentor?" dark-haired Sarah Graham asked during a lull in the music.

Smiling, I nodded to the slender man, with his solemn face and shock of curly red hair. "Yes, Mentor, I saw you working on our house," I said. "You're the teacher here, aren't you? My father is a teacher, too—a professor at the college in Cincinnati."

Just then Ann approached with a well-dressed man at her side. "Carrie, this is John," she said, the excitement of the evening glowing in her cheeks. "John McNeil. You know, Sam Hill's partner in the general store."

"Welcome to New Salem, Mrs. Strauman," John said carefully, speaking with an Eastern accent. He had a handsome, even-featured face, but somehow his polite smile failed to reach his pale green eyes.

"Thank—thank you," I stammered, feeling strangely uncomfortable with this urbane man, so different from the hearty Southerners who filled the room.

Old Joe struck up another tune, and once again dancing feet took up the rhythm of the clapping hands. A thunderous roar echoed from the stomp of shoes upon the puncheon floor. Finally, one by one, couples began to drift away, calling out their good-byes at the door.

"So long! Good luck to you folks!"

"Right glad to have you with us!"

Their voices faded in the distance as they strolled on down the road or drove off in their wagons.

Soon we were left alone with Old Joe. With loving care he packed his fiddle in its leather case. "Well, looks like we got the house all warmed up proper for you young folks," he said. "Guess I'll take my leave."

In a moment our new house was silent. It seemed much bigger now that I saw it empty in the flickering candlelight. The pungent smell of fresh-cut wood enveloped me as I stood in the center of the room and looked around me, unbelieving.

"Do you like it, Carrie?" Josh stood beside me, smiling, his arm around my waist. "There's still a lot to do. I have to set in doors and windows, and build a fireplace. But at least it's a shelter."

"It's a lovely little house! I just can't believe it's this far along already. And I can't believe those men could work all day and still have energy to dance all night."

He laughed. "They'll probably feel the effects tomorrow."

When he went to get our bedding from the wagon, I thought of all the whiskey I had seen consumed that night. Some of the men would surely feel the effects of that, too.

"I'll build us a bed as soon as I can," Josh said as he laid the feather mattress on the floor. He draped blankets across the open doorways. "First thing in the morning, I'll build the doors."

"This is fine for now," I said, smoothing out our sheets and pillows. "Just think, Josh . . . our very own home."

With quick, impatient puffs, he blew out all the candles and crawled in beside me. The darkness intensified the odors that surrounded me like fog. The new wood. Melting tallow from the candles. The dank, sour whiskey stink on Josh's breath as he drew me close to him. I should scold a bit about that whiskey. But not tonight. Not this very special night—the first night in our own home.

Next morning after Josh unpacked our things, he made and hung the front and back doors. Then he left with the oxen and wagon, headed for the creek bed to get a load of stones for a fireplace.

Humming to myself, I arranged our belongings around the house. It didn't take long—we had no furniture. A trunk of clothes would have to serve for a table, with a stool at either end. My books and pretty wedding dishes I left packed in the barrels. Josh's tools and supplies lay in the corner, wrapped in quilts, looking like some oddly shaped late sleepers.

Now, let's see, I thought. We need a cupboard and some shelves. A bed, of course.

"Hello!"

The voice broke into my thoughts. I glanced up and saw Ann Rutledge at the door, wildflowers clasped in her hands. "I brought a bouquet for your new house," she said. "Oh, Carrie, won't this be a nice place for you?"

"I'm afraid it's pretty bare right now. Josh is going to build some furniture as soon as he gets the fireplace done. I have to finish the chinking, too, before we get a hard rain."

"I'll send my little brothers and sisters down to help you. They'll think it's a game."

I shook my head, amazed. "I just can't believe how helpful everybody is."

"I'm glad to have new neighbors . . . especially someone who has traveled." She studied me with clear, intelligent blue eyes. "You can tell me all about the world outside Sangamon County."

The world outside, I thought, with a surge of sympathy. These women are so isolated. "It seems a long time since I left Cincinnati," I said. "So many things have happened— the boat, the wagon trip. And now, our new house."

Recalling last night's party, I began to tease, "I must say, Ann, you certainly have your share of beaus. John McNeil, and who was that other young fellow ready to fight for a dance?"

Her cheeks flushed crimson. "Oh, you mean Billy Berry. Well, dancing is all right, but I'm in no hurry to settle down to hearth and cradle. I'd like to get more education." She paused. "I guess that sounds silly, doesn't it?"

"Not to me. My father is a teacher. I'll always be grateful he gave me some decent schooling. Lots of people think it's a waste of time for girls."

An intent expression clouded her face. "There's so much I'd like to learn about. Sometimes I lie awake at night and think about all those different places the people at the inn come from. Papa was born in South Carolina. He's always talking about his family there. He told me one of them signed the Declaration of Independence. And one was appointed by Washington to the Supreme Court." She slowly shook her head. "I wonder what those South Carolina relatives would think of Miss Ann Rutledge of New Salem, Illinois. I guess they'd think I'm just some ignorant backwoods girl."

"They'd think you're a princess, Ann. Princess of the prairie."

"Oh, Carrie, don't tease me." She laughed. "Well, I'd better go back and help Mama now."

I watched her as she walked down the road with a light and graceful step, her head held proudly, long auburn hair blowing in the breeze. She could not have been lovelier if her plain brown dress had been of ermine. Truly a prairie princess, I thought.

Sometime later Josh returned with the wagon filled with creek stones. With my unskilled but willing help, he began the tedious job of laying stones. By the end of the third day, we had completed our fireplace, and I was cooking my first meal inside our new home.

That whole summer flew by, days crowded with activity. Josh traded gun repair for some seasoned walnut boards and built a bedstead, a table and benches, and a handsome corner cupboard. At night he sat and rubbed these with linseed oil until the wood grain gleamed, while I scribbled in my journal or wrote a letter to Papa or my sister, Eliza.

I told them of our cabin where one room served as kitchen at mealtimes, bedroom at night, and parlor when we entertained guests. I didn't like to boast, but we had turned that bare room into a cozy home, with red-and-white checked curtains at the three small windows and a new patchwork quilt across the bed in the corner. My cooking tools hung beneath the mantel of the fireplace on the side wall, and my pans and kettles lined the hearth, next to the woodbox. We had a food safe, and a washstand for our water bucket with its gourd dipper and our washbowl with its little dish of lye soap. Josh had made a chest of drawers for socks and linens. Our heavy clothes lay folded in the trunk at the foot of the bed, our winter blankets in another trunk beside the door under the row of wooden coat pegs. Yes, it was a cozy place, and when we sat down at the table in its center, we could proudly survey our whole domain.

Our garden flourished under the blazing summer sky. Early each morning I put on my sunbonnet and went out to hoe and weed my vegetables. As the heat and humidity rose, warm rivulets of sweat ran down my scalp beneath my bonnet, down my back until my dress was damp and clinging. Then I went inside to cook and clean and sew. Our little cabin blossomed under my loving hands.

One morning after breakfast Josh said, "Today I'm going to find a bee tree and lay in a good supply of honey for us. Then I'm going to do some trading. I heard about a farmer who needs another yoke of oxen. Maybe I can work out something with him."

I felt saddened as I watched Josh lead our oxen down the road. Those patient beasts had pulled us all the way from Shawneetown. They seemed like old friends who had shared hard times.

Just as I was starting supper, I heard him call, "Carrie, come outside!" My mouth flew open when I stepped through the door. There sat Josh, astride a fine chestnut horse. Behind him stood a milk cow, contemplating me with mournful brown eyes.

"What do you think of my horse?" he asked. Sitting tall and proud in the saddle, the sunlight glistening on his blond hair, he looked like a Teutonic prince.

"Oh, Josh, what a beauty! And a cow! Now we can have milk and cream and butter every day."

"That's not all I got for the oxen. He's going to give me a

dozen laying hens and a rooster as soon as I get a coop built. I'd better get to work right now.''

"Chickens, too! We'll have eggs enough to trade. I'm beginning to feel rich! We may not have much money, but we can trade for just about everything we need.''

Josh jumped down and fondly ran his hand along the horse's shining neck. "I want to make money, too. I want to buy land—as much as I can get my hands on. That's where the future is—in land.''

Unconsciously I shook my head. Sometimes his ambitions overwhelmed me. "I don't know when you'd find time to farm. You're always busy now, and so am I.''

"Well, I'm going to be busier for a while. I have to build a barn and a chicken coop and cut some rails to fence in our backyard. Then I'm going to build myself a workshop.''

He worked with his ax until dusk that night. After a late supper we carried our stools out into the yard. The sky was dark, lit only by a scattering of stars and a thin slice of pale-gold moon. The air smelled sweet and green; a peaceful hush hung over all the world. From the distance we could hear faint sounds of water bubbling over the dam.

I felt content, serene. And I had a secret it was time to share. "Josh?" I began, overcome by sudden shyness.

"Yes?"

"Well . . ." I swallowed and began again. "It may be a little early to be sure . . . but I think I might be in a family way.''

Silence.

"Josh, did you hear what I said?"

He took my hand and squeezed it tightly. "Yes . . . I'm just trying to take it in. Our baby . . . It's a kind of miracle, isn't it?"

I breathed out a long sigh and nodded. "I hope it's a boy—a tall blond boy who looks just like you."

"Either one is fine with me," he said, slipping his arm around me. Then he chuckled softly. "A boy would be nice, though—especially when he's old enough to heft an ax. I sure could use his help."

# Chapter 4

"Lucky" was the name of Josh's horse. "Couldn't have picked a better name myself," Josh said. "I was lucky to get him. Lucky in a lot of things since I came here."

The cow was "Missy," although I felt "Missus" might have been more appropriate for this dignified matron.

I didn't name the chickens. I just called them "chick, chick, chick," and they all came to me with their waddly little run, clucking impatiently until I tossed shelled corn and sunflower seeds to them. The hens quarreled over each grain as they scratched the ground and gobbled down their supper. They paid me back in eggs—more than we needed—and I used the extra eggs like money, trading them at Sam Hill's store for sugar and coffee and bacon.

One day in early October I carried two dozen eggs down to trade for coffee. As I turned to leave, an Indian walked into the store, followed by an Indian woman with a tiny baby on her back. Josh had told me there were still some Indians around. Scattered remnants of former tribes, they lived hidden back in the hills, coming into town at times to trade for the white man's treasures: an iron pot, a piece of calico, a bit of candy.

I stopped, fascinated by the copper-skinned trio. My heart raced as I stared from one pair of piercing black eyes to another. I had never been so close to Indians before. The man wore buckskin clothes and a necklace of strung claws. His face, with its leathery brown skin, hawklike nose, chisled cheekbones, and grave expression, seemed inscrutable to me. Should I be afraid? I wondered. My skin pricked up in icy goose bumps.

He laid four deer hides on the counter, while the woman held me in an unflinching gaze. She seemed as curious about my gingham frock and sunbonnet as I was about the beads and decorations on her short buckskin dress and moccasins.

"Help you, sir?" Sam Hill asked, his Yankee face as solemn as his customer's.

The Indian nodded silently and pointed to a keg of gunpowder.

I made a feeble attempt at a smile, then scurried out the door and down the road for home. All my life I had heard horror tales. Maybe these Indians were harmless—everybody said they were—but their presence nearby was just one more thing to disrupt my sleep at night.

Sleep had become elusive enough this past month. A greenish haze of nausea hung over me. Even the smell of food could send me into violent spasms of vomiting. Pregnancy did not agree with me.

Other women seemed to thrive on it. I saw them growing plump and rosy, still keeping up their endless chores—cooking, churning, gardening, spinning, weaving, sewing, chasing after broods of children.

My work too often lay neglected. And I was worried. I knew little about having babies. I was becoming gaunt as the odors from the food I cooked made me retch and retch, until nothing came but greenish bile.

The nausea soured my disposition, too. I complained to Josh, "These people here are really ignorant. Some of them can't even read. When Mentor Graham picks up his newspaper at the store, he stands outside and reads it to the others. Can you imagine not being able to read?"

"It's not that people are ignorant," Josh said, frowning impatiently. "They're plenty smart when it comes to trading or farming or inventing ways to solve their problems. But a lot of them never had a chance to go to school. Even now it's hard, with the school in session just three months a year. And people have to pay for every kid they send."

"I suppose they'll all grow up illiterate, too." My stomach cramped with nausea. "Our baby has to have a good education. I'll teach him myself at home if I have to . . . if I can find time, with all the work around here."

"There sure is a lot of work." He sighed. "At least I got the barn and gun shop built, Now I'll have time to hire out and help farmers with the harvest. Every dollar I earn is that much more for our savings. This winter I'm going to make some guns for Sam Hill to sell for me."

Hoping to quell another wave of nausea, I bit into a piece of dry corn bread. If I could only concentrate. "It's easy to save here," I said, "living off the land and trading for the other things we need. We seldom spend any money."

"We'll spend a lot when we buy a farm."

On Sunday afternoons, when I was able, Josh and I took long walks around the village and through the wooded path back to the schoolhouse. The forest flamed with autumn leaves, scarlet, gold, wine-red, and the slender tongues of orange sassafras. The rustle of our footsteps through the fallen leaves exhilarated me, and for a time, I was free from threats of a queasy stomach.

The days were getting shorter. In the evenings we sat beside our hearth fire, listening to the crackle of the flames as I knitted a shawl to wrap around the baby and Josh rubbed linseed oil on his gunstocks.

At times a nervous, fearful mood came over me. One evening I suddenly glanced up from my knitting and said in a quavering voice, "I hope I don't die when the baby's born."

Josh's jaw dropped. He stared at me in shock. "Carrie, don't even think things like that! You're young and healthy. You'll be fine."

I looked down at my thin arms and hands. "Do I look healthy to you? If my stomach stays upset much longer, there won't be anything left of me. I can't help worrying. My cousin Rose Ann died in childbirth . . . And you know there's no doctor here."

"There's a midwife in Clary's Grove."

"Granny Spears." I stared into the flames. "They say she was stolen by the Indians as a girl and learned the Indian healing ways. Herbs and salves and things. I don't know how much good they do."

"You'll be fine, Carrie. Just try to rest and take care of yourself. I'll help you with the heavy work."

I tried to absorb some of his unfailing optimism. "Mrs. Rutledge told me I'd feel better after the third month. She should know. She's had nine."

"And look how healthy she is," he said, nodding assuredly. "My mother had eleven, and she could work in the fields all day if she had to. Try not to worry about it. That can't be good for you."

My needles clicked again and I clenched my jaw tightly. Sure, it's easy for a man, I thought. How much harder for a woman, to sit helpless while events grip you, changing the familiar territory of your own body into something strange and threatening. I wished I knew more about what was going on inside me. Maybe if my sister had lived nearby, we could discuss these embarrassingly intimate details. I still felt a little like a foreigner among these hardy pioneers.

The next Saturday I had to ignore my queasiness long enough to walk to Sam Hill's store and trade for more yarn. As I strolled down the road, shouts and raucous laughter drifted from the grassy field near the bluff. The noise grew louder with each step I took.

People milled about outside the store. "It looks like everybody in the county is in town today," I said to a husky farm woman on the porch.

She grinned at me, her weathered skin crinkling. "Well, the young fellers like to get together for their fun on a Saturday afternoon. Just look at them down there—racin' and wrestlin' like there's no tomorrow. The Clary Grove boys and Sand Ridge boys and Island Grove boys—all havin' a big time today. Goin' to have a shootin' match later on, I hear."

"They seem awfully noisy to me."

She smiled indulgently. "Now, honey, keep your fur down. You know they work hard all week long. They deserve to whoop it up a little on Saturday."

"I suppose you're right," I muttered and stepped inside the store. "Sam, is there any mail for us?"

"Now, let me see. Yes, here's a letter from Ohio. That'll be twenty-five cents, please."

Twenty-five cents, just for a letter! I dug into my little bag, thinking that Josh worked all day harvesting for a dollar, or a dollar and a half. It seemed a crime so much of it must go for a letter. But, however reluctantly, I paid.

The letter was from my sister, Eliza. Everyone was fine, she wrote. She had gone to our cousin's wedding in late August and had worn a new gown of pale blue gauze, trimmed in satin of the same shade. Leg of mutton sleeves and flounces on the full skirt. She was quite the fashion plate that day. Papa was anxious for more news from us. Was our health holding up? He had enjoyed the description of our house-raising.

That letter, that little touch of home, brightened my whole day. As I tucked it in my bag, Sam Hill held up a bolt of cloth. "Just got in some new printed goods. Could I interest you in a dress length?"

"No, thanks, Sam. I'd just like to trade these eggs for yarn. Nothing else today."

While we made the trade, I scanned the dark shelves, crowded with enticing merchandise. The big white stoneware platter, the gleaming brass kettle, the spice mill—all beckoned to me, begged me to buy them. Most of all, I loved the handsome walnut mantel clock with little gold leaf rosettes painted on the glass door.

I turned from them and hurried out the door. No need to spend our precious money for things we can do without, I told myself. We'll have to make do and save our money for a farm.

* * *

The next week Sarah Graham invited me to an all-day quilting bee. I stayed home in the morning, adrift in a sea of nausea. It was after noon when I finally walked down to her big brick house just outside town. The quilt on the big frame in the center of the room showed evidence of a busy morning's work. A dozen thimbled hands were stitching nimbly, while a dozen women's mouths chattered without pause.

"Come on in, Carrie," Sarah called to me. "I was afraid you wouldn't make it." Her calm, warm voice, her pleasant smile, made me glad I'd come. After studying my face, she said, "You still look a little green. Could you be in a family way?"

I nodded, blushing. It hadn't stayed a secret long. Sarah's swelling belly told me she was in the same condition.

"Come sit by me," Ann Rutledge said. "Don't you like this quilt pattern? It's called 'bear paw.' "

"Oh, yes. You've made a lot of progress this morning." I pulled my thimble from my pocket and undid the threaded needle I had fastened to my dress front.

Ann's mother viewed me with a frown. "I'm goin' to bring you down some wild-cherry-bark tea to build up your blood. You look peaked, and you've lost a lot of flesh."

"I always use sassafras-root tea," Sarah said.

Another woman spoke up. "If she's got the mornin' sickness, she should make a tea with a bit of oats."

"Down home we use columbo root and chamomile flowers. Just sip some now and then, whenever the sick feelin' comes."

With that, the women began a conversation that continued all afternoon. They knew a cure for every disease of man and beast. The air bubbled with talk of poultices and salves and teas made from all kinds of leaves and roots.

Personally I thought the remedies sounded too gentle to do much good. Our Cincinnati doctors relied on a harsh regime of bleeding and purging. Of course, their patients often said the cure was worse than the disease.

"How did you learn all that?" I asked the women. "How do you remember which herb cures which sickness?"

"We learned it just the way you're learning now—by hearin' other folks tell about them."

Sarah pointed emphatically at me. "Now, when your baby starts to come, you make sure somebody puts an ax under your bed and a knife under your pillow. That'll cut the pain."

Her remark opened a discussion of all the possible complications of childbirth. On and on the women talked, engrossed in their dramatic tales of horror. Breech births and hemorrhages. Cords wrapped around babies' necks. I listened until their voices seemed to blur and new waves of nausea swept over me.

I ran outside and retched in the yard until I was weak and trembling. The sour smell of vomit made me retch again. Some women followed me out, still giving advice, but I could only hear the roaring in my head.

Sarah took my arm and gently led me back inside. Murmuring soft words, she helped me to her bed, where I lay down gratefully and closed my eyes. All the while the world spun madly.

Tears welled up in my eyes, as weakness and despair

blanketed me. I was ashamed. This was a sorry way for a frontier wife to behave.

Last May I had been a joyous bride, eager to begin the long trip west, my mind filled with thoughts of romance and adventure. But now, just five months later, I was thin and sick, too weak to clean my house or cook for Josh.

Sarah tiptoed to the bedside. "Here's some sassafras tea. Just take a few sips, honey. You'll feel better."

"Thanks," I murmered, struggling to sit up.

"I'll have Mentor drive you home in the wagon, and I'll send along some stew, so you won't have to cook tonight."

I took a cautious sip of tea and lay back. "You're so good to me."

"Well, Carrie, you're a young girl, and you're a long way from your family at a time when a body needs a family most. We'll just have to be your family now."

Her kind words brought a flood of tears streaming down my cheeks. I felt foolish. Pregnancy seemed to control my emotions as well as my body.

The sassafras tea must have helped, for the next day I felt a little better. Gradually, day by day, the nausea faded. By the end of a week, I could bake and cook a proper meal again.

Neglected chores surrounded me. "Josh, if you'll bring me enough water for the big kettle, I'll wash clothes today," I said one morning as he came in from milking.

Outside, the sun shone amber through the trees, all trimmed in their flamboyant autumn colors. I dug through the mantle of fallen leaves for kindling, and my fire was crackling merrily by the time Josh returned from the well.

He hung the big iron kettle over the flames and filled it with water.

I sliced some lye soap into the water and, after it had dissolved, added a big pile of dirty clothes and linens. No time for sickness now, I told myself. I threw more logs on the fire, and the water soon began to bubble. As I stirred with my long-handled paddle, I daydreamed, looking up to watch the flocks of wild geese flying south. Their urgent cries seemed to call to me, begging me to fly away with them to new exotic lands.

The clop of Lucky's hooves broke through my dreaming as Josh rode up. "Look at what I got for that repair job this morning." He jumped down and lifted a large brown crock from his bulging saddlebag. "Apple butter. And here's some eating apples, and a ham, and a big venison roast." His voice rang proudly as he laid out his prizes.

"That's a good morning's work," I said, smiling at the boyish expression on his face. "It looks like enough food for a week."

"He wants me to help him pick corn for two or three days, too. That's cash money."

Josh was always busy these days, but he seemed to thrive on it. Since he had finished his shop and small forge behind the house, the rythmic clanging of his hammer accompanied my daily chores. Besides his gun work, he repaired plows and kettles and kitchen utensils and did a score of other minor blacksmithing jobs. People usually paid him in goods: garden produce, pork and lard, cornmeal, or homespun yarn. We got our wooden tub and bucket that way, and some soft sun-bleached flannel I was saving to make baby gowns.

I let the fire die and the lumpy, soapy mass of wash

cool down. Then, one by one, I rubbed each piece between my hands, then rinsed and wrung them all again. By this time, my arms and back and shoulders were tired and painful.

But the clothes looked and smelled so clean, I glowed with pride when I hung them on the fence to dry. There's no smell quite as fresh and sweet as clean clothes with the sun's warmth clinging to them.

"Hey, Carrie! Looks like you're feeling better," Sarah Graham called to me from the road, as I laid the last dish towel across the fence.

"Yes, thank heavens. You're looking well, too. Out for a walk this lovely afternoon?"

She came into the side yard and sat down on a stump near me. "I'm just going down to the store to see if we have any mail. Mentor gets riled at Sam Hill, 'cause he always serves whiskey to the men before he waits on the ladies. But Sam is the postmaster, and that's the only store in town. Guess we don't have much choice but to trade with him."

"He has some nice things down there. Someday I'd like to have that big walnut mantel clock."

"Someday you'll have it, honey. Your man's a worker, like mine. He'll do all right. You know, I'm just thankful to have a store so handy. When we first came here, the closest store was in Springfield. I tell you, it was a welcome sight when I saw them laying out the town lots."

"I'd say you're really lucky your farm is just outside town. The women who live farther out don't get into town much."

Sarah turned and looked out to the west, to the boundless prairie. "It's a lonesome life, and that's the truth. Not everybody is cut out for it. I've heard tell of women going mad from loneliness." She rose with a long sigh. "Guess I'd better get on down to Sam's."

"Do you feel all right, Sarah?" I asked hesitantly. "I mean, you still feel like walking and doing all your work around the house?"

"Oh, I slow down some when I'm expecting, but I keep up with chores. You just have morning sickness. When are you expecting, hon?"

"Not till next April. How about you?"

"I guess this one will be a Christmas present. We're hoping for a boy this time."

I chewed my lower lip nervously. There were a hundred questions I wanted to ask her. About having babies. About the changes taking place in my body. About the spots of blood. But my shyness held me back. A lifetime of prohibitions was ingrained in me. One didn't mention body functions. My stepmother had taught me well.

When I get to know these women better, I thought, maybe then I'll ask about what I need to know. All my fine education and reading didn't teach me the things these unschooled women learn at quilting bees when they're still young girls.

I shook my head regretfully as I watched Sarah walk on down the road.

The next Saturday afternoon the men held another shooting match. Josh seldom missed one. "It's not just a chance to show off my shooting," he told me. "I can demonstrate the kind of rifle I build. Those two guns I made brought a good price at the store."

"What's the prize for the match?"

"It's a beef again. The first four places win quarters of beef, and the fifth place gets the hide and tallow. Maybe I'll win all the prizes, like last time." His mouth curved in a boyish grin.

"And we'll lead the steer home on a rope."

Shortly after noon we ambled down to the spot deep in the woods where the matches were held. A crowd was gathering. Men nodded solemnly to Josh, then dropped an envious glance to the fine long rifle at his side.

I could feel the anticipation stirring in the air as I walked toward a group of women sitting along the side. Ann Rutledge smiled and waved to me. "Hi, Carrie. Sit by me. Feeling better now?"

"Yes, a little better. A person doesn't have time to be sick around here."

"Now, isn't that the truth of it?"

Twenty men or more had paid the entry fee and were waiting for their five allotted shots. They were all smiling, trying to look casual, but their eyes shone with the raw gleam of competition.

The shoot moved slowly; no man would be hurried. Everyone craved to be the best. One by one, with great deliberation, each stepped up to the mark, some sixty feet away from the target.

In his turn Josh inhaled deeply and faced the target with his slender Kentucky rifle, that long and awkward-looking weapon. He loaded his gun with meticulous care, each movement refined to an art. First, he measured the powder from a scraped translucent horn and delicately placed it in the charger. Then he poured the charge into the muzzle and gave a few light taps. Next he laid a greased patch across the muzzle, forced in the lead bullet, and rammed it into place with the hickory ramrod. What a theatrical production it was!

Finally, the gun was loaded. Josh took his place, cocked the gun, aimed, and pulled the trigger. The audience jumped. The blast seemed deafening after the long, tense silence of the preparations.

Josh won the first two places in the match. He was brimming with pride. "Two hind quarters of beef! Well, Carrie, how do you like that?"

"It's great!" I said, my smile as broad as his, "You make it look so easy."

"We'll trade off one quarter, and I'll dry the other, Indian style. We'll be eating these winnings all winter."

High-spirited, laughing at our good fortune, we strolled back home amid a shower of falling leaves. The woods looked wide and open now, as the trees shed the last of their brilliant autumn garments. Squirrels chattered to us from the highest branches, and the scent of leaves and wood smoke drifted on the gentle breeze. But as we neared our cabin, nestled snugly beneath the spreading maples, a sudden chill in the breeze whispered of winter coming on.

By morning the sky was swollen, the color of lead bullets. Finally, a slow, mournful drizzle began that lasted for days. The cabin was dark, with a dampness that clung to walls and furniture despite the blazing hearth fire.

My spirits clouded like the dreary weather. I was sick again. It seemed I couldn't bounce through pregnancy unscathed, as these other women did. Perhaps I was just not strong enough.

From the bottom of my trunk I pulled forth the blue-lacquered jewelry case, and with trembling hands, I lifted out my mother's cameo. Sinking down on the side of the bed, I stared at the lovely profile on the brooch.

Had my mother looked like this? I strained to recall her face. It seemed unbearable that I could not remember.

Overhead, thick wooden shingles muffled the gentle weeping of the rain. Out in the gun shop Josh's hammer clanged an echo to the labored pulsing of my heart. A mist, like silvered fog, hung in the dark corners of the room. I blinked aside the tears that clouded my eyes.

Well, Mama, I thought, wherever you are, I hope you can hear me. I have a big surprise for you. Come April, you're going to be a grandma.

# Chapter 5

Cold rains began to fall again a few days before Christmas. I stirred the fire constantly, trying to coax more heat and light into our damp cabin.

"I'm afraid the cold is really settling in now," I said, clutching my shawl closer to my shoulders and pulling my new rocker near the fire. Josh had just made the rockers, two of them, from burnished maple. Once settled, I reached for my brown wool and needles from the wicker basket at my side and took up where I had left off last night, knitting heavy socks for Josh.

He sat down in the other rocker and ran his hands along the satin-smooth arms. "When I finish the gun I'm working on, I'm going to start a new project. I've just enough cherry wood to make a cradle."

Our smiles met with shared anticipation. "It's hard to wait so long," I said. "I want to see what the baby looks like. I can't wait to hold him and rock him and dress him in the little gowns I've made. And I want to be done with all this sickness."

He gazed at me intently. "You're feeling better now, aren't you?"

An instant's hesitation came before my silent nod. I was embarrassed to tell him of the spots of blood that sometimes stained my underclothes. Anyway, what would a man know of such things? I knew so little myself about these mysterious female problems.

I looked about the cabin and its sprinkling of homemade Christmas decorations—a wreath of milkweed pods and bittersweet, and some paper stars I'd made and hung above the mantel. Next year I'll be feeling better, I thought. I'll decorate the whole house with bright, shining things to make the baby's eyes sparkle.

The chill in the air steadily grew harsher and more cutting until the day before Christmas, when I awoke early and pulled back the curtain to see a strange and unfamiliar world. It was snowing, huge flakes covering everything with thick white frosting.

That evening Lucky picked his way around the snow drifts as we drove the wagon down to celebrate Christmas Eve at the Rutledge Inn. A group of neighbors had congregated there, the Onstots and Asbells, Camrons, John McNeil, and all the Rutledges. Ann was bringing out her dulcimer to play for us when we heard the stomp of boots out on the porch. The door flew open, and a blast of frigid air invaded us as a red-cheeked Sam Hill hurried inside.

"The population of Sangamon County has just increased by one," he announced, warming his hands before the crackling fire. "Mentor Graham stopped by the store and said his wife had a baby boy. Black headed, he said. Great big eyes, like Sarah's."

"A Christmas baby!" Beaming broadly, Mrs. Rutledge

handed Sam a cup of mulled cider. "Now, that's something really special, isn't it?"

Ann began to strum the dulcimer. Her father stood and boomed out the first words of "Deck the Halls," waving his hands exultantly until we all joined in the singing.

I thought of Cincinnati. I could see Papa leading us in singing carols, his rich baritone carrying above our light sopranos. My sister Eliza's rosy cheeks, her blue eyes gleaming over crystal cups of fragrant spiced wine punch. The smell of crisp fresh popcorn as we strung it for the tree, the crunch between my teeth as I bit into kernels of it. The strong, clean scent of pine wreaths, beeswax candles glowing with a steady, smokeless flame.

All through that evening, I ached with memories of Christmases long past. Papa, Eliza, Lydia. Somehow they seemed more real to me than the people at the Rutledges'.

The next day, Christmas, dawned cold and white and clammy. I rose early, dug down in the trunk, and brought out the heavy checked wool shirt I had made for Josh with cloth from traded eggs. "Merry Christmas, dear," I said, kissing his forehead as I handed it to him.

He wore a broad smile as he slipped it on. "Umm, nice and warm. Just the thing for days like this. I have a surprise for you, too."

A gust of wind blew a thin sprinkling of snow over the floor, like sugar on a doughnut, as he opened the door to go outside. When he returned, he handed me a gift—the big stoneware platter I had seen in Sam Hill's store. A warm glow filled me as I traced my finger lovingly around the pattern on its surface—a delicate scene with castle and trees, a tiny boat on a pond—all in ginger brown on white. When I placed the platter on the mantelpiece and stood back to admire it, a lump formed in my throat. "Oh, Josh, it's beautiful."

Our first Christmas dinner was a sumptuous affair. We had wild turkey, corn bread dressing, sweet potatoes, and pumpkin pudding for dessert. But again I thought of Cincinnati. I just knew they were preparing a lavish dinner at home, with Eliza humming carols as she set the table and Papa carving turkey or ham. Candles would be shimmering in silver holders, casting soft and gentle light throughout the dining room—a room as big as our whole cabin here. How far away Cincinnati seemed that day.

And Josh's family. Did Josh get homesick, too? Who would ever know? He kept his feelings under lock and key.

Shrill shouts of children's voices outside brought me to the window after dinner. Two little boys, looking plump in their layers of heavy clothes, were building a snowman in an empty lot nearby. Their shrieks of glee rang through the icy air, their eyes gleamed above red-apple cheeks. Another boy, carrying a wide greased board, called to them, "Come, go sledding with me!"

"Only children can enjoy this weather," I said, as Josh came in with still another load of firewood.

"I like the cold myself. It's invigorating!" The logs dropped into the woodbox in the corner with a heavy thud.

But even Josh got sick of the snow that kept falling day after day. By New Year's Eve the stuff was three feet deep. The world looked strange, a huge uncharted sea of white, beneath a leaden sky. Few people passed by our house now, and those who did resembled snowmen, with white frosting covering their hats and bulky coats.

On New Year's Day a gale blew down from the north. It rained, chilled, and then froze to form a thick crust on the snow. The winds continued, and the rain changed to snow. It snowed and snowed, white flakes blowing sideways in the winds. Drift on drift piled up, carving fanciful shapes against each windbreak.

The temperature fell. Day after day the blizzard continued. Day after day I stood by my frosted window and watched my little world become entombed.

Keeping the chickens' water from freezing was a major problem. Three times a day I braved the cold to place heated rocks beneath their water tray and to collect the eggs before they froze.

January crept along painfully. "Phew! It's almost twenty below zero!" Josh slammed the door behind him when he came home from the store one day. Face blue and pinched from cold, he hung up his coat and went to the fire. Never once did he look at me.

"Were there any other people at the store? It seems so long since I've seen anyone." Seated in my rocker, I had been trying to knit, struggling to hold the needles firm in my stiff, icy fingers.

He stared into the flames and rubbed his hands together slowly. "Oh . . . a few."

"Who was it? Was there any news?"

"News? Oh . . . nothing much," he mumbled in a strained and husky tone. His chin was buried in his collar as he poked at the fire.

"What is it, Josh? Tell me," I pleaded. "I know there's something wrong."

His gaze lifted, pained and questioning. He opened his mouth to speak, then stopped and cleared his throat. "The Grahams' baby died."

My breath seemed suspended as I sank slowly back into

my chair. A numbing wave of hurt washed over me. Instinctively my hand dropped to clasp my swollen belly.

I struggled to speak. "Poor little thing . . . born in this blizzard." I could see that unknown baby clearly in my mind with his big eyes, like Sarah's, blue as the morning glories outside her door. He'd had thick dark hair, someone had said. Tears welled up in my eyes.

"They're going to bury him tomorrow." Josh was speaking quickly now. "A bunch of us are going to the cemetery tonight to build a fire on the snow. By morning the ground should be thawed enough to dig the grave."

"Oh, Josh . . ." My hand held my belly tightly. I felt devastated, as if Sarah's loss were my own.

"Don't think about it. It's not good for you," he said in a taut voice.

"That tiny baby, out there in the cold . . ." My tears spilled over and traced hot lines down my cheeks.

"Don't talk about it anymore. Sometimes babies just aren't strong enough to live. The cemetery's full of babies . . . kids of all ages. It's part of this life, Carrie. We have to learn to live with it."

I turned away from him and wiped my eyes. Sucking in a deep breath, I tried to knit again with shaking hands, but my mind was whirling. Josh, Josh, I thought, what about our baby? How can you help but wonder if we'll ever see him walk and talk and smile at us? What are the limits of your granite strength?

The days crawled by, a dull monotonous dirge of cold. The sky was low and swollen; arctic winds blew relentlessly across the prairie. At night we lay in bed under a mountain of blankets and coats and shawls, hot bricks wrapped in towels down by our feet. We stared into the darkness, listening to the howling gale outside. It seemed an insane monster, intent on shaking our house from its foundation. It whistled around the doors and windows, crept down the chimney, slid past the fire to chill each pan and plate and piece of furniture.

Mornings, we dressed beneath the blankets, our breath puffing out in frosty clouds of white. It took a special kind of heroism just to climb out of bed.

"Did anybody ever warn you about these Illinois winters?" I asked Josh one freezing morning, unable to hide the bitterness in my voice. "Did you know what we were getting into?"

"This is the worst winter they've ever had around there," he said, calmly. "Everybody says so. The farmers have always left their cattle in the fields all winter. Now they have to dig in the snow all day just to find enough corn for a few days' feed."

"I don't care about the cattle. It's the people—you and me—I'm thinking of." I thought of Sarah's baby boy. "Do you think we could go down to the Grahams'? I never even got to pay my respects. It's been so long since I've seen them . . . or anyone."

"Well . . . I guess the snow on the road is fairly beaten down." I could see he was anxious to please me. "I'll hitch up Lucky and we'll try out the new sleigh I made."

After wrapping myself in several shawls and sweaters and draping myself in my long woolen cloak, I stepped out into the silent white world. Nothing looked familiar. Outbuildings were buried, forming exotic shapes. They looked like temples of the Orient, their snow roofs sparkling like opals.

Snow began to fall again as we drove outside town toward the Grahams' house. Feathery drifts shook from the trees and flew through the air like little white birds. I pulled my hood up closer to my face.

Mentor's dogs announced our arrival, and he met us at the door. He smiled wanly, a haze of hurt lingering in his eyes. "Such a winter!" he said, as we stepped inside. "I've been here since twenty-six and I've never seen the likes of it. I hear the inn is filled with stranded travelers."

We pulled off our boots, and in our stocking feet, followed him over to the fire. "How are your cattle faring?" Josh asked.

Mentor pulled an extra chair up to the fireside. "I've enough feed for a while. A fellow wonders how long this can last."

Don't they think of anything but cattle? I wondered. Then I sensed the abnormal quiet in the house. "Can I see Sarah? Is she lying down?"

"Yes." Mentor looked forlorn. "She's been doing poorly since we lost the baby. I'm glad you've come to visit, Carrie. It will do her good."

When he led me into the bedroom, I tried to hide my shock at the sight of Sarah. Her wide blue eyes, usually so clear and vivacious, stared blankly at the wall. Her face looked gaunt, her cheekbones jutted sharply beneath shrunken, pallid flesh. A faint sour smell of sickness clung to her.

"Sarah," I said, taking her listless hand in mine. "I'm so sorry I couldn't come sooner. The weather kept me . . . but I've been thinking about you every day."

She turned to me, her eyes questioning, trying to focus through some inner fog. "Carrie?" Her chest heaved with a deep cough.

"Yes, it's me, Sarah. I've finally come to visit you. It's the first time I've been out for a month."

She coughed again. A bone-thin hand lifted and absently wiped her mouth. Her labored breathing echoed in the chilled air of the room. She spoke slowly, as if in a trance. "My baby died. My baby boy. He was so frail. The wind just blew and blew. I held him close to keep him warm. But he died. He's gone."

Overcome with sympathy, fighting back my tears, I put my arms around her and felt her trembling. "Oh, Sarah, I'm so sorry."

She lay stiffly, staring at the wall behind me, at the cross-stitched sampler hanging there. Her face was so pale against her dark hair. "My baby died. My baby boy."

I sat with her for a long while, speaking of many things, trying to pull her from the quicksand of her loss.

Later we drove home, our heads bent against the sting of the blowing snow and the prairie winds. I sat silent on the sleigh seat, full of dread. My secret fear had been that I might die when my baby was born. Now I faced the chilling truth of the other danger. I might lose the baby.

Those days the fire blazing on our hearth was never adequate. When I set the table, the plates and cups and forks were slabs of ice. Mornings, we woke to find the water in the pitcher by our washbowl frozen over. What did it matter? Washing only irritated my chapped hands and face.

Out in the barn the animals huddled together, munching icy bites of hay, looking up with doleful eyes when Josh went out to tend them.

Josh and I holed up like two bears in a cave. No one came to see us. The world outside loomed frozen and forbidding, and inside, there was only Josh and me. I wanted a woman to talk to. The blood, the spotting—was it normal? God, I knew so little about having babies. If only I could talk to

Granny Spears or Mrs. Rutledge . . . I longed so much to have a healthy baby, many babies. The need in me was deep and basic, as for food and water.

All I could do now was wait and try to endure the cold and isolation.

Then the wolves began to howl close to the house. One night I woke abruptly, torn from my dreams by their mournful plaint. Despite the cold I broke out in a sweat. I drew close to Josh's side, shivering as the howls continued, monstrous and threatening.

"Damn wolves," Josh muttered, his voice hard and angry. "I don't know why they should be howling. They're not going hungry. They eat all the deer caught in the drifts, and I know they've eaten frozen cattle."

At first their cries came from far off, but each night they seemed a little closer. It sounded like a pack of them, maybe a dozen, howling with agonizing hunger. I lay awake and trembled as the wails carried through the dark and icy night.

Later the howls seemed to come from our own yard, out near the barn. Josh jumped out of bed and grabbed his rifle from its antler-holder above the door. After loading it, he opened the back door, aimed, and fired in the direction of the howls.

A sharp yelp cut the frozen night, followed by an unearthly silence.

I began to shake. As he crawled back into bed, my shivering changed to heaving, convulsive sobs.

"Now, Carrie, it's all right. The wolves are gone now." he said, slipping his arm around me.

But still I sobbed. "Oh, Josh, can't you see I'm freezing to death? It's been months since I've seen the sun, and I never see any people. We're all alone here."

He patted my heaving shoulders. "Just hang on a little longer, Carrie. It's almost the first of February. Just a few more weeks till spring. You'll feel better then."

"I don't think I can last till spring. Look at me! I'm thinner than I've ever been, and with a baby coming, too! I'm afraid."

His arms enfolded me. "You'll be all right, Carrie. You'll be fine," he murmured.

I laid my head against his chest, but I felt little comfort. "Next winter we'll have to go through all this again."

"No. No. Everybody says this is the worst winter they've ever seen. Next year will be better. And next year you'll have the baby to keep you company."

If I live through the birth, I thought. And if my baby does.

I tossed about until dawn, thinking of the pack of wolves still roaming outside somewhere. Then, finally, I resigned myself. This is the frontier, after all, I thought. No place for weaklings. Did I expect fine homes and hired girls to do the washing? I'd just have to make the best of things.

In the morning, after breakfast, Josh dressed himself in extra layers of woolen clothes. "I'm going hunting. People may be running short of meat. I can probably sell some game and pick up extra cash."

"It's cold. It's just too cold to be outside." I stared down at my cracked and bleeding hands and began to clear the breakfast table.

"I won't be long. I might as well get the game before the wolves take all of it." He waved and left the house.

I cleared a spot in the frost on the window and watched as he dragged the dead wolf from our yard into the woods behind. The beast, with its matted, dirty fur and daggerlike incisors, was ferocious looking even in death.

Before he left Josh brought in a kettleful of snow to melt for water and made two trips in from the log pile. "There. That should keep you in firewood. I'll be back by noon."

Long rifle in hand, he started off, struggling through the high drifts, lifting his long legs and sinking into the snow with every step.

I made the bed and swept the hearth and reluctantly endured the sting of water on my sore hands as I washed the dishes. I put a pot of bean soup on to cook. Then I sat down by the fire and began to embroider a tiny christening gown. Several times I stopped to stir the soup. The fire devoured log after log, but still the chill hung in the house. The air itself seemed white and frosted.

The day dragged on, its winter silence broken only by the crackle of the fire and the gurgle of the soup. The rich aroma of beans and bacon drifted slowly through the room. I knew that it was long past noon. Josh had always seemed invulnerable, but now I began to worry. Time after time I walked to the window and scraped away the ice to peer at the arctic world outside. Where was he? How could anyone survive for long out in this cruel weather? Maybe he had fallen. Maybe the wolves had found him and taken their revenge.

He must surely be dead, alone out there in the cold, I thought. With trembling hands, I pulled my shawl closer to my shoulders as a cutting chill ran up my spine. How long should I wait? Where could I go for help? But, of course, he would be back. Yes, any minute now I would hear him stomping the snow off his boots out on the step.

I added water to the soup and stirred it, grateful for the bit of activity. The beans simmered in their pinkish liquid, thick, hot, and fragrant. Then, as I reached for wood to feed the fire again, I saw that I was down to the last log. I knew I must brave the cold myself to bring in more wood.

My boots and mittens, shawl and cloak, seemed poor protection from the icy blasts of wind that whipped around the house when I stepped outside. I thought again of Josh, walking for hours in this cold. The few steps to the woodpile seemed like miles. Ice had glued the logs together, and I struggled to separate enough for an armful. As quickly as possible, I gathered what I could, and then started running back to the house. The cold air made even breathing painful.

Clumsily I hurried up the frozen path. Just as I reached the door, my feet slipped out from under me on the icy stoop. I fell forward—hard—right on the pile of logs.

"Oh, God!" I cried in agony, when the sharp wooden edges jabbed against my swollen stomach. The bitter sting of cold gave me strength to rise and kick the logs away, so I could close the door.

And then I felt something warm and sticky ooze down my legs. I moaned and went to the bed, pulling off my mittens and throwing them down with my cloak. A thin trail of bright red blood followed me across the room.

"Josh, where are you? Please come home," I pleaded, as I crawled into bed. Giant hands seemed to seize my midsection, tearing me apart. I was losing so much blood.

The baby! Oh, no, it couldn't be the baby. Just some blood, that's all. I had lost blood before. It was nothing. My pulse was racing, pounding hard against my temples. A roaring in my head kept rhythm with the beating of my heart. Something inside me gave way, and blood began to pour from me.

The room spun around me as I pulled myself up and stumbled to the chest to get some towels. Then bending over clumsily, I pulled the chamber pot from beneath the bed. I nearly fell as I sat down on it. I leaned against the side of the bed and listened to the deafening roar in my head. Cramps, the worst I'd ever felt, tore at me. The world was reduced to pain and pounding heart and roaring head. My body had a being and a purpose of its own.

I lost my baby in a flood of blood and matter. It was too horrible to comprehend. Our longed-for baby, the firstborn of our family, heir to Josh's family name and trade. And there he lay, covered with blood, in the bottom of the chamber pot. Trembling, I stared down at his tiny head, his minature fingers clenched into a fist.

I struggled into bed and stuffed towels against my body to quell the hemorrhage. The roaring in my head grew louder. I was too weak even to cry. My eyes were dry and gritty and cold as the room around me.

The roaring slowly faded, and the dizzy swirl dissolved into a pool of black.

I drifted in and out of consciousness as the hours crept by. The fire died and the cold was now complete. I lay there, too weak to care, imprisoned in a world of ice.

At last the door opened. I raised my leaded eyelids and gazed up to see a stranger who vaguely resembled Josh. But this man's lips were huge and blue, his eyes squinted with a tortured look of pain.

He eased himself into a chair and began to stomp his feet, beating his hands against his knees. Then he lifted up his hands and blew on them.

"I got lost," he said, his voice thin, his swollen lips barely moving. "Everything looked so different . . . Snow blowing . . . Drifts so high . . . Couldn't tell which direction I was going . . . Don't know how I ever found my way home."

He bent his stiffened fingers around the poker handle and

stirred the ashes until a few embers began to glow. He looked over at me, frowning. "What's wrong? Are you sick? Why didn't you throw those logs on the fire?"

Suddenly alert, he rose. "My God, that's blood on the floor!" With a few steps he was over by the bed, staring down at me.

I looked up through a haze of weakness. Josh stood there, tall and bulky in his heavy clothes, silhouetted in the dim light. I could hear his labored breathing, and the crackle of the fire as it caught life again. The smell of beans and bacon lingered in the air.

As we looked at each other, a single tear rolled down my face. I forced myself to speak. "I lost our baby."

# Chapter 6

Every day for a week afterward my good New Salem neighbors dropped by with pots of food and pans of bread and soothing words of understanding. I survived my loss, as people do, and yet I knew I would never be the same. I felt older now, and scarred. The whole world was a harsher, crueler place.

In early March the snow began to melt. The river raged, tossing about chunks of ice and uprooted trees like straws. For weeks we listened to its angry roar. Outside our door the yard lay wet and swollen, a sea of oozing mud. In the road a layer of hard-packed ice lingered long after all the snow was gone.

"Would you believe it? Two whole days of sunshine!" Josh said one morning, as he came in from milking. The boots he left beside the door were caked halfway up with mud.

I smiled. I think it was the first time I had smiled since Christmas. "Today would be a good time to start catching up with my work. Maybe I'll wash out a few things."

He hung a rope across the room for me, and all day I ducked around the line of dripping clothes. I didn't mind. The washing seemed a welcome return to normalcy. I must try to put aside my loss, to think about the chores, cooking and cleaning. I must not think about the baby . . . those tiny, tiny hands . . .

By now the road out front looked like a busy highway. Country people battled the mud to go do their trading and, especially, to see other human beings. Their faces were thin and deathly pale, portraits of the ravages of winter.

Spring sunshine brought back warmth and hope. I lingered in the yard to feel its healing hands upon my face and shoulders. As I listened to the birds singing in the treetops, I sensed the stirring of life in the fertile soil around me. Soon the mud would disappear. Soon the wildflowers would blossom once again.

Josh came and stood beside me. "Well, we made it through that beastly winter, Carrie," he said softly. "Things will be better now."

"I saw some green leaves on the bushes in the woods. Maybe spring is really here to stay."

"Why don't you walk down to the store with me? It will do you good to do some visiting there."

The walk was tiring. The thick mud seemed to suck on my booted feet with every step. I had to lift my skirts and walk over to the side of the road, fearful that each passing horse would splatter me with muck. As we approached the store, however, the pleasant drone of mingled voices made the trip seem worthwhile.

Mentor and Sarah waved to us from the porch outside the store. Sarah's eyes met mine in a bond of shared loss.

Josh surveyed the throng of people milling around the store. "Looks like Sam's doing a booming business today."

"I don't know how many are buying things, and how many just want to get out and see their neighbors," Mentor said, a grin warming his angular features.

The sound of human voices was like music to me. Enthralled, I listened to snatches of conversation.

"Powwow days. That's what the Indians called this time of year. They always held war councils in the spring."

"Law me! Almost time to take my spring bath and change these scratchy wool duds for tow cloth."

"Makes a body feel just like a butterfly leavin' the cocoon."

"Did y'hear tell we're fixin' to get another store? Yep. Them Herndon brothers raisin' the cabin down the road— they're fixin' to build a store right soon."

"Don't see how a body can build anything in this mud. Can't even get my garden in."

"Say, y' lose many cattle last winter?"

"Yep, a heap. Illinois is mighty hard on cattle."

Under my breath, I muttered, "Illinois is hard on women and babies, too."

Sarah looked at me, nodding solemnly.

Just then, a hardy-looking farm wife stepped up on the porch. She carried a year-old baby boy, a knitted shawl wrapped around his legs.

"My, how that little feller's growed!" The neighbors oohed and aahed.

I stared at the baby, my breath caught in my throat, as a flood of grief washed over me. My arms ached to hold that little body close. I lowered my head and clenched my hands, struggling to fight back the tears.

"You have to be strong, Carrie," Sarah said firmly, holding my arm.

"I can't." The words choked through my locked jaws. My eyes pleaded for her understanding.

"You must. It's the only way a woman can survive."

Days passed slowly. The mud began to dry, but the river still was high and swollen.

One day in the middle of April Josh stuck his head in the door and called to me, "There's a flatboat hung up on the milldam. Want to walk down and see it?"

"Sure," I answered. I needed an excuse to get out of the house for a while.

The road was jammed with people scurrying down to the river, chattering with circuslike excitement. By the time we got there, the whole side of the bluff had filled with spectators of the little drama being played out below.

A long flatboat, loaded with live hogs and barrels of cargo, was stuck tight on the dam. The front of it hung over, raised up in the air, as the back slowly filled with water. Three young men and an older one all labored mightily to unload the cargo on the bank before the boat sank.

"Did ya ever see an ark in such a fix?" the man beside us asked.

"Would you look at that tall kid?" Josh said, laughing. "He looks like he was chopped out with an ax and needs a jack plane taken to him."

The man guffawed. "Made for wadin' in high water, that one was."

The rawboned, gangly youth they spoke of stood a head taller than the men around him. His outlandish arms and legs dangled from ill-fitting homemade clothes. His movements were clumsy, yet he heaved the full barrels with great strength.

Shouts of advice and encouragement rang from the crowd along the banks as the men continued to unload the cargo. Finally the tall youth called out, "Anybody up there got an auger?"

"The cooper's likely got one," an onlooker answered.

The youth jumped off the boat and disappeared up the hill with the man. When they returned, he bored a hole in the stern, and we all watched as the water slowly drained out. Then he plugged the hole with a piece of wood, and the crew eased the boat over the dam.

A wild burst of applause rang from the audience. Cheers and shouts and laughter filled the brisk April air.

The crew then poled the flatboat to the bank and came ashore to reload their cargo.

"Dennis Offutt's the name," the older man said in a bold and earthy voice. "I'm the owner of this boat, and I'd sure like to thank you folks for your help."

Someone called out, "And who's that long tall drink of water? He's the hero of the day."

"This here's Abe Lincoln. He's one smart boy, he is."

As Offutt and his crew started up the hill toward town, I looked again at the ungainly homely youth. When he passed, I saw his eyes—a deep, dreamy gray. His was a face you would not soon forget.

The men spent the rest of the day in New Salem. "Fine town you got here!" Offutt repeated several times as he walked about. "Place has real possibilities, what with the river and all."

"We're growing fast," Jim Rutledge said, radiant with pride.

Offutt's words came faster now, loud and enthusiastic. "Won't be long till steamboats will be coming up the Sangamon. Bet I could build a boat with rollers to get over the shoals. Might even put on runners and use it on the ice. Yes, sir, this country's openin' up so fast it makes my head swim!"

The citizens of New Salem beamed.

"When I get back from New Orleans, I think I'll build a store here," Offutt announced. "Young Abe can help me run it." With that, he and his men boarded the flatboat and continued their journey.

The old settlers said the fruit trees were three weeks late in blossoming that spring, but finally the fields and gardens were dry enough to be plowed. The air rang with the "gee-haw" of ox drivers turning up the rich black earth. The pungent scent of fertile soil hung over the land. Out in our barn lot, newly hatched chicks cheeped frantically as they scurried after the mama hen.

Helping Josh plant seeds in our big garden, I felt a new serenity, a sense of oneness with nature. I paused to look at the woods, blossoming now with redbud and wild cherry trees. Wildflowers—white Dutchman's breeches, violets, pink phlox, and lavender sweet Williams—bloomed beneath them.

"Josh, can we plant flax this year?" I asked. "I'd like to make some linen."

"Sure. I was planning to get a few sheep, too. We can always use the wool."

"We're going to have a farm right here in town!"

He nodded eagerly. "Yes, and pretty soon we'll have enough money saved to buy us a real piece of land."

"But, Josh," I said hesitantly, "we're just getting everything fixed up here. You have your shop and all."

"We'll see. Maybe if we're lucky we can get land close to town, so we can still live here. I could ride out every day to do the farming and be back in time for supper."

My cheeks burned, and my throat felt tight as I looked over to him. "Oh, I hope so, Josh. That long winter taught me I'm not made for much isolation."

I said no more. A woman is supposed follow her man—everybody knows that. But it was my life, too.

New homes went up all over town that first spring. The sounds of ax and log chain echoed through the woods. House-raisings, housewarmings, dances, and festivities gave us a lively social life.

I tried hard to join in the celebrations and put my grief behind me. Surely there would be other babies. Surely I would be able to bring the polished cherry cradle and the tiny gowns down from the loft, where Josh had so hastily stashed them that awful February day.

At one housewarming dance, Old Joe, the fiddler, was joined by a banjo player, while another man clicked out the rhythm with the "bones," some sticks held loosely in his hand. Their cheery tunes bounced off the walls, and the crowd was caught up in an infectious joy.

Looking over Josh's shoulder, I saw Ann dancing with Sam Hill. Her sunny face and bright eyes made an odd contrast to his stern Yankee features. Hill was a successful businessman. Ann could do worse. But his hot temper was legendary, and there were those who called him stingy.

For the next tune Ann was holding hands with John McNeil, Sam's business partner. Sam stared red-faced while his handsome young partner danced the pretty belle up and back between the facing rows of laughing men and women.

When the reel was over, I joined Ann beside the cider

bowl. "I think John is sweet on you." I teased. "I can see it in his face."

The flush in her cheeks deepened, and she lowered her head. "Do you really think so?"

"Most definitely. But you could have your choice of any bachelor in the county. I suppose before too long we'll be dancing like this at your wedding."

Ann laughed and I squeezed her arm. Then John McNeil came and claimed her for another dance.

# Chapter 7

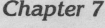

When summer came, I found I was expecting another baby. My old companion, nausea, was back again, and I walked on eggs, fearful that something would go wrong. The ease with which other women seemed to have their babies filled me with envy.

New Salem was growing fast. Homes sprang up all over town, and businesses prospered. The mills were anthills of activity. From far out on the prairies, farm boys brought in wagonloads of corn. While they waited for the grain to be milled, they fished and swam and played games along the river banks. Their shouts and laughter drifted through the town streets.

If only the Sangamon River were to prove truly navigable, the promise of a new metropolis would be a reality.

"We're going to have a doctor—Dartmouth educated," Josh told me one summer day. "I met him at the store. Yankee type from Vermont. He bought two lots, and he's building a combination home and office."

"A doctor! What good news!"

"To tell the truth, he doesn't look like he's in the best of health himself." Josh chuckled.

I, for one, was very pleased to have a doctor settle in New Salem. Surely he would see me through to a safe delivery this time.

Josh was always busy. When he wasn't making or repairing guns in his shop, he helped the farmers. Afternoons, he fished and hunted to provide a wide array of food for our table. From the river we had catfish, bass, perch, and pike; from the woods, deer, squirrel, rabbit, turkey, prairie chicken, and quail. For a treat he would present me with a duck or goose. Every evening a different aroma sifted through our little cabin as I stewed and fried and roasted the day's catch.

On the first day of August, Josh said, "Come with me while I go down to vote. I've got some deer hides out back. We'll stop by the store and see what Sam will give us for them."

I untied my apron and hung it on a peg, always eager to get out of the house for a while. Smoothing the skirt of my old dress, I noticed how faded and threadbare it had become. "Maybe I could get a piece of goods to make a new housedress," I mused.

"Sure. We need a spinning wheel, too. When I shear our sheep, you'll want to spin the wool."

"Yes. We're going to be ready for winter this time."

"Don't worry. It will be a lot milder this year. Last winter was just crazy. Of course, this summer has been crazy, too—with that bad hailstorm in May and the heavy rains we've had. The crops were all beaten down—some of them ruined. The old-timers say they've never seen the likes of it."

Frigid winters, scorching, stormy summers—that was my impression of Illinois. The August sun bore down mercilessly upon us as we walked to the store. The humidity was thick enough to squeeze between your fingers. Each step was an effort, and by the time we arrived, my dress was soaked with sweat.

Hill's store and its porch were the meeting place for the whole community. Talk of the elections filled the air, mingling with speculation about crops and new neighbors.

"That Dennis Offutt's fixin' to open up his store right soon."

"Well, so's the Herndons. And George Warburton's buildin' a store, too. 'Fore long we're going to have more stores than people."

Inside, we traded the deer hides for a piece of yellow calico and a fine new spinning wheel. I tingled with pleasure as I ran my hand along the satin wood of the wheel, admiring its craftsmanship. "Oh, Josh, it's beautiful! Let's hurry home! I can't wait to try it out," I begged, like a child with a new toy.

Josh chuckled. "Just let me go and vote. It won't take long."

Carrying my new spinning wheel between us, Josh and I walked down to the polling place, a neighbor's house, where a few men mingled aimlessly out front. Over to one side, a tall, homely young man was talking to another group.

"Look, there's that clever fellow from the flatboat," I said.

Josh glanced over at him. "Abe Lincoln. Yes, he's back in town—waiting for Offutt to start up his store. He's boarding here, doing odd jobs around town. But the thing he does best is tell funny stories.''

Abe's audience seemed mesmerized as he spoke to them in his slow and easy drawl. He had a flair for drama and a gift of mimicry, taking on the voice and movements of the characters in his tale.

''This fellow they called Old Jake had a special knack for huntin' prairie chicken,'' he said, grinning. ''Never came home without a bagful, though his rifle was old and rusty, and his huntin' dog was half-blind and whole-deaf. Well, as you know, prairie chicken are mighty wary game. It nearly drove the other fellows wild, tryin' to figure out how Jake could bag so many. Finally, one of 'em took Old Jake aside and said, 'Look, I've got to know your secret. If you tell me, I swear I'll never tell another soul.' Jake looked him square in the eye and said, 'You promise you won't tell?' 'Cross my heart three times,' the man said. Well, Old Jake bent in real close and whispered, 'First, you have to hide back in a fence corner.' 'Then what?' asked the fellow. 'Then you stand stone still,' Old Jake answered. 'Stone still. Got it. What next?' asked the man. 'Now, listen close,' Old Jake continued. 'When you're all set up, you breathe in deep and make a noise just like a turnip. That'll bring 'em every time.' ''

The men burst into laughter, slapping their thighs and guffawing noisily. Abe laughed, too, his craggy face beaming with good nature.

I stood in the yard while Josh went in to vote. No other women were around; voting was strictly a man's business. Yet, like all the other women, I knew the local candidates well, and I felt a bitter frustration that I could not cast a vote.

"It's not fair!" I said when Josh returned.

My anger caught him by surprise. "What's that, Carrie?" he asked with a puzzled frown.

"Why can't I vote? It's my town, too. I'll bet I know more about what's going on than most of these men standing around here."

He gave me a penetrating gaze. "That's the truth. You do. And, Lord knows, you're better educated than most of them." With a shrug he lifted the spinning wheel and prepared to leave. "You know how it is, Carrie. Men hate to admit that women have brains, too. Though I suspect many a man's vote has been swayed by his wife's opinion." He grinned, trying to placate me.

"That's not the same at all," I said under my breath. The stubborn streak my stepmother had tried so hard to smother reared its head. I clenched my hands into fists as I hurried down the road.

On the way home we met Susan Onstot, the plump, no-nonsense wife of the cooper. Her blue gingham dress and matching sunbonnet looked fresh and crisp despite the heat. "Carrie, I've been hoping to run into you," she said. "There's going to be a camp meeting at Rock Creek next week. We'd sure like to have you come."

"Would you like to go?" I asked Josh.

He pondered for a moment, wiping his sweaty brow. "I can't get away right now. You go, Carrie. You can pray for both of us."

Susan Onstot threw him a disapproving glance. "We'll be glad to pick you up and take you along with us, Carrie," she said through pursed lips, patting my hand solicitously.

"Thank you," I murmured.

As we strolled down the road, I shook my head at Josh. "She thinks you're an infidel."

"I'm not an infidel. Far from it. I believe in God. I believe in the Ten Commandments and the Golden Rule. But these churches here are so different from the ones back home."

"You keep telling me I have to learn the ways here, to fit into this life," I scolded. I had already had to change so much.

His voice was low and somber. "Sometimes a man just has to follow his own conscience."

"Well, you can't escape," I said in a lighter tone. "You're going to be prayed *for* whether you like it or not!"

At home we gave the new spinning wheel a place of honor near the fire. Josh sheared our sheep, though it was not the season. I worked the wool, with every minute I could spare. First I washed it and, after it dried, I separated the fibers with breaking cards. With the finer cards, I combed the wool into rolls for spinning.

Once I filled a basket with the fluffy rolls, I sat down at the wheel and began to spin. The wheel sang to me with a pleasant whir that made the work go faster. My fingers tingled with the pull of the spinning bobbin against the slender strand of wool.

"Look at all this wool I've spun," I said proudly when Josh came in for supper. "We may be sweltering now, but I remember last winter. I don't ever want to be that cold again."

"When the walnuts ripen, we'll get some hulls for dye."

"No! I'm sick of brown for everything. I'm going to dye this wool yellow or red or purple or green. Anything but brown."

Amusement flickered in his eyes. "Whatever you like, my dear. But plain old brown suits me just fine."

I ran my fingers over the spun wool and smelled its clean fragrance. "Sarah said she'd show me how to use her loom. I'm going to make us another blanket."

"Are you feeling well enough for all this?" He studied my face. "You need to take care of yourself. The baby is the most important thing right now."

"Oh, I'm all right. I'm only sick first thing in the morning. Everything seems better this time."

"Are you sure?"

I nodded. He reached out for me and we clung together silently, sharing our unspoken hopes for the coming baby.

Sarah's husband might have taught at the school, but Sarah was a teacher, too. She showed me how to roll the wool from bobbin to reeler, to make skeins for dyeing. Then she helped me find wild broomstraw, and we fixed a dye bath in the iron kettle outside.

"Always put the dye plants in a cloth bag so they won't get mixed in with the wool," she said, as she dipped a skein into the pot of steaming yellow dye. "And don't forget to add some salt and vinegar to set the color." She smiled at me, confident in her craft. "Oh, I can show you plants and leaves and roots that will give you every color of the rainbow—for instance: bright red—you'll need madder root for that."

Soon the rail fence was lined with skeins of yellow wool, drying in the sun.

The next day we warped and dressed the loom at Sarah's house. It took hours to get everything prepared, but when I started to pass the shuttle back and forth across the loom, I basked in newfound pleasure. The joy of creation elated me as I watched the golden cloth take form before me, inch by inch.

The hours flew by. I glanced up, surprised to see the sun hanging low in the western sky. "I have to go home and fix supper now," I said regretfully.

"Goin' to the camp meeting?" Sarah asked.

"Yes, Susan Onstot's taking me. Are you going?"

"Sure! It's a good chance to get out and see the other folks and to listen to a powerful preacher, too."

I hadn't realized how powerful a preacher could be until I took my place on the log bench down by Rock Creek. Wide-spreading branches overhead enclosed the congregation, shielding us from the blistering sun.

The traveling preacher looked like a rugged man, mud stained and smelling of wood smoke and saddle leather. His deep voice thundered through the wooded glen. "You are vile! Corrupt! Immersed in sin!" he ranted. "You are doomed! You're only fit for hellfire! Repent! Repent!"

Stunned, I glanced about me. The people sat awestruck, staring at the preacher. Tears glistened in the women's eyes.

Sinners? I knew these harried settlers hadn't time for sin. A little whiskey drinking was the worst of it. They slaved from the first rooster's crow until after sunset in their homes and fields. Then, long after dark, they spun and wove, cobbled and carpentered. Their calloused hands and gnarled fingers told the story of their lives.

Here were faithful, hard-working wives and husbands, hoping only that their children's lives might be a little better than their own. If the devil couldn't find worse than this, he'd soon be out of business.

But the preacher would not relent. He raved on and on, pounding on the rough pulpit, until a few of the women stood up, their bodies twitching violently. Their first jerks shook loose their bonnets and combs, and their hair flew out behind them. Some danced about, eyes glassy and unseeing. Others fell to the ground, shouting and writhing convulsively.

My body tensed, my throat felt tight with panic. "What is it?" I asked, staring in amazement at the spectacle..

"It's the spirit of the Lord. Gives some folks the jerks," Susan Onstot whispered.

Just then I heard a dog's sharp yip. Over to one side, a freckle-faced boy threw walnuts at the pack of hounds that lurked near the huge iron pots of stew cooking over a fire.

The preacher raged on until late afternoon. When he finished, all the faithful gathered on the banks of the river to immerse the converts. Caught up in the excitement of the pageant, I went along and joined in the singing of old hymns.

A little upstream several boys yelled and splashed, disrupting the religious ceremony. I turned to Susan. "Who are those rude fellows? I'd think they'd play their games somewhere else."

"That's the village rowdies, out in force. Not an ounce of respect amidst the lot of them."

The youths immersed each other and then, giggling mischievously, set about baptizing their dogs.

A group of angry men shouted and started after them. "Get out of here, you scalawags! We know who you are, every one of you! We're goin' to tell your folks! You're in real trouble now!"

The boys leapt from the water and scrambled up the hill toward town.

After the ceremony the people slowly walked away, subdued and thoughtful. Susan Onstot took my arm and led me up the hill. At the crest she stopped to catch her breath, then tensed and pointed up the road. "Look! John McNeil is walking Ann home. Guess he's officially courting her now." She paused, then clucked and added, "Well, what do you know!"

# Chapter 8

The New Salem community was like an extended family. Everyone was involved in the milestones of each other's lives—their births, deaths, and weddings. And so we all watched with intense interest the courting of Ann Rutledge. She was a great favorite, and we demanded the best of the lot for her.

"That John McNeil's a puzzle," people said. "You never know what's going on behind those eyes."

"Cold as the multiplication table."

John was a college-educated man from New York state, courtly with the ladies, but famous for running a hard bargain in his business deals. With his sharp instinct for profit, he loaned out money at high interest and bought farms from distressed neighbors at low prices. When he sold, he demanded cash or land. No promissory notes would do for John McNeil. His partnership with Sam Hill was highly profitable, and the townsfolk knew him as a man of property.

And yet, there was an air of mystery about him. They

said he didn't vote—a most unusual habit in a place where politics were vitally important to all.

That fall, Ann and John went together to all the corn-shucking dances and house-raisings. At other times they sat and talked on the porch outside the inn or strolled along the road beneath the autumn-painted trees.

John walked tall, proud of his lovely companion. Ann's face radiated a special glow, and filtered sunlight shimmered off her auburn hair. Her cheeks were pink, her eyes wide and shining, and her lips curved in a constant smile. Ann was in love.

As for me, my pregnancy advanced. I fought to quell my anxieties. The baby will be fine, I told myself. I'll have no problems. By the time spring flowers bloom again, a healthy baby will lie in Josh's polished cherry cradle. My arms will be filled, and the haunting ache will go away.

Autumn was a hectic season on the frontier. There was food to put away for winter, precious seeds to be preserved for next year's garden, hogs to butcher, corn to pick and shuck, logs to stockpile against the coming cold. And there were new activities in town.

"Things sure are changing in New Salem," Josh told me.

"I know, it's growing fast."

"Well, now the doctor's trying to organize a temperance society. Can you imagine that?"

"I don't suppose he'll get too many members from the fellows who hang out at Clary's Grocery."

"No, that's a rough bunch. They'd rather drink than eat. Their brawls and cockfights can get pretty gory."

The previous Saturday afternoon the rogues had

swarmed into town again—fifteen or twenty of them on horseback, galloping through the streets single-file, yelling war whoops. They stopped at the saloon for drinks and chewing tobacco, then moved on to the edge of town, where they wagered on wrestling and jumping matches. Their raucous voices filled the air. After they passed the whiskey jug around a few times, they raced their horses, wild earsplitting shouts cutting through the thunder of the pounding hooves.

"A little temperance wouldn't hurt this town," I observed.

"That's not all. There's going to be a debating society, too," Josh said. "Jim Rutledge and his boys will be in it. Mentor Graham too, of course, and others. I thought I might go down some night and see what it's all about."

A strange, nagging dissatisfaction came over me. "They should have something like that for women, too. Men are so lucky. All I have is a borrowed newspaper and a few books to keep me in touch with the world. Sometimes I feel like I'm living on an island, totally cut off from everything."

He turned to me, and I could see his concern. "Yes, I'm sure you must often think about the differences between this place and Cincinnati," he said, slipping his arm around my shoulder. "But New Salem's growing fast. Pretty soon it'll be a real city. We have a doctor now, and two new stores."

"I like Offutt's store. There's not a lot of drinking and rough talk like at the others, and you know Abe Lincoln will give you honest weight. I heard he walked ten miles—way out east of Fish Trap Ford—just because he'd made a mistake in weighing out some tea."

"I like to go there just to hear his funny stories," Josh said, grinning. "I never knew a man with so many tales."

Our second winter set in early. People feared a repeat of the last year's vicious weather, and town talk centered on the signs of nature.

"Gonna be another bad 'un. Squirrels gatherin' up the nuts early, and their tails are big and bushy."

"Yep. There's heaps of woolly worms, too. Their coats are powerful heavy."

"Shells on the hickory nuts is thicker; and bark on the trees is heavier. Gonna be a bad 'un. That's gospel."

I couldn't bear to listen to the talk. I dreaded the dreary days of winter, when shadows darkened the cabin and the wood smoke hung outside in a smothering fog.

This year will be different, I told myself. I'll get out of the house more. I won't spend so much time alone, fretting about myself and the baby.

"Can you feel him move?" I asked Josh one night, taking his hand and laying it across my swollen belly.

"I don't know . . . Wait a minute. Yes! I felt it! Frisky little fellow, isn't he?" Our eyes met in awe as our fledgling made his presence known.

"Everything is going to be all right this time," I promised him.

Sometimes in the afternoons I wrapped up warmly and walked down to weave with Sarah. It was a pleasant way to pass the dark days, chatting, listening to the whir of her spinning and the dull thud of my shuttle through the loom. I could always count on Sarah to keep me abreast of the news.

"How does Mentor like the new debating society?" I asked her.

"Oh, fine. You know Mentor. He thrives on new ideas. He reads both newspapers, and I swear he spends most all his money on books."

"It could be worse. He could spend it on whiskey, like some do."

Sarah glanced up from her spinning. "I suppose you're right. He really is a good man, but he surely spends a heap of time and money on those books."

"Josh is good, too, but he's so busy all the time. I don't think he realizes how much time I spend alone in that little cabin. Oh, I'll be so glad when the baby comes," I said wistfully.

"I know you will, Carrie." With a sigh, she lifted up the filled bobbin of wool and slipped on a corn shuck for a new core. Then, as she began to spin the wheel again, she said, "Mentor's tutoring Abe Lincoln nights—with grammar. At least, they start with grammar. Once they get to talking, they keep on till after midnight. You know, that boy's got quite a mind behind that homely face."

I nodded. "I see him reading books in the store whenever he isn't waiting on a customer. Papa would have loved to have a student like him."

"Well, he'd better learn to do something besides clerking. I hear tell Offutt's store is about to go under."

"Oh, that's a shame. I was afraid they were opening too many stores for such a little town."

"That Offutt! Big business tycoon! He has his fingers in so many pies he can't keep track of all of them. There's sure some mix around here, isn't there?" Sarah said with a wry laugh. "Lots of folks can't even read, and then there's Doc Allen, graduated from Dartmouth, no less, and John McNeil, Bowling Green, Jim Rutledge, Josh—there's plenty of other educated people, too."

"This time of year, I guess what matters most here is how much food you've put up and how many logs are on your woodpile, not how many books you've read. Still . . . sometimes a person likes to think beyond survival." Cincinnati's impressive museums and libraries flashed through my mind.

Sarah reached down into her basket for another roll of carded wool. "I hear there's a new college for women in Jacksonville. Going to train girls to be teachers. How's that for progress?"

"Really? Jacksonville's not far, is it?"

"No, just twenty-five miles or so. Some of the young fellows are talking about going to Illinois College there, too."

"Everything is changing so fast," I said. "I didn't know what to expect when I rode up here with Josh through all that open prairie. I'll admit I was pretty scared."

"So was I, when we came up from Kentucky. Women have a hard lot, that's the truth—following their men around wherever they decide to travel next. But plenty have it worse than we have here."

"Oh, yes! I like New Salem. And Josh says they'll even be running steamboats up the Sangamon soon," I said.

"Well, I don't see how they can do that. It's just a trickly little river."

"He says they can straighten out the bends and deepen the channel. Wouldn't that be a great thing for this whole area?" I glanced out the window at the sun, a fuzzy orange ball sinking low into the hazy horizon. "Oh, Sarah, it's getting late. I have to go now."

A brisk wind hurried me home. Its icy fingers crept beneath my cloak and slapped angrily at my flannel skirt and linsey-woolsey petticoat. Visions of last winter rushed through my mind. I walked faster, breathing heavily, anxious to reach the secure haven of my little home.

As I approached our yard, I saw the faint glow of Josh's lantern out by the barn. It must be milking time already, I thought, walking toward the light. The barn was a snug place even in cold weather. Lucky and Missy looked cozy in their shaggy winter coats, and the warmth from their bodies drove away the nagging chill. The hay they chewed smelled of sun and summer and fertile earth.

Josh sat on a low stool, milking Missy. The squirt and splash of the warm, foamy milk into the pail sang a rhythmic little tune. "Hi, Carrie," Josh said, looking up from his task. "How's Sarah doing these days?"

I leaned back against the barn door, watching the flicker of the lantern light against his face and Missy's bulky side. "Oh, she's fine. We were talking about how fast things are changing. Tell me, Josh. What do you think it will be like around here five years from now?"

He pondered as he finished milking. "Well, I think we'll have a real city here by then," he said. "I think we'll have a new schoolhouse—a free school, like the state promised. Steamboats on the river, and a regular stagecoach line. And maybe the mail will come two or three times a week, instead of only once."

He stood and walked over to me, carrying the full wooden pail. "Now, aren't you glad we came?" he asked, reaching his arm around my expanding waist.

I smiled up at him, looking at the chiseled lines of his square jaw. He seemed strong and invincible. "Yes, I'm glad," I said. "Sometimes I miss Cincinnati, but I have you, Josh, and I know I'll be content when the baby comes."

"Hang on, my pretty Carrie. Just hang on through this winter. Spring will be here soon, and then we'll have our baby."

# Chapter 9

In early spring the river ran high with melting snows and New Salem bubbled with excitement. A steamboat was coming! The boat, the *Talisman*, had left Cincinnati in February, and the whole town eagerly awaited its arrival.

Late in March, when we received word that the boat had reached Beardstown, just forty miles away, New Salem prepared to celebrate.

"Come, let's go see the *Talisman*," Josh urged, the morning the boat was due to arrive.

"I wouldn't miss it for the world!" Huge with pregnancy now, I found it difficult to walk far with my awkward off-balance gait. Still, I wanted to be part of this special day in New Salem history. The first steamboat. The navigation of the Sangamon, providing cheap, convenient transportation. Maybe someday I'd be able to take a steamboat from here to Cincinnati!

Ignoring my discomfort, I joined the noisy throng that surged toward the river. Josh and I climbed down the bluff and found a place to stand along the crowded bank. Flags

flew from tree branches, flapping in the breeze, adding their
bright colors to the festive spirit.

The children, unable to contain their bursting energies,
shouted and raced up and down the hill. Animated conversations rang through the moist spring air.

"Did y' ever see a steamboat before?"

"Sure thing! Over to Beardstown. Noisy contraptions.
Where's the durn thing at?"

"Jest set tight in your saddle. It'll be along directly."

Just then a loud blast of musket fire exploded downstream.

"There she comes! Around the bend!" I called out excit-
edly to Josh.

"Look there in the pilothouse! What's Abe Lincoln doing
there?" Josh asked, amused.

"Not only is he piloting steamboats, Sarah told me that
he announced for the legislature. I hope he'll be all right if
Offutt's store goes under, the way they say it will."

As the ornate steamer approached, glistening with fresh
white paint, barefoot boys waved wildly from their perches
in the trees along the banks. Then they slid down and ran
downstream to climb other trees, to wave again at Lincoln
in the pilothouse. Chores were forgotten as everyone listened
to the angry hissing of the steam engine and the slapping of
the paddle wheel churning thickly through the murky water.
When the steamboat blew its thin, high whistle, everybody
cheered.

The *Talisman* slipped easily over the dam, which had disappeared in a river swollen with spring floods. As it stopped
by the mill to take on wood, the crowd followed each movement of the boat and crew with avid interest.

"This here's sure a great day for New Salem!"

"They'll have to build a port here."

"We'll be shippin' hogs and corn and everything. Yes, sir, this little river's gonna connect us to the whole durn world."

Josh was caught up in the same enthusiasm as we strolled back home. Words tumbled from his mouth like water from a spring. "Springfield's going all out to celebrate when the boat gets there. Fireworks, cannons, speeches. Even a fancy dress ball at the courthouse. And people said it couldn't be done. They said you couldn't run steamboats on the Sangamon." His grin seemed to cover his whole face.

Less than two weeks later, the *Talisman* returned to quite a different scene. The flood waters had receded, and the boat got stuck on the milldam.

The red-faced captain shouted angrily, "Why in hell would some fool dam this river?"

"We had permission from the legislature," Jim Rutledge said, iron jawed.

"To hell with the legislature! We're goin' to have to tear it down!"

"Tear down our dam? You're plumb crazy, man!"

Again a crowd of onlookers rimmed the bank. One of them stepped up, speaking in a calmer voice. "Now, don't you fellers get your fur up. We'll all pitch in and tear down enough to get that boat on over. Then we'll build it back up. There's enough of us right here to get that chore done."

As they worked on the dam, the men from town muttered among themselves. "What earthly good are steamers if you can only use them during spring floods?"

"Huh! Mighty short season, if you ask me."

Josh told me about all the problems of the *Talisman*'s return. I wasn't able to go down to the river with him; my time was drawing near. Each day I grew larger and more uncomfortable, until the simple task of climbing out of bed became an ordeal.

One day at dawn it began. A harsh cramp seized my abdomen. I lay wide-eyed, excited yet fearful. My pulse raced wildly and I wondered what would come next. Should I wake Josh?

Outside, a rooster crowed—a thin halfhearted squawk.

And then it came again. The pain. Again. This was it—my baby's birthday!

"Josh! Josh!" I shook his shoulder nervously.

His eyes opened. He blinked and looked around the room. "What is it?"

"You'd better go get Dr. Allen. The baby's coming."

"Oh, my God!" He sprang up, staring at me with a furrowed brow. "Are you all right?"

"Yes, yes. Just get the doctor, please. The pains are coming pretty fast."

He threw on his clothes and ran down the road to the doctor's house. Within a short time, they returned together. The sight of Dr. Allen's kindly, dignified face, his big black leather bag, comforted me. He was Dartmouth educated, I remembered through the pain. Surely he would be prepared for any kind of problem.

As the sun rose, I lost all sense of time. I felt caught in the grips of some unseen monster bent on tearing me apart. Excruciating pains ripped through me, time and time again. Would they never end? Just when I thought I could relax from the torment, another came, worse than the last.

I was out of my head—an animal given up to animal endurance of the racking pain. Low moans issued from deep inside my throat, unconscious, uncontrollable. A final wave of agony, and then . . . I heard a cry. A weak and sickly sort of cry. A little kitten mew.

"It's a boy!" the doctor said, his voice cutting through the haze inside my head.

I looked up at the tiny moist creature he held so carefully. He was all skinny arms and legs and his little face was wrinkled in a scowl. My baby boy!

"Can I hold him?" I asked weakly, reaching out my hands.

"Just another minute."

I lay back and closed my eyes. A miracle! I couldn't believe he was really here. I smiled and lay in beatific ecstasy.

"Here he is, little mother." Dr. Allen laid the baby, wrapped now in a flannel blanket, in my arms.

As I ran my fingers tenderly over his soft hair, I marveled at his miniature perfection. "He's so tiny!"

"Yes, he's very small. I'll go call Josh now."

Josh stepped over to the bedside and proudly gazed at his new son. Then he drew a quick breath, and his body stiffened. His face tensed as he asked, "What's wrong? He's hardly breathing."

Dr. Allen turned and placed his hand on Josh's arm. I heard the hint of sympathy in his voice. "He's very small and weak."

I gasped. A sob caught in my throat. "Will he be all right?"

"We'll do the best we can for him."

I looked down at my baby through a blur of tears. He seemed so helpless, lying there beside me. Slowly I traced my finger over his tiny, perfect features. His chin was cleft, like Josh's. His hair was fair and soft as down. He had beautiful long fingers on his doll-sized hands, with little specks for fingernails.

I couldn't contain the flood of love that surged through me. This is my son, I thought. I am his mother.

We named him Robert. By the time he was twelve hours old, he had turned a sallow yellow color.

"I'm afraid he's jaundiced," Dr. Allen said.

I looked again at Robbie's sweet little face. Jaundiced. His breathing was slow and shallow and he was barely able to cry.

Panic overcame me. "Oh, no! Oh, please! I can't stand to lose him. Please," I begged.

Dr. Allen gently patted my hand. "Now, Carrie, we'll do everything we can. Sometimes a jaundiced baby comes around."

"Oh, God," I sobbed, and hugged my baby close to me.

Little Robbie lived two days. He died in my arms. I held on to him for hours, refusing to let him go, even after his tiny body had turned cold.

I could hear Josh in his shop, hammering steadily. I sat in bed and rocked my lifeless baby, singing in his ears, trying to will him back to life. I sang lullabies and hymns and ballads—every song I knew. I sang and sang and rocked my baby, holding him against my engorged breasts.

Finally Josh came in. Barely filling his hands was a tiny box of oiled oak, lined with the little flannel blankets I had sewn. I looked at Josh and shook my head.

His jaw was tightly clenched, his eyes were red. "It's time, Carrie."

I shook my head again.

Josh sat down on the bed beside me, and something long controlled in him broke loose. A tortured moan escaped his lips as he threw his arms about me. His shoulders heaved convulsively. Our baby lay between us.

Then he released me and reached down to the baby. I could not let my baby go. My arms clutched him ever tighter to my breast.

Josh's red-rimmed eyes burned into me. All my agony was mirrored there, and in them I read the truth. Nothing I could do would ever bring my baby back.

Slowly, tenderly, he took the baby from my arms. He held his tiny son close one last time, then laid him in the little wooden box and covered him with a blue flannel blanket I had hemmed one winter's night.

I turned my head and stared at the wall. I stared at that wall for hours. Logs. Hand-hewn logs with clay mud chinking. Log on top of log on top of log. A slow rain pattered on the roof, a steady, weeping sound. But my hurt was too deep for tears.

They took my Robbie to the cemetery and buried him beneath the tall oak trees. Part of me was buried with him.

# Chapter 10

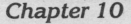

Lost days. Lost weeks. Gone in a blur of agony and tears. Was it grief that brought the fever and stabbing pains that racked my body? I was deathly sick and didn't care.

Neighbor women flocked in with pots of stew and pans of hot bread. Were there ever neighbors as good as those in New Salem? I had long since stopped concerning myself with who could read and who could not. These people had a wisdom not found in books, a wisdom of the heart. They swept our floor and washed our dishes, but more important to me were the hugs and handclasps that spoke of their sympathy and shared pain.

My fever broke, and as time went on I grew stronger. I went outside to putter in the garden Josh had planted, drawing a mysterious strength from the promise held in that rich dark soul.

Weeks later, when I felt well enough to walk down to the store with Josh, I was struck by the changes in our town. New homes seemed to have sprung up overnight.

"What's Abe Lincoln doing, now that Offutt's store

closed?'' I quizzed Josh, feeling a renewed interest in the world around me.

"Don't you remember? Abe's been gone since April to the Black Hawk War up north. Most of the other young fellows from town are gone, too. But they're coming home now.''

"Yes . . . I do remember.'' I looked about me in amazement. "Josh, all these new houses! I can't believe my eyes.''

"Yeah, one house-raising after another. New Salem's really on its way now. See, there's Miller's new blacksmith shop across the street. That's Miller and Kelso's house next door.'' Josh slowed to point out another new cabin at the end of the block. "That's Bob Johnston's. He's a cabinetmaker and a wheelwright. Going to build a workshop out back.''

I looked around at the village, trying to take everything in at once. "It seems like I'm just waking from a long sleep.''

"We have to grit our teeth and go on, Carrie,'' he said, giving my hand a gentle squeeze. "There will be other babies. We have our whole life ahead of us.''

I looked into his eyes, grateful for his warm hand on mine. "You're right. I'm ashamed to have been such a weakling.''

"The gun shop's my salvation. When I'm working there, I don't have time to brood.''

"I was thinking . . . maybe if I had a loom . . . I'd like to learn to weave those fancy patterns. But a loom is awfully big. Sarah has hers in a separate room.''

He pondered for a moment. "There's space over in the corner by the chest. We could push it back when you're not using it. I'll go down and draw a pattern off Sarah's. Then I'll start tomorrow and build you one."

When we reached the Herndon brothers' store and stepped inside, I noticed Billy, Reverend Berry's son, standing behind the narrow wooden counter.

"Well, hi there, Billy!" Josh called out. "Back from the war, I see."

The quiet, slender young man glanced up from a column of figures he was adding. "Mornin, folks. I'm back, all right, and I've bought a half interest in this store. Just learnin' all the merchandise. What can I do for you today?"

My eyes played over the well-stocked shelves lining the walls of the little store. "I'm out of everything. We need coffee and tea and sugar and some spices. And some madder root, if you have it. I want to make some red dye for my wool."

Billy gave a slight, one-sided grin. "Goin' to make Josh a new red hunting shirt?"

"Could be," I said, returning his smile. It was good to smile and talk to people again. I had stayed a recluse long enough.

As Billy gathered up our supplies, I noticed a copper teakettle on the shelf behind the counter. Even in the dim light, its polished metal gleamed. Josh pointed a thumb toward it. "Hey, Billy, how much for that kettle?"

"Oh, Josh . . ." I knew we couldn't afford anything so fine.

"That one is two dollars," Billy said, sounding apologetic. "But I've got others that aren't quite so steep."

"We'll take that copper one," Josh said firmly, laying the precious cash out on the counter.

"Thank you," I whispered as he handed me the parcel. I couldn't have been more pleased if he had given me an emerald. The kettle was a special gift, I knew. A symbol of the things we shared. Our hearts were broken, yet we still held firm to our dream of a brighter tomorrow. We would survive, my Josh and me.

Though still weak, I began to clean the house and tackle all the work I had neglected for so long. I even made a batch of soap. I made lye by pouring water through the wood ashes we had saved in the big hopper in the yard. This I added to grease in my iron kettle, and proceeded to boil it down over an outdoor fire.

As I stood and stirred the bubbling mixture, I watched a nervous wren search the yard for insect tidbits. One by one she fed them to her cheeping babies in the gourd birdhouse hanging from our maple tree.

"We frontier women are like you little wrens," I told her. "Life is a constant struggle to provide food, clothing, and shelter for our families. At least you have feathers. You don't have to spin and weave and sew."

Two chattering squirrels chased each other round and round a walnut tree, then leapt over to an oak. I laughed, savoring the scent of wood smoke blended with the sweet perfume of locust blossoms in the woods. Putting my face up to the sun, I felt its warm healing strength.

The soap thickened. I ladled it into flat pans to cool, and later that evening cut it into bars. Those creamy bars of strong lye soap would last for weeks, cleaning dirty hands and dishes, pots and kettles, and mountains of dirty clothes.

My hens gave me dozens of extra eggs with which to trade. Our small flock of sheep grazed in a field just outside town, in a space we leased for a share of their wool. My garden thrived. Delicate blue flowers formed on the flax, and we could almost hear the sweet corn growing.

I laid out an herb garden, with plants donated by my neighbors. Peppermint, Saint-John's-wort, lobelia, goldenseal, horehound, lamb's ear's, bee balm, and feverfew took root and flourished. I now had herbs for teas to prevent or cure almost any ailment. At least they were better than the whiskey some folks used.

In his shop behind the house, Josh worked for hours every day, building and repairing guns. Men came from miles around, asking him to make new stocks or to fresh out their rifle barrels. While they were there, they looked with avid interest at the new guns he was making.

"Fine piece, that," they would say, eyes gleaming. "Sure would be proud to own that. Brass mounts, brass patchbox. Mighty fine work."

Most of the guns Josh made were simple "poor-boy" rifles, without decoration, made to sell cheaply. But when time allowed, he added some of the fancy scrolls he loved to carve. At night he carved on powder horns and sold them, too, along with bullet molds and leather bullet bags.

"Damn fine gunsmith," the men said. He wore the title proudly.

One evening in late July, Josh looked up from his plate at supper and announced, "I've used up all those gun barrels I brought with me from Ohio. Guess I'm going to have to make a trip to Saint Louis to get a new supply. I can take the steamer down from Beardstown."

My eyes widened; my pulse quickened. "Saint Louis! Can I go with you?"

"I hate to disappoint you, Carrie, but I don't see how.

Right now we can hardly spare the money for me to go. Someday, Carrie . . . someday we'll both go, and we'll make the trip in style.''

My mind buzzed with the thought of being alone. Could I handle the cows, the sheep, the constant need for firewood?

Josh left at dawn, when the first light lay in pink streaks and the trees behind the house were still shrouded in black. The empty wagon rattled down the road behind him. As I watched him disappear, a silhouette against the hazy dawning sky, a huge lump caught in my throat.

Our little cabin suddenly seemed deathly quiet. I stood in the doorway, looking out over the wide circle of the horizon, and I listened to the deafening sound of silence. For the first time in my life, I was completely alone.

With Josh away, I worked hard all day on the house and garden chores. Sometimes neighbors helped with the heavy outdoor work, but my back still ached from chopping kindling and carrying in great stacks of firewood. In the evenings I spun wool, humming to the whir of the wheel to keep myself company. I thought of Josh in the big city, among stylish, well-dressed people, passing by museums and theaters. Would I ever see those things again?

At night I lay alone and wide-eyed, listening with new awareness to the mysterious noises in the dark outside my door. The tall trees down by the creek rustled under the weight of wild turkeys flocking in to roost. Then the night was quiet, the silence broken only by the mournful ''whoo—whoo—''of an owl.

One night a sudden crack of gunshot woke me. I ran to the window and peered out. Silvery moonlight outlined the figure of our neighbor, Bob Johnston, rifle in hand, standing out near his henhouse in his nightshirt. His old hunting dog was close beside him, yapping fiercely.

"That fox again!" I muttered. "Sneaking up on our chickens. He'd better stay away from mine, after all the work I've put into them." Angry now, I grabbed Josh's weighty gun from its antler holder the way I'd seen him do it, and flung open the back door. "Get! Get out of here, you varmit!"

I paced the floor for a while, thinking of the unseen threats outside. When I finally settled back into bed, I took comfort in Josh's gun and my good neighbors. I knew I could always depend on them. But what if we lived on a farm and Josh went away, leaving me alone for weeks at a time?

Long before daylight I was awake again. The rooster crowed cheerily out in the henhouse as a golden flush spread behind the tall trees, heralding the sun. Time to begin another busy day.

First I hurried out to the henhouse to make sure the fox had not harmed my chickens. The pungent smell of straw and feathers met me as I stepped through the low doorway. In the half light, I could see all my black-and-white hens perched cozily upon their roost. The cocky rooster strutted back and forth a few times, stretched his long neck to its fullest, and crowed ceremoniously for my benefit. All was well.

Just after breakfast Ann Rutledge stopped by, her face radiant. "I wanted you to be the first to know, Carrie," she said, clasping my hand. She looked like a child who just couldn't keep a secret.

"Know what? Now, let me guess—John asked you to marry him."

She nodded, beaming. "Oh, Carrie, I'm so happy!"

"Then I'm happy, too," I said, and gave her a quick hug. "Come in and have some coffee. Tell me all about it."

While she talked, her voice vibrant with enthusiasm, I felt a strange sense of foreboding. John seemed such a lone wolf, without family or ties of any kind. I prayed he would be good to this dear girl.

Later that morning I sauntered down the road to Susan Onstot's quilting party. I walked with a light step, eager for the company and conversation. The air was cool and sweet; a soft breeze fluttered through the trees.

As I approached her house, I heard the familiar rhythmic clang of a hammer. Henry Onstot's cooper shop out back was flourishing. People needed his wet barrels for shipping whiskey and brine-packed pork, his dry barrels for flour, his wooden tubs, buckets, and churns.

Inside the house the bulky quilting frame sat in the center of the room, surrounded by chairs and benches. The colorful quilt was pieced in a sawtooth star pattern.

"Come on in, Carrie," Susan Onstot said. "We've a heap of women comin'. Lots of new neighbors these days. Here comes Becky Waddell. Her husband's a hatter, you know."

"I can't believe how fast this town is growing."

Within a half hour the room was filled with neighbors, new and old. Outside, the sun baked the earth, but a cooling breeze blew through the open doors and windows. A dozen women were already stitching when Ann Rutledge arrived, eyes sparkling. A faint smile played about her lips as she squeezed in on the bench beside me and began to sew with nimble movements.

"Got the date set, Ann?" Sarah asked, smiling at the girl's sudden flush of color. Nothing stayed secret too long in this town.

"No, no date set yet." Ann's eyes never strayed from her stitches. "John has a lot of business to attend to, and I'm still in school."

"He'll probably want to build you a fine big house before you marry," Nancy Camron said. "Lord knows he can afford it."

"Lord knows she'll need a big house if she takes after her mama and has nine young'uns," Mrs. Onstot jested.

Ann's cheeks flushed a deeper crimson. "There will be so much to get ready. I'll have to start weaving linens and stitching quilt blocks in my spare time."

"Oh, let me help," I said eagerly.

Ann smiled in response.

"When you get married, Ann, we're going to have us a wedding party to beat all," Nancy said, and all the other women murmured in agreement.

The excitement of Ann's engagement enlivened our group, and everyone had bits of advice to contribute. We sewed all day, stopping at noon only long enough to eat the chicken with dumplings Mrs. Onstot had simmered over the low fire. By late afternoon the quilt was finished, and I knew all the new people's family histories and more remedies for the varied maladies of mankind. What a wonderful afternoon, I thought as I walked home. There's nothing quite as satisfying as being all talked out.

A week later Josh returned with a wagonload of gun barrels. He was eager to get back to work. "In Saint Louis, they're changing over lots of rifles—switching flintlocks for percussion caps," he said. "You can use them even in the rain. If the men around here go for that, I should be busy for a long time."

"Do you think they will?"

"I can't say. These men get real attached to their flint-locks, but it's hard to keep the powder dry in wet weather. They won't have that worry with the percussion cap. I'll just have to wait and see if it catches on."

But that wasn't what I really wanted to hear about. "Tell me about Saint Louis," I begged. "What were the women wearing?"

He laughed. "Well, I can't say for sure. The biggest change I noticed was the bonnets—big wide brims and high crowns with flowers and feathers all over them. And Saint Louis—what a city! The river's full of steamboats, coming and going all the time. Everybody's in a hurry, just like in Cincinnati."

"I'd love to go there sometime. I don't like being left behind." I paused, then added with a touch of pride, "I took good care of everything while you were gone, though."

"You did fine. And someday, I promise you, we'll both go. The boat trip was pleasant and it was fun to be in a big city again for a while. But I'm glad to be back to the peace and quiet here in New Salem." He pulled me to his lap and held me close. "I'm glad to be back with my pretty Carrie."

"And I'm so happy to have you back," I whispered in his ear, burying my head against his warm, broad shoulder. "You can't know how much I missed you."

Josh was home. My world was complete once more. But I felt a new sense of maturity. For the first time in my life, I had been on my own. I loved Josh and loved having him to depend on, but I knew now that I could take care of myself, if necessary.

Josh had returned just in time to cast his vote for Abe Lincoln for the legislature. Abe lost, but there was always next time, and everyone knew Abe had other things to think about—like earning a living.

A few weeks later, we heard that one of the Herndon brother's, Rowen, had sold his interest in the store to Abe. Now Abe would have his own business, with his own partner, Billy Berry.

# Chapter 11

That fall Andrew Jackson was elected to serve a second term in Washington, D.C. The activity in our little town continued at a fast pace. Alex Trent bought Clary's Grocery, Isaac Burner built a house. Camron and Rutledge sold their mill to Jacob Bale, and Sam Hill and John McNeil dissolved their partnership.

We had another doctor, Dr. Regnier, who came from Marietta, Ohio, our home state. A young man about Josh's age, he burned with zeal to bring health to the Illinois frontier.

We needed all the help we could get. A new fear had us in its grip—cholera. Reports of deaths from that dread disease filtered down from Chicago, Rock Island, and then Saint Louis. We soon learned there was a case as close as Springfield.

Cholera. Spotted fever. We heard horror tales about it. Purple blotches appeared on the throat and chest. Victims experienced watery discharges, and agonizing cramps, beginning with the limbs and spreading until they seized the whole body. Within twelve hours, the patient was dead.

"Cholera is a disease, the first symptom of which is death," one doctor reported.

For us it was just another illness to add to our long list: malaria, typhoid, ague, diphtheria, tuberculosis, summer complaint, and smallpox. Not to mention epidemics of scarlet fever. It's a wonder any of us survived.

"Chew garlic to ward off disease," the older women advised me. I put garlic in almost everything I cooked. I even made up bags of camphor for Josh and me to wear around our necks to keep the sickness away.

There were other problems, too. By late fall the prairie grass in the unplowed fields outside town had dried to tinder in the Indian summer sun. It seemed to be waiting expectantly for a single spark to set it aflame.

I woke at midnight one night to see bright lights flickering through the window. "Fire! Josh, wake up!" I shouted.

"My God! A prairie fire!" He leapt from bed and threw on pants and a shirt. "Our sheep are out there in the field. That fence I made to keep the wolves out has them trapped. I've got to get to them before the fire does."

"Careful! Please be careful!" I called after him as he ran out the door.

I threw a shawl about me and stood frozen in the doorway, staring into the distance. Far to the north a fiery orange brilliance rose and fell and rose again in flashing waves on the horizon. A roar like distant thunder shook the earth about me as high winds blew the charging columns of flame closer.

Shouting their alarm, the townspeople dashed out of their houses, armed with shovels, rakes, rags, and buckets. They looked like scurrying ants silhouetted against the fiery wall of flame that devoured the prairies.

Frantically I slipped a dress over my gown and ran outside,

drawn along toward the fire with the others. "Can we save the town?" I shrieked, hoping to be heard above the noise and confusion.

"There's firebreaks," Bob Johnston answered as he ran by, "wide furrows plowed in the fields near town. But with that wind, it could jump over easy enough. We've got to be ready to beat it out."

I became part of the faceless crowd of frightened people, screaming, shouting, running. Swaying clouds of smoke loomed closer, then exploded into flame. The air felt hot as at midsummer, though the fire was still some distance away.

I stared, fascinated by the awful power of the fire. I was struck by the beauty of it, roaring and ravenous.

Then I had the heart-stopping realization that Josh was out there somewhere. I yelled frantically, "Can't we do anything? What about the farmers? What about their livestock?"

As if in answer, I heard the screams. A wall of shrieking birds approached, fleeing from the fire. Then came the howling of wildlife, rabbits, foxes, squirrels, wolves. All were racing blindly from the certain death that chased them across the prairie. Within moments they had come and gone.

The fire surged closer to our village. Women and children ran with buckets of water, dousing the barns and haystacks at the northern edge of town.

"Hurry! Grab your pail!" someone yelled. I raced home and back and joined the bucket brigade.

The men brought torches and ignited a row of fires along the edge of the wide plowed furrows. They stood guard with shovels as their fires quickly spread and burned back toward the fast-approaching wall of flame. Two great frenzied lines of fire burned toward each other, irresistibly, until they merged in a mad clash, with an explosion that shook the earth.

The grass alongside town was burned black. Men and women with sweaty, blistered faces waited grimly in a line, wet rags ready to beat out any stray lick of flame that dared invade our ground. The town was saved, but still we stood, not daring to go home, not daring to believe the fire was really overcome.

I was afraid to think what might have happened to Josh.

Trudging slowly down the road, I started for home. The heavy smoke in the air burned my eyes, and its sour acrid smell clung to my clothes and hair. I heard the sheep first, their plaintive baas drifting above the rustling confusion in the street. Then I saw Josh riding toward me, leading those few sheep. I broke into a run, joy coursing through me at the sight of him.

We met in front of our house. His face was blackened, and his shoulders drooped. His eyes were dull with exhaustion.

"Here they are. All safe," he said wearily, as he dismounted.

My trembling fingers clutched his arm. "You're home. Thank God you're here," I said, feeling drained and numb.

"I'm home. I ran the sheep over to Asbells', and helped him backburn to save his house and barn."

"Is everybody all right out there?"

"Yes. Some haystacks are lost, but all the people and the livestock escaped."

"Thank God."

He led his horse into the stall and began to pat its back in long, soothing strokes. "Lucky here gave me the biggest scare. He went crazy—almost bucked me off. If I'd let him have his way, he'd be in Springfield by now."

For a week the acrid smell of burnt things clung to the town like fog. A strange unnatural hush clung, too, with our realization of our close brush with death.

One disaster overcome, another rose immediately in its wake—scarlet fever. People woke up hoarse, with violent fevers and throats clogged with phlegm. They couldn't breathe and feared choking to death. Sometimes throats swelled with enormous lumps that had to be lanced by the doctor. For weeks some of the children lay near death.

One gray November morning a sharp knock at the door interrupted my weaving. I lifted the latch and saw Bowling Green, our justice of the peace, standing on the stoop. He was a huge man, with bright blue eyes and a ready smile, but that day he wasn't smiling. He looked somber as he stood there, cradling a little girl in the curve of his hefty arms.

"Good morning, Bowling! Who's your little friend?" I ran my fingers through the child's honey-colored curls.

Huge dark eyes stared up at me; her delicate features were pinched with fright. She clung fiercely to Bowling and hid her face against his massive neck.

"This is Miss Betsy Brown." He stepped inside, placed her gently in my rocker, then took my arm and led me toward the door.

I frowned up at him quizzically. "Who is she?"

He shook his head and gazed far off into the distance. His voice was low and grim. "Another tragedy in this year of tragedies. The family lives out in the country. Her mama and baby sister were real sick with scarlet fever. Her daddy, Jason Brown, was heading into town, probably to get the doctor, when that thunderstorm blew up last night. The lightning must have spooked his horse. He bucked up, and poor Jason fell off and cracked his head against a stump. The horse bolted, and nobody found Jason till this morning. He was dead.''

"Oh, no!'' I uttered with a gasp.

"The man who found him went back to the farm. Jason's wife and baby had both died of the fever during the night.'' He paused and shook his head again. "There was little Betsy in the cabin, trying to wake up her poor dead mama.''

I was speechless. A choking feeling tightened in my throat.

Bowling patted my shoulder. "When they brought Betsy to me, I thought of you, Carrie. I thought you and Josh might take her in.''

"Oh, yes!''

"The Browns have relatives in Kentucky. I'll have to write them and see what they want to do about Betsy and the farm. But in the meantime . . .''

My pulse quickened. "Let her stay here. Please.''

"Thanks, Carrie. I knew I could count on you. I'd better go find Josh and let him know.'' He started on the path that led behind the house.

I rushed back and knelt before the rocker. Slowly, tenderly, I reached out and drew the child into my arms.

She began to sob against my breast, a mournful cry of utter desolation. "Mama! Where's my mama?''

What could I tell her? Choking with emotion, I sat down and began to rock her, humming softly in her ear. It felt so good, so right, to hold that little body in my arms.

When Bowling and Josh came in the back door they stood and gazed wordlessly at me. My husband's eyes glistened as he watched me rock the child.

"How old is she?'' he asked quietly.

"Around two and a half, according to the neighbors out there," Bowling said. "Isn't she a pretty little thing?"

I hugged her tightly to me. "She's beautiful. Oh, Josh, we can fix a little bed for her. I can make her dresses. I'll knit her some little socks and mittens."

He reached down and gently patted her silky curls. "She's welcome to stay here," he said cautiously. "But you know, Carrie, she has family in Kentucky. She's just here for a while. Don't get too attached. It'll be that much harder for you later on."

I could hardly hear him for the pounding of my heart. The warmth of her small body in my arms filled me with boundless joy.

All the love I had planned to give my two lost babies came pouring out of me. I was powerless to hold it back.

# Chapter 12

For weeks Betsy woke during the night, screaming out, "Mama! Daddy!"

I jumped up and ran over to the little trundle bed Josh had made her that slid under ours by day. "Don't cry, darling. I'm here. I'll take care of you."

Gently I lifted her from sweat-dampened blankets and tried to comfort her. As I carried her to the rocker by the fire, I could feel her tremble, hear her short, sharp breaths. I wrapped my big wool shawl around us and began to rock, patting her back rhythmically while I sang a lullaby.

Her trembling stilled, and she looked up at me. Flickers from the fireplace lit her face with a muted golden glow. Her brow furrowed, her eyes filled with questions.

"Mama?" she asked, reaching up a tiny hand to touch my cheek.

"I'm here. I'll take care of you," I whispered, holding her close, feeling the soft tendrils of her hair against my face.

"Mama," she repeated with a contented sigh.

My eyes filled with tears. Poor little girl! What will she do when she has to go away from me, after she has come to think of me as Mama? What will I do?

Bowling Green had written to her aunt and uncle in Kentucky telling them of the tragedy and that we had taken Betsy into our home. We doubted they would come for her before the spring.

In the meantime she was ours. Her charm was irresistible. Each time she looked at me with those huge sad eyes, I stopped whatever I was doing to hug her.

She followed me around the house and yard, never letting me out of her sight. She helped me churn the butter and set the table, and handed me my rolls of wool, staring mesmerized as the spinning wheel quickly spun them into yarn.

At Christmastime she helped me decorate the doors and mantel with pinecone wreaths tied with red and green bows. The scent of spices filled the house as I baked cakes and cookies heedless of the cost of the precious sugar.

"We'll make this Christmas something Betsy will always remember," I told Josh.

Next year she won't be here, a voice inside me warned. I hadn't really accepted that and didn't allow myself to dwell on it.

At night I worked on her present—a rag doll. My needle flew as I embroidered big brown eyes for the doll, just like Betsy's. I used yellow yarn for her hair and made a miniature blue gingham dress to match one I'd sewn for Betsy. My excitement mounted. I could hardly wait to give Betsy her gifts.

Josh took time out from his gun making to prepare for

Christmas, too. "I'm making her a wagon," he confided, "so she can take her doll for rides."

Josh had a special love for Betsy, and she adored him. Her squeals rang through the house when he picked her up and held her high in his strong arms, almost to the ceiling.

"Daddy! Daddy!" She laughed as he lowered her and clasped her in a bear hug.

She called us "Mama and Daddy," now. We dared not try to stop her, fearing her reaction. But always in the back of our minds the specter of her Kentucky relatives remained.

The day before Christmas, Ann Rutledge stopped by the house, bringing Betsy a knitted red woolen sweater with a cap to match.

"What a nice surprise!" I smiled as I slipped the child's arms through the sleeves. "There! Don't you look pretty? Say 'thank you', Betsy."

"Fank you," she repeated, struggling to button the new sweater over her tan ankle-length linsey-woolsey dress.

I beamed with pride.

Ann reached out and embraced Betsy, murmuring softly, "What a dear girl. Such a little sweetheart."

There were dark circles rimming Ann's eyes. "John is taking a trip back East," she said suddenly.

"Oh, Ann! Will he be gone long?"

She slowly raised her eyes to mine. Her face looked drawn and pained. "I'm not sure." She hesitated for a moment. "And Carrie? His name isn't really McNeil. It's McNamar."

"That's so strange. Why would he use a false name?"

"His father had a lot of debts back east, so John came

west to try to make some money," she said in a tight, defensive tone. "Now he's going home to pay off the debts and bring his family out here."

To me the story seemed improbable. Why would an honest man live for years with an assumed name? "So, you think he'll be back by spring?" I ventured cautiously.

She cleared her throat. "I expect so. He's bought one hundred and sixty acres near Sand Ridge, and Daddy's going to rent a part of it from him." Her voice now had a nervous edge.

"Maybe this winter will be mild. Then John can get his business settled and get back soon," I said. "You may be a spring bride, Ann." I hoped to cheer her with my confident smile.

She shrugged. "I just take one day at a time. But I trust John. I don't care what anyone thinks. What difference does it make if someone wants to change his name?"

"I'm sure it will all come out right," I said, patting her arm consolingly. What else could I say?

But as I waved from the doorway, watching her trudge slowly through the snow, my heart ached for her. Where was the light, graceful step of last summer? She suddenly seemed older, no longer a happy girl, but a careworn woman.

On Christmas morning Betsy shrieked with excitement when I handed her the new rag doll.

"Baby! Baby sister!" she cried, kissing and hugging the doll. Then her eyes turned melancholy. She gazed up at me, and I knew she was remembering the baby sister she had lost.

"Look, Betsy! See, a new blue dress for you, just like

the dolly's.'' I held it up against her. ''Won't you look pretty?''

Josh brought in the little wooden wagon he had made. ''Put the dolly in the wagon, Betsy,'' he said with a tender smile. ''We'll take her for a ride around the house.''

She laughed and began to play with her new toys. For a while the sadness was forgotten.

I treasured every minute of that winter and refused to think of the day someone would come to take my little girl away. All day long she stayed beside me, following me in her high boots through the snow out to the henhouse and to the woodpile when Josh was away. We built whole families of fat snowmen in the yard.

I sang as I worked, and she sang along. Her dark eyes glimmered with excitement at the fairy tales I told her while I sewed. She was a bright child, and we carried on long conversations while I cleaned and cooked and spun.

During the gray winter afternoons, I wove at my loom while she lay napping, and the sound of her steady breathing comforted me. I realized how lonely I had been before she came.

One day during Betsy's nap time, Josh came in from his shop looking stricken. He sank down in a chair and stared at the floor.

''What's wrong?'' I asked, alarmed.

''You won't believe what I just heard.''

''What is it?'' I hurried to him, knelt, and studied his face.

He ran his fingers roughly through his thick blond hair. ''Rowen Herndon accidently shot his wife. He was cleaning his gun . . .''

''Oh, no! How badly is she hurt?''

Josh swallowed hard and slowly shook his head. "She's dead."

I stared at him. My blood had turned to ice.

That evening Josh and all the other neighbors walked over to Herndon's house, where Elizabeth's body was laid out for the all-night wake. I stayed home with Betsy, sitting by the fire, thinking of sweet Elizabeth.

The men built a fire to melt enough frozen soil to dig a grave, and they buried her in the morning. As I stood in the cemetery, shivering from the biting cold, I knew that I was close to my little Robbie. Betsy's parents rested here. And her baby sister.

Fighting waves of desolation, I joined with the townsfolk as we sang hymns. Death was no stranger to us. It seemed to lurk around every corner, making life all the more precious.

That winter a brazen pack of wolves vexed the farmers, seizing their sheep and hogs. One Saturday a wolf hunt was organized. Boys and men from town and country met early at the outskirts of the village. From my house, I could hear their hearty shouts and laughter. It sounded like a party. Once again, these rugged frontier men had transformed a grim job into play.

"We'll go out in the country and make a big circle," Josh told me. "Then we'll beat the bushes, and raise a ruckus. We'll gradually tighten the circle until the wolves are trapped. And then we'll kill them with clubs."

"You don't shoot them?"

"No, not in that crowd. One of us might get hurt."

Hours later he returned home, his face reddened from the cold. "Well, we got them," he announced as he walked to the fire, rubbing his hands together briskly.

"How many?" I stirred the rabbit stew and began to mix corn bread for supper.

"A whole pack of them. The farmers should rest easier tonight. Us, too. Those devils come right into town if they get hungry enough."

I shuddered at the thought. "Remember how they howled out back during the winter of the big snow?"

His eyes saddened as they sought mine. "Nobody will ever forget that winter, will they?"

When my corn bread was mixed, I spooned it into a heated pan, set it on hot coals, and packed more coals on its lid. It would not take long to bake. "Betsy, come and help me set the table."

She put her doll on the bed and skipped over to me, stopping for a kiss from Josh. As I handed her the plates, I was once again aware of how her small presence seemed to fill the house, brightening all the dark corners. Her sunny smiles, little songs, and grown-up conversations had brought joy back into my life.

This year the dark, gloomy winter days lost their power to bring my spirits down. Betsy was my sunshine.

The long-awaited letter from Betsy's uncle in Kentucky finally came—just a note, really, though written with painstaking care. I gripped the wrinkled sheet with trembling hands, and read the penciled lines:

> We have a new baby at our house, and my wife is feeling poorly. Thank you for looking after my niece. I will come for her as soon as the roads are fit to travel in the spring.

In the spring. He would come for Betsy in the spring. I stood and stared at those three words. My heart caught in my throat.

I'll run into the woods with her and hide, I thought crazily. I'll take her down to Sarah's, where she'll blend in with the other girls. Her uncle doesn't even know her. He could never pick her out.

Each day I loved her more. Each day I felt more certain I could never give her up.

# Chapter 13

Once more we watched the miracle of spring transform the land. Long Vs of ducks and geese flew north. Saucy robins, feathers bright and new-looking, appeared, scratching impatiently through last fall's matted leaves. Out in the barn, ewes struggled through the throes of lambing. And the greening rain came, that slow, persistent rain that coaxes the land to turn suddenly, astonishingly, green.

With Betsy's chubby hand in mine, I strolled the woods and showed her where the shy spring flowers hide. We savored that special spring fragrance of awakening earth and new grass and clean air. We watched the tree leaves slowly unfold, changing naked limbs to wide green sheltering canopies.

Missy, our cow, had a new calf. Late each evening, we went out to the barn to see that Missy and her babe were safely bedded down for the night. The little calf lay curled up in the straw, while the protective mama stood vigil over him, gravely chewing her cud. We poised there in the circle of lantern light, surrounded by earthy barn smells of milk and hay and harness leather, and two pairs of soft liquid eyes held us in their trusting gaze.

All spring I waited and wondered, and each day the tension built higher, the coil wound itself tighter. One day, as we were standing in the yard, I voiced my anxiety again to Josh. "When do you think they'll come for Betsy?"

His face clouded. "You know what that letter we got in January said. They just had a new baby, and the mother wasn't feeling well. I don't suppose they're in any hurry to make the long trip up here."

"I hope they never come! Maybe they'll just forget about it."

He kicked at a clod of dirt and shook his head. "No, Carrie, they won't forget Betsy. There's the farm to think about, too . . . just sitting idle. I think I'll ride out there this afternoon and look things over."

"How far is it?" My eyes turned to the broad sweep of greening prairie to the west.

"Ten miles, I'd say. Want to come along?"

I glanced over at Betsy, playing on the front stoop, dressing her doll in the nightie I had made. "No, I don't want to remind her of what happened there. I think she's finally beginning to forget about it. She hasn't had a nightmare for a month."

Josh's eyes met mine. "Poor little thing," he murmured.

"She's so happy here with us, and they're going to come and uproot her again. I just can't stand to think about it." My eyes began to fill with tears.

"Now, Carrie, you always knew she didn't belong to us."

Angrily I raised my head and glared at him. "I never knew it! From the first, I felt like she was mine."

A tense silence closed around us.

When Josh left, I settled Betsy down for a nap and took out my pen and paper. Slowly, thoughtfully, I began to write a letter to her aunt and uncle. I poured out my heart to them, told them how we loved her, and how she called us Mama and Daddy, and how she brightened our whole life. I told them about our two lost babies, and how Josh was doing well and was more than able to provide for her.

Finally, I lost all pride and implored them to let us keep her. By the time I had finished the letter, I felt completely drained.

"It's not a bad farm," Josh said when he returned. "Eighty acres, part of it in timber. There's a tight cabin, and a barn and smoke house."

A shudder ran though me as I thought of that tragic, empty house. "How can you stand to go there? Is everything just like they left it?"

"Pretty much. The squirrels got down the chimney and chewed some things up pretty bad. Field mice got their share, too. Bowling Green arranged for the neighbors to take care of the hogs and cattle until the relatives come."

He cleared his throat and shifted nervously from one foot to the other. "Carrie . . ." He hesitated. "I was thinking I might buy that farm. I could probably get it for a good price."

My mouth fell open. "You wouldn't! You wouldn't expect Betsy to move back to that house, would you? All those horrible memories . . ."

"Remember?" His voice was husky. "Betsy's not our little girl. Her aunt and uncle are coming for her. I was afraid you'd get too attached to her. It's going to be hard. . . ."

"Look." I handed him the letter. "I've written them and asked if we can keep her. I told them we'd lost our own babies, and we'd take good care of her and—"

His anguish was plain. "Yes, but they're her family. I'm sure they'll want her."

"It's worth a try, isn't it?"

"Yes. Sure. I want to keep her as much as you do, but I know they'll take her."

Betsy had come in from the stoop. She stared at us with some alarm. Sometimes we forgot how much she could understand. "Mama! Mama!" she pleaded, lifting up her arms to me.

I swept her up and held her close. "Mama's here. Don't you worry, honey. Mama's here."

"Carrie . . ." Josh hesitated, then picked up the letter from the table. "I'll take this down to the post office. It's worth a try."

The days rushed by, busy days, occupied with planting our big garden. Down from the barn loft came the bags of carefully preserved seeds—tomatoes, cucumbers, squash, and pumpkins. The previous fall I had squeezed the seeds out on a cloth and let them dry, and now it was time for them to begin a new life.

We dug out seed potatoes from the hay in the root cellar. The cabbages and beets we saved over winter would make their own seeds when we planted them. We had green beans, turnips, peas, and carrot seeds to plant. And the onions to set out. There was flax to spin for linen. The rich black loam lay soft and hungry for the seeds, and the fertile green perfume of spring hung over all the land.

In spring we sheared the sheep, too, bringing in a fresh supply of wool to spin and dye and weave and knit.

Food and clothing, warmth and shelter. The work of our hands provided for all our basic needs. It was a simple life, in tune with the ageless rhythms of the earth.

"Look, Betsy!" I called one morning. "The baby chicks are starting to hatch! Come quick and see!"

With her long dress flying out behind her, she raced out to join me in the henhouse. Betsy's face glowed with delight, and her squeals of laughter greeted each tiny ball of soggy golden fluff as it picked its way out of its shell.

New Salem still churned with activity. One sad day, we helped the Rutledge family pack and move out to the farm eight miles from town. I sorely missed seeing Ann's smile and friendly wave when I walked by the inn. Henry Onstot was innkeeper now.

The store that Abe Lincoln was now running with Billy Berry was doing poorly. Sam Hill's store carried a fuller line of merchandise, and while Billy Berry slowly succumbed to the wiles of whiskey, Abe lost himself for hours in the books he loved to read. He borrowed books from anyone who had them, propping his long legs in strange positions as he read.

One day I went into his store to get some tea, and there he was, stretched out on the counter, reading, as usual. He looked a mile long, lying there. He didn't even hear me come in.

"Morning, Abe." I said loudly.

Slowly, reluctantly, he drew his eyes from the page and looked over at me, blinking his way back into our everyday world. "Oh! Mornin', Carrie. Mornin', little Betsy."

He unfolded his ungainly arms and legs and stepped down from the counter. "What can I do for you today?"

"Well, I need some tea and a piece of bacon, if you have it." I glanced down at his open book. "What on earth are you reading now, Abe?"

"Just somethin' I borrowed from Colonel Rogers over at Athens."

"You walked all the way to Athens to get a book?"

A slow, broad grin creased his face. "Well, now, I've walked lots farther than that. I always say my best friend is the man who brings me a book I haven't read." Chuckling, he reached up on the shelf for tea and bacon. "Anythin' more today?"

"Let me see those printed goods. I might make Betsy a new Sunday dress."

Just then two sloppily dressed brothers from out past Sugar Grove entered the store, talking loudly. They had obviously been sampling their whiskey jugs early. My cheeks reddened as they continued their cursing and rough talk.

Abe frowned and spoke sternly, "That's no way to talk with ladies present."

"I reckon I'll talk any damn way I damn well please," one shouted drunkenly.

Shaking his head in disgust, Abe turned back to me. "Would you like to see that calico?"

"Not today, thanks." Quickly I counted out the coins for the other items, grabbed Betsy's hand, and left.

Stopping to pick some violets outside, we heard the loud voices coming from the store. Abe carried the foul-mouthed man bodily out the door, threw him on the ground, and rubbed smartweed in his eyes.

Then Abe stood up to his full six feet four, and calmly studied the man writhing on the ground. "From now on, remember your manners when you come into my store," he said.

Abe had been appointed postmaster, so each Tuesday I walked down to his store, expecting another letter from Betsy's uncle. A strange mixture of hope and fear enveloped me during these anxious vigils.

When the weekly mail delivery arrived, a big crowd gathered around the store, waiting for Abe to read the newspapers aloud. No matter whose papers they were, Abe always read them first, so we could all keep up with the news from Springfield, Saint Louis, Louisville, and even Cincinnati.

As I waited for a letter from Kentucky, I noticed Ann Rutledge standing close by. "Nice to see you, Ann," I said, hurrying to her side. "Any news from John?"

Her sad face gave me the answer. "Well, he wrote when he got to Ohio," she said. "He was sick and had to stay there for three weeks."

"But he did get to New York all right?" I asked, wishing it could be different for her.

"Yes, I had a letter from him after he got there."

That had been months ago.

Chewing her lip nervously, she watched while Abe passed out the mail. I stood beside her, certain that a letter from Kentucky would make that day the happiest, or the saddest, of my life.

Abe handed out the last letter, and the crowd began to drift away. He turned and looked at her sympathetically. "No letter today. I'm sorry, Ann."

She gazed up at him, stricken, then quickly lowered her head. "Maybe next week," she said with a nervous shrug.

Moved by the glimpse of her raw pain, I reached out to her. "Yes, next week."

"I'm sure he has a lot of business to tend to out east," Abe said gently. "Don't worry, Ann. He's not goin' to forget you."

"I guess not!" I exclaimed, "Why, Ann's the sweetest girl in Sangamon County. Isn't she, Abe?"

He gave an embarrassed chuckle. "Well, yes, I reckon she is."

One by one, the days crept by. Out in the country farmers plowed their fields and planted corn. When the crops were in, they went on with the endless task of clearing more land. They rented extra oxen, until they had the six or seven yoke needed to break up the dense, stubborn roots of the prairie grass.

Always there were stumps to grub, brush to burn, and rails to split for fence. And by then the corn was up, ready to be hoed by hand. Men prayed for sons in these parts.

The letter from Kentucky never came. Instead, an old wagon pulled by a tired-looking nag stopped in front of our house one day. A dust-covered, trail-worn man knocked at the door.

"This Joshua Strauman's house?" he asked.

I nodded numbly. My heart leapt into my throat, and its pounding echoed through my head.

"I'm Ezra Brown. Come to see about my brother's things," he drawled.

My hands were shaking as I motioned him to step inside. "Just a minute. I'll call my husband."

I hurried out to Josh's shop, my mind racing with impulsive plans. I could run away with Betsy. I could hide her in the woods. I knew I would not let him take her.

Josh looked up from his workbench as I rushed in. "What's the matter?" he asked.

"Betsy's uncle is here!" I burst into tears. "Oh, Josh, don't let him take her!"

He blanched. "We'll see," he said slowly. "We'll see what happens now."

I darted back to the house and grabbed Betsy in my arms,

holding her protectively as Josh trudged in. His jaw muscles stood out in a hard ridge; his hands were clenched into fists.

"I see you finally made it," he said curtly.

The man wiped a rough hand across his sweaty brow. "Mind if I set down a spell? It's been a powerful long ride."

"Sit down. There's still some coffee in the pot," I said, not moving from the doorway, where I stood holding Betsy.

Mr. Brown dropped into a chair and exhaled a long, weary sigh. "I jest couldn't come no sooner. Now that's the gospel truth. The wife's been poorly ever since the baby came in January. That makes four young'uns for us now, and a sickly mama to boot. Why, she ain't even got the garden in yet."

My heart raced. "Did you get my letter? We want to keep Betsy here. See, we have a nice house. Josh is a gunsmith. He does real well. And we don't have any other kids. . . ." Words spilled from me uncontrollably.

"You'd be doing us a big favor," Josh added in a strained voice. "You can ask about us around town. I know the people here will vouch for us."

The man looked up at me as I stood in the doorway, Betsy locked in my arms. I tried to read his eyes. All the while, my pulse pounded madly in my head.

"Well . . ." he said hesitantly, wiping his hand against his mouth. He looked at me again. "Well . . . she is our kin. Purty little thing, ain't she? It don't seem natural to leave her. But seein' as you don't have no young'uns and I've got four, and seein' as you're so set on her . . ." He paused again. "Well, I reckon she might just as well stay here."

I sank down on a stool, finally exhaling a long-held breath. My arms still clung to Betsy, and she looked up at me, her little brow furrowed with questions about these strange adult negotiations.

Josh stepped over and shook the man's hand heartily. "Thank you, sir! You don't know what this means to us."

"I can see you're real attached to her. I reckon my poor brother would want it this way." Ezra Brown stood up, stretched, and hitched up his loose-fitting trousers. "Now, about that farm . . ."

"I'll drive you out to look it over," Josh said. "And we'll stop and see about some legal adoption papers."

I could not stop smiling as I watched them drive away. The joy and relief after months of anxious waiting made me feel like dancing in the streets. Bending down every few minutes to kiss Betsy, I smiled and sang and laughed aloud as I swept the floor and scrubbed it with the corn-shuck brush.

"Betsy, you know what?" I knelt down before her, light-hearted as a child myself.

Silky golden curls flew out like a halo when she shook her head.

I captured her and hugged her close against me. "I'm your mama now."

"Mama?" Her hands reached around my neck.

The sight of her gleaming face and huge dark eyes was blurred by my tears. I nodded joyfully. "Yes, Betsy, I'm your mama. I'm really your mama now."

Several hours passed before Josh returned. I had been recording the day's happy events in my journal when he walked into the house, his brow etched with frown lines.

"Carrie, I need to talk to you," he said solemnly.

My whole body tensed. "What is it? He didn't change his mind about Betsy, did he?"

"No, it's not that. I—I'm going to buy that farm."

Slowly, I exhaled, then tensed again. "Oh, Josh."

"He's willing to sell me the eighty acres for eighty dollars. That's less than his brother paid for it, and he put up the cabin and barn and cleared the land. I just can't turn it down."

"You know we can't take Betsy back out there to live. She's bound to have memories. Besides, we have a nice house here. We have friends . . ."

A conflict of emotions struggled behind his eyes. "We always talked about a farm. You know that's what I've always wanted."

I turned away to hide the disappointment in my face. I didn't want to leave my home, my friends, my town. Through the open door, I heard the clop of horses' hooves on the dirt road out front and the voices of children playing and laughing. The clang of the blacksmith's hammer drifted down the street. And from the distance, I heard the merry tune the river sang as it spilled over the dam, turning the wheels that ground the corn and cut the wood at the mill.

Suddenly I knew with deep conviction that I did not want to move out to the isolation of a farm.

Josh's voice softened. "We don't have to move right away. I can ride back and forth from here and farm the land."

"How can you do that? It's a ten-mile trip each way. You have your gun work and everything here. And what about the livestock? Can you leave them out there alone? The wolves are sure to get them."

He laid his hands firmly on my shoulders. "I'll work everything out. You know I can do twice the work of most other men. I just can't pass up eighty acres of prime land for eighty dollars."

I looked into the eyes of this man I had loved for as long as I could remember. "It's all right," I said, breathing out a heavy sigh. "Betsy's going to stay with us. That's the only thing that really matters."

# Chapter 14

We celebrated Betsy's third birthday in July. She was growing taller and slimmer now and no longer seemed a baby. She had learned to sing my favorite ballads with me as we worked around the house and yard. "Sing 'Annie Laurie,' Mama. Sing 'Barbara Allen,' " she begged, and joined in with her clear, true voice.

Josh wore new ruts in the dusty country road with his daily rides out to the farm. He bought an ox and an iron-pointed bar share plow. After plowing all day he worked out in his shop at night, making a wood-toothed harrow to smooth the soil. Then he planted corn by hand, covering the kernels with a hoe and scattering pumpkin seeds among them.

When he finally rode home after sundown, his eyes were clouded and the ache of fatigue lay heavy upon him.

"I hate to leave the ox out there all night, but he's too slow to bring back and forth," he said one evening after supper.

His constant talk of the farm irritated me. I knew it only

as the scene of the tragedy of Betsy's family. "We don't have room for an ox here," I said. "We already have the cow and calf and horse and chickens. When are you going to move the sheep out there?"

"Just as soon as I can build a fence to keep the wolves out." He leaned his head back against the rocker. "There's so much to do. The house needs a lot of repair."

A tightness gripped my stomach. "Josh, we can't move Betsy back into that house. She's doing fine now, but that might bring it all back."

Wearily he sighed and laid his fingers on his temples. "I suppose I could build a new house . . . but I just don't know where I'll find the time."

"Don't worry about that now. We have a good house here. What you really need is someone to help you with the farm work. Three men came by today and left their guns for you to fix. You've been doing so well with your gun work, Josh. I hope you won't leave it all to be a farmer."

"I'll take time off to fix those guns. But I can see so many possibilities out on the farm." He sat up straighter and his eyes began to gleam. "I can raise a fine crop of corn and wheat, and livestock, too—hogs and cattle and sheep. I'd like to put in an orchard out behind the house. And I could build a bigger gun shop there."

"Josh! You're only one person!"

He threw me a crooked grin. "Yeah, and I'm one tired person tonight. Guess I'd better get some sleep. Sunup comes mighty early this time of year."

I lay awake that night, staring at the eerie shadows cast through the windows by the moonlight. Why couldn't Josh understand how I felt? I didn't want to move out to the farm. Solitude always weighed heavily on me, dragging my spirits down. I needed to have neighbors nearby, people to talk to, to call on in emergencies. It wasn't just for me, now. Betsy needed playmates, schooling.

Could I just flatly refuse to move? No, I thought not. I didn't want an all-out war with Josh. But I could try to forestall it as long as possible, I thought, snuggling down for an uneasy rest.

One summer day we invited Sarah's daughters, Almira and Minerva, to spend the day with Betsy. They brought along some tiny china cups and saucers to play tea party. Then Betsy got out her dollhouse and the corn-shuck doll family I'd made, and the girls played with them for hours on a quilt under the maple trees outside.

Later we all wandered through the woods behind the house, where the wildflowers and wild strawberries grew. Three baby squirrels performed for us, chasing each other up and down a tree, while the three little girls giggled and frolicked through the flowers below.

Betsy followed the older girls around, imitating the way they walked and talked. Her pretty little face beamed with delight. I chuckled to myself as I watched them play.

How could Josh think of moving us out to the country, away from all our friends? I wondered. We would be lucky to get into town for an hour or two a week, even in the summer. In winter, we would be snowbound for weeks on end.

In late afternoon Betsy and I walked the Graham girls back home. Sarah, glowing in another pregnancy, greeted me at the door. "Come in and sit a spell. I just made a pot of tea."

"Sounds good. How are you feeling, Sarah?"

"Oh, I'm fine, but I could use more sleep. Mentor and Abe Lincoln keep me awake half the night. When they start talking about some new book, they never want to stop."

I sank down on a cane-seated chair beside the table. "I heard Abe's been staying here with you since he signed his interest in the store over to Billy Berry."

"Yes, I guess Abe's just not cut out to be a business-man," she said, as she filled two cups from her rose-patterned ironstone teapot.

"What's he doing now?"

She shrugged. "Well, he's still postmaster, of course. He clerks in Hill's store part-time, and he does odd jobs for people."

"It's a shame he can't find some way to use that mind of his. He's just wasted here."

"He's been studyin' a lot with Mentor," she said. "He got hold of a law book, so he's workin' on that. And he's still studyin' grammar. He and Ann Rutledge."

My hand hesitated with the teacup halfway to my lips. "Ann?"

"Yes. She's talkin' about going over to the new Jacksonville Female Academy, and Mentor's tutorin' her in grammar." Sarah stepped over to poke the fire.

"I take it Ann hasn't heard from John McNeil yet. Or McNamar, or whoever he is."

"Not a word. I wonder if he didn't leave a wife or a girl in trouble when he moved out here and changed his name."

"A lot of people wonder about that," I said. "Poor Ann."

"You can tell how miserable she is, just by lookin' at

her. Abe feels real sorry for her, too. And I think her daddy lost a lot of money on the mill and inn. Things are pretty tight for the Rutledges right now.''

"What a rotten shame! Do you think she'll just sit around and wait for John forever? She could have her choice of all the bachelors around here.''

"Well, right now she's studyin' and tryin' to save money to go to school in Jacksonville. She's workin' as a hired girl for Jimmy Short. Abe always walks her out there after class.''

"Maybe she and Abe will get together," I said, grinning. "They'd make a good pair. Of course, he's not much to look at. John McNeil was such a handsome fellow, and he had that Eastern polish.''

"He had the money to support a wife, too. Abe's just this side of a pauper.''

"Tell him to talk to Josh if he's looking for some work. That farm is about to do my husband in." Reluctantly I stood up. "I'd better be on my way now, Sarah—if I can tear Betsy away. She loves to play with your girls.''

"She's such a dear," Sarah said with a tender smile. "You've done real good with her, Carrie. Nobody could guess all that poor little thing has been through.''

Suddenly an image flashed into my mind—Betsy's frightened, bewildered face that day when Bowling Green had brought her to us. My hand trembled as I reached out and touched Sarah's arm. "Oh, Sarah! Josh keeps talking about moving us out to that farm. I can't bear to think what that would do to her . . . to bring back all those memories.''

Sarah's eyes met mine, warm with understanding.

"I can't move out there," I said grimly. "I just can't.''

"You know, Carrie, that's exactly how I felt when Mentor brought me up here from Kentucky. It seems we women always have to follow along behind our menfolk. Like the cattle."

"Sarah, what a thing to say!"

As I walked home with Betsy, our long shadows stretching out on the road before us, I thought of Sarah's words. And with each step my resentment grew.

We're nobody's cattle, I thought angrily. We're people, too, and we deserve some consideration. I've worked so hard, learned to take care of those dumb chickens, hoed that huge garden for hours, out in the scorching sun.

Gone were the soft white hands of the city girl I had been. My chapped hands now rubbed our clothes with lye soap, churned our butter, cooked and baked and preserved all our food, spun and wove yards and yards of wool and linen. They sewed every stitch of clothes we wore.

All I ask is to stay in the house I helped to build, I prayed silently. Even the chinking was packed in by my own hands.

But when Josh came home, tired and covered with dust, I forgot my anger. He was carrying an orphaned fawn he found in a grove of trees near the farm.

"Look, Betsy! Look what I brought for you!" he called as he neared the door.

The spotted fawn lay cuddled in Josh's arms. When he ran a gentle hand along its soft smooth hide, the fawn lifted its head and studied us with large wondering eyes.

"Oh, Daddy, can I touch him?" Betsy begged.

We followed Josh outside, and he helped the fawn stand on its long thin legs. After a few wobbling steps, it stopped and sniffed curiously at the hand Betsy held out.

She wrapped her arm around the tawny neck and patted the quivering spotted back. "Look, Daddy! He likes me!"

"Sure he does. Let's milk Missy now and see if he'll drink."

Together we coaxed the fawn to suck some milk from our fingers, and fixed a straw bed for it out in the barn.

The next morning Betsy was up at the first rooster crow, eager to feed and pet her fawn again. "What's his name?" she asked.

Josh chuckled and ruffled her silky curls. "He doesn't have a name yet. We'll have to give him one."

She gazed up at Josh, eyes bright and inquisitive.

"Look at his long skinny legs—like stilts," he said. "Let's call him Stilts."

Betsy glided her hand along the fawn's velvet throat. "Your name is Stilts," she whispered into an alert pointed ear.

Stilts soon learned to follow Betsy around the yard. He frolicked and played tag with her, licking her hand as she picked blades of tender grass and flowers to feed him.

While Betsy played with Stilts, I experimented with my wool, trying to learn to dye the wool all the different colors. I asked advice from everyone I know.

Soon the wall pegs that held my skeins of yarn looked like an artist's palette. Boiled sumac berries gave me a deep red. Peach, oak, and hickory bark, and goldenrod gave varied shades of yellow. Maple bark for rust-brown, and cedar berries for gray. I tried pokeberries, blackberries, and grapes for red and pink, and pokeberry roots for purple. Green oak leaves made green, and witch hazel bark made black. For browns, from light to dark, I used walnut hulls and roots and bark.

When I could snatch the time, I worked on the coverlet I was weaving. I had learned to make twill weaves, herringbone, and bird's-eye. Now I was working on an overshot weave in a delicate rose pattern.

I sat at my loom by candlelight until the late hours of the night, caught up in the hypnotic rhythm of the movements: press the treadle, throw the shuttle, pound the beater—over and over again. Outside, a chorus of summer insects sang to the rhythm I had set. Inch by inch, a coverlet took shape beneath my fingers.

Josh's extra load of work and travel finally exhausted him, and he gave in. "I have to find someone to help me on the farm," he said one humid night in late summer.

"I'm glad to hear you say that," I told him. "You know, there's been a cholera epidemic as near as Jacksonville. If you're worn out all the time, you might get sick."

"I'm thinking of that gun shop out back. The men are after me to get my gun work caught up."

"They need those guns for hunting."

"Yeah, and more important, they need them for the Saturday shooting matches," he said with a laugh. "I'm going to get a man to help me on the farm. Then I'll work out there in the mornings, and in the gun shop in the afternoons. At least until I get things caught up here."

After that Josh could relax a bit. He even took a day off to drive us all to Springfield so we could see the circus. What a day that was!

We left home with Lucky and the wagon before dawn so we could arrive in time to see the big parade through town. The road was jammed with people traveling to Springfield. Horses' hooves and wagon wheels raised clouds of dust that lay in the air like heavy fog. Most of the people had never seen a circus, and the air crackled with excitement.

Inside the mammoth circus tent loud voices droned in unison as the performance began. Oohs and aaahs spilled out in liquid surges at the courage of the lion trainers and high-flying acrobats.

A daring-looking woman with flaming red hair and a pink satin costume covered with flashing spangles swept into the center of the ring. She jumped up on a handsome white horse, stood upright, and rode around the ring at full gallop. The sharp slap of the horse's hooves echoed through the sweltering tent.

Betsy jumped up and down, shrieking with excitement. "Oh, look! Pretty dress! Pretty lady!" she said, pointing a tiny finger.

"Now, see here, Miss Betsy. Don't you be thinking you can ride like that," Josh teased.

Next, a smooth-talking showman came into the ring with a giant anaconda at least eighteen feet long. He let it crawl around his shoulders, its head extended far above him. Its long forked tongue darted in and out; its evil eyes seemed to burn holes in the crowd.

Then the man, teasing us with a malicious grin, carried the slimy snake up close to the audience. Women screamed. Children burst into tears. Yet when the show was finished, the subdued but fascinated crowd crept close to the snake's cage to stare.

Josh, Betsy and I returned home very late that night, tired and covered with dust. It had been a good day and a well-deserved respite from work and worry.

The next day I was back in my garden, and Josh was back working the farm under the cloudless August sky.

There were beans to be picked, hay to be scythed, eggs to be collected, and firewood to be chopped.

From the wide horizon the scorching west wind blew and blew. I listened to the endless mournful song it sang and made myself a promise. Never, never would I move out to that windswept prairie. I would remain here always, beneath the wide arms of my maple trees.

# Chapter 15

In September I stole time enough to make Betsy a new Sunday dress of the finest linen, dyed to a soft rose. It was a lot of work. To make the linen, I pulled the flax plants just before they ripened and soaked them in water to rot the woody part and free the fibers. Then I dried them in stacks and beat them with a mallet. Finally I scraped the fibers from the stalks and hackled them to separate the linen from the tow. I combed and combed with fine hackles until I had the longest, finest fibers to spin for Betsy's dress. I sewed tucks across the bodice and a ruffle around the skirt, and I trimmed it with yards of crocheted lace. When I saw how pretty she looked in it, all the work seemed worthwhile.

"Is this the dress I'm going to wear to church this Sunday?" she asked as I measured the hem.

I sat back on my heels to admire her. The rose color of the dress matched the sun-kissed flush in her cheeks. "Yes, honey. And Mama will wear her good blue silk."

A flood of memories inundated me as I lifted that old dress from the trunk and shook out its wrinkles. I had been so young, so naive, when I twirled before the dressmaker's mirror in Cincinnati, imagining how my new blue dress would impress a boyish Josh, my beau.

How we've changed, I thought. Here I am, with chapped hands and an aching back, rushing from one chore to another, never quite caught up.

And Josh. Josh craved land as a drunk his liquor. He slaved out on the farm until he was numb, then came home and talked of buying more land.

I couldn't understand this need in him, this obsession with land. All I wanted was some degree of comfort, food, and warmth, and shelter, and those dearest to me always near at hand. Bit by bit, this conflict was building a wall between Josh and me.

Life went on. Josh fixed a little room for Betsy in the loft and built a walnut chest for her clothes. At night I helped her climb the ladder and listened as she sang her dolls to sleep.

One day in late September I came home from the store with news. "The Camrons are moving up to Fulton County. New Salem just won't seem the same with them and the Rutledges gone. After all, they started this town."

Josh was bringing in water. He grimaced and abruptly set the bucket on the stand. "I hate to see the old settlers move away. I'm afraid the town has stopped growing. People are still buying land, though. Good farm land will always be valuable, no matter what happens to the town."

"What can happen to the town?" I asked. "It's all settled now. We have our houses and stores and the mills and doctors and the school. What could happen?" Shrugging my shoulders impatiently, I sat down at my loom.

"Well, it's sure not growing as fast as people thought it

would. If the state would spend some money on the river—
straighten out the bends and all . . .''

"As far as I'm concerned, New Salem is a fine town. You
couldn't ask for better neighbors anywhere. And there's always something going on—barbecues and husking bees and
taffy pulls and dances. You have your debating society and
shooting matches."

He reached out to stir the fire. "I haven't had much time
for those things lately."

"Josh, you'll work yourself to death on that farm," I
said sternly as I treadled the loom and threw the shuttle
one more time. "You have enough gun work to keep
busy right here."

"Why can't you understand I'm doing this for all of us?"
he demanded, anger flaring in his eyes. "That land will be
worth a mint one day."

When we're too old to enjoy it, I thought, biting my tongue.
Remember a woman's place. The silent follower. Like cattle.
What a galling thought.

The trees soon changed color, and their leaves began to
fall. Within days, the ground was covered with thick layers
of red and wine and gold.

Betsy ran laughing through the rustling leaves, kicking
them before her, chasing after Stilts, her fawn. She and her
little friends built up great mountains of leaves, then ran and
jumped right in the middle, giggling deliriously. They were
drunk with fall, intoxicated with the joy of being young.

We gathered walnuts in the woods, and by the time our
buckets were filled, the tarry hulls had stained our hands
black.

Out in our garden, huge orange pumpkins sprawled about.
I laughed as Betsy tried to pick one up, her round cheeks

reddened from the strain. "It's too heavy for a little girl," I said. "Daddy will carry it in for us, and I'll make you some pumpkin pie."

The air was crisp and clean. I was content—almost. I longed for a baby. Betsy was such a joy; I felt another child would make my life complete. A son, to carry on the Strauman name and gunsmithing skills. I thought of Robbie.

"Don't worry," Sarah had told me. "I lost my first two babies, and I was childless for quite a while after that. I tried everything the doctors and old grannies could think of—poultices, pills, leechings. Even snake oil ointments. Something must have worked. I'm turning out quite a goodly litter these days."

I waited. Each time our passions rose, I felt that would surely be the magic night. Each month my hopes built up anew, only to meet with disappointment. The dark fear haunted me that I would never have another baby.

But it was fall, the time of glorious golden days and I had no time to be sad. It was time for corn shuckings, and celebration. One by one, the farmers made immense piles of picked corn in their barnyards. After burying a jug of whiskey in the center of the pile, they invited all the neighbors to come help strip the corn.

How those men could work! They slipped on their husking gloves, pulled out their husking tools, and their rough hands flew. Corn shucks scattered in all directions. Ears of shucked corn soared in golden arcs and plopped into the wagon at the side, while good-natured ribbing and laughter filled the air.

Inside the farmhouse we women stitched quilt blocks, stopping to lay out a potluck supper. Ham and beans, fried chicken, cole slaw, raisin cake, and pumpkin pie covered a table that groaned beneath the weight of the food. We all shared the bounty of the harvest season.

When the pile of corn was shucked and laid up in the crib to dry, the men passed around the whiskey jug. Old Joe got his fiddle from his saddlebag, Jack fetched his banjo, and the dance was under way. Far into the night the rafters rang with "Miss McCall's Reel" and "Weevily Wheat," as our stomping feet wore down the floorboards to a glowing smoothness.

During a break between tunes at one party, I saw a melancholy figure in the corner of the room. "Look at Ann, sitting there by Granny Spears," I remarked to Elizabeth Asbell, as we dipped mulled cider from the kettle. "She looks so sad, it could break your heart."

"I know. She's turned down every invite to dance."

"How long will she keep waiting for John McNamar? It's been over a year now. It just doesn't seem right . . ."

But then Old Joe struck up another reel, and I was caught up with the music as if a gust of wind had lifted me up to the clouds.

Finally we gathered Betsy from the cluster of drowsy children on the side. Josh carried her out to the wagon, and we began the long drive home.

"Wasn't that fun? I do so love to dance," I bubbled, covering Betsy with a warm woolen blanket.

The crisp air held a special autumn scent, of harvest time in the fields and orchards. A full moon bathed the prairie with a dreamy golden haze. Out in the fields the shocks of corn stood like wigwams in a ghostly Indian village. I sighed and leaned back, lulled by the beauty of the night.

Silently Josh reached over and took my hand. We had no

need for words; the bond was there between us. For better or for worse, as we promised on our wedding day.

Next morning Josh was up at dawn. "I have to go out to the farm," he said with a gaping yawn.

"I was hoping you could stay around here for a while. You've finished all the harvesting."

"I want to clear more land. Jack Kelso's coming out to help me saw down some trees and cut them up for firewood. I'll be home with a wagonload by supper time."

It was not yet noon when I heard the rapid thudding of horses' hooves out front. Our weaving, rattling wagon flew down the road in a fog of dust as Jack Kelso whipped Lucky along to full gallop. The wagon jerked to a halt at Dr. Allen's house.

I gasped. My heart seemed caught in my throat as I grabbed up Betsy and ran to them.

Josh lay in the back of the wagon—white-faced, tight-lipped, his eyes squinting with pain. My voice croaked when I tried to speak. "Josh! What is it?"

He pointed to his leg, lying in a twisted, grotesque position. "That tree! That damned tree!" he spat out, weak but still angry. "It fell just like I planned it, but it lit on a branch and bounced. Caught my leg under it."

Betsy began to whimper, big tears streaking down her face. I tried to comfort her as I looked at his injured leg. "It's badly broken, isn't it?" I said.

"Yeah," he muttered, grimacing with pain.

Dr. Allen hurried out and helped Jack Kelso carry Josh into the office. After he examined the leg, the doctor laid it between two wooden splints and covered it with thick layers of bandages.

''He must stay off this leg completely for two months, at least.'' Dr. Allen's face was solemn as he handed me a packet of powder to give Josh for pain.

Stunned from shock, I stared into the doctor's kindly eyes. ''Two months! Josh can't sit still ten minutes. I don't know what I'll do with him.''

''It's a nasty break. His leg was twisted under that tree. Then Jack had to lift him up on the wagon by himself, and make that rough trip into town. I'm just counting on Josh's strong constitution to knit everything back together right.''

''Can he walk on a cane? Or crutches?''

''Not for a while. I'll be down to check on him.''

Dr. Allen and Jack Kelso carried Josh on a litter to our house and cautiously installed him on the bed. His eyes were dazed; he winced with the pain of being moved again.

It seemed so strange to see Josh, my rock, lying sick in bed. ''Would you like me to make you some soup?'' I asked him in a choked voice.

Clenching his jaws tightly, he shook his head and glared out the window.

''How about some bread and jam? I have some strawberry preserves I've been saving. What would you like?''

''What I'd like is to get that land cleared.'' His voice was bitter. ''I want to plant wheat there next spring. I can't lay around this house. I have work to do.''

I smoothed back his sweat-dampened hair and kissed his brow. ''It's a shame, Josh. It's really rotten luck. But you'll just have to rest and take care of yourself for a while. You'll have to learn to be patient.''

''Patient!'' he exploded. ''Do you think nature is going to

be patient? Do you think winter will wait if I don't get my fall work done? I don't have time for patience in my life.''

I turned from him and walked over to the hearth. My heart felt heavy as I stirred the fire and put the kettle on for tea.

# Chapter 16

While Josh was recuperating, I learned to milk the cow and harness up the horse and wagon. I carried our water in from the well and shoveled manure from the barn. I chopped and hauled firewood until my back and arms were cramped and stiff. Our neighbors helped, but they had their own chores, too.

Josh bore his pain and sleepless nights with fortitude, but the inactivity and helplessness were frustrating for him. He quickly tired of lying in bed, looking at the same scene every day. Each separate piece of furniture engraved itself indelibly in his mind: the table and benches in the center of the room, the rockers by the fire, the spinning wheel, the walnut corner cupboard with its display of dishes, the chest of drawers, the washstand, the loom over in the corner. Each pot and kettle by the hearth, each iron utensil hooked beneath the mantel, each basket and wooden bowl hanging on the wall was scrutinized. He brooded. He stared holes into the gingham window curtains and the roses in the coverlet on the bed.

One chilly morning in late November our neighbor, Bob

Johnston, brought over a pair of crutches he had made in his woodworking shop. According to Dr. Allen, Josh was ready for them. Josh grabbed them eagerly and stuck them under his arms, grinning as he hobbled around the room. "This is fine, Bob," he boomed. "I'm much obliged to you."

"Oh, come on, you'd do as much for me. That's what neighbors are for," Bob said, a pleased flush creeping up his big, bearded face. "I'll haul in a load of firewood before I go."

I reached into the cupboard for a mug, eager for Josh to have the distraction of company. "Stay for a while, Bob. Have a cup of coffee. Tell us what's going on in town."

Bob hesitated, rubbing his beard. "Well, just for a bit. I've got a heap of work to do today."

"Don't talk to me about work," Josh grumbled. "I've been stuck in this house for weeks, just thinking about everything I should be doing. At least now I'll be able to get around with these crutches."

"Take it slow till you get the feel of them," Bob said.

"Oh, I'll be fine now. Tell me, what's new in town? I feel so left out of everything."

Bob sat at the table and took a long sip of coffee, then scratched his head. "Well, now, let me see. I hear Doc Allen's fixing to get married in the spring. You knew Abe Lincoln got on as deputy surveyor, didn't you? He got hisself a horse on credit, and a chain and compass. He just rolled up and waded in."

"He's out surveying already?"

"Yep. Got the north part of the county. Say, I hear the settlers are just pouring in up north. This latest wave is mostly Easterners. New towns are springing up right and left. It's been that way ever since they got that Black Hawk trouble settled."

Josh nodded. "They're bound to come. We have the best farmland in the world, right here in Illinois. The price is cheap enough, and all they really need is a gun and a plow. Carrie and I didn't bring much more than my gun tools and the clothes on our backs." He glanced at me, a proud gleam in his eye. "I guess we've done pretty well in these last four years."

"The greatest thing about the frontier is the freedom." Bob's voice rang with conviction. "We're nobody's lackeys here. We don't have to bow to any man for meat. That's what brings the people swarming west like bees to a patch of clover."

"You hit the nail right on the head, Bob," Josh said. He paused. His face closed in a brooding look. "If only this damned leg would heal . . ."

"Hey, Josh," Bob interjected quickly. "Did you hear Abe tell the one about the horse trader?"

The two men exchanged stories for half an hour. After Bob left, Josh clumped around the room on his crutches. He was grinning and happier than I'd seen him for a long time. "Maybe tomorrow I can go out to the shop," he said. "And figure out a way to chop wood."

I clucked and shook my head at him. "Josh, don't be silly! You shouldn't be worrying about anything except getting your leg healed."

"I hate to see you doing my work. There's Missy to milk and feed. Good thing we sold the calf. And then there's Lucky and the ox, now that Bob brought him here from the farm. Is there enough hay down from the loft for them?"

"Everything is taken care of, Josh. I don't mind milking

Missy. Betsy is learning to do it. She likes to help. Why don't you just sit here by the fire? You can tell her all about her grandma and grandpa and all her aunts and uncles back in Ohio. Tell her about when you were a little boy.''

When she heard this, Betsy's dark eyes gleamed. She ran to him and patted her little hands on his arms. ''Stories! Tell me stories, Daddy!''

He shifted in his chair, wincing with pain. ''All right, little girl. Climb up here beside me. Careful, now. Don't bump my bad leg.''

At least he would be occupied for a little while, I thought, relieved. Poor Josh. He tosses the whole night through, from pain and from worry about unfinished projects.

''Josh, would you like me to bring in some tools from your shop?'' I asked when he became quiet. ''Maybe you could work on some things in here.''

''With these crutches, I'll be going out there myself in a day or two,'' he said evenly.

''You have to be careful. The doctor said your leg has to be completely immobile until it heals. Don't take any chances.''

''Don't nag me, damn it!'' he yelled in a burst. ''I won't be treated like an invalid!''

With each day that passed his rage and frustration deepened. He was angry with his clumsiness, with the pain, and with the rains that transformed the yard into a sea of mud.

Abe Lincoln stopped by, and for a while Josh forgot his ill temper. He laughed until tears rolled down his cheeks at Abe's boundless supply of funny stories.

''Stay for supper, Abe,'' I urged. ''You're the best medicine I've seen so far.''

Good humor shone in his deep-set gray eyes. ''Well, thank

you kindly, Carrie. Don't mind if I do. Is that roast venison I smell?''

"Yes, Jack Kelso brought some over for us. Everybody's been so thoughtful. New Salem people are the best in the world.''

Abe nodded. "That's the truth," he said. "They've sure been good to me.''

My days were busier than ever now, with bringing in water and firewood, and caring for the animals, in addition to my other work. I didn't mind. I was used to hard work, and I seemed to grow stronger with the years. But it hurt me to see the frustration simmering in Josh's eyes. "I'll make a sled,'' he told me. "I can load it with logs from the woodpile and pull it back to the house.''

I chuckled at the image of Josh on crutches pulling a loaded sled through ankle-deep mud. "I keep telling you I don't mind bringing in the wood," I said.

"It galls me to see a woman doing my work.''

"Josh, remember when I was sick after I lost the babies? You helped me with my work then. Now it's my turn to help you. That's what marriage is all about.''

Glumly he pulled himself upright, hobbled over to the window on his crutches, and stared out at the sullen sky. He turned then and looked at me, a pained expression on his face. "I just can't stand to be an invalid.''

Again he gazed into the distance. The leafless trees allowed a wide view through the woods, where everything lay still and breathless, waiting for the first snow. His voice sounded husky and strained as he said, "What I wouldn't give to go hunting today.''

"It won't be much longer now. Why don't you let me go out and bring in your gun tools?''

Anger flared in his eyes. "You don't know one tool from the other. I'll get them myself."

"You can't go outside. The yard is full of mud."

"Leave me alone, for God's sake! I'm not completely helpless!"

He grabbed his crutches and clumped out the door, down the step, and through the rain-soaked yard to his shop. I watched tensely out the window, powerless to help him, as his slender crutches sank deep into the oozing muck with every step. He started back, struggling to manipulate the crutches while he carried his tools in one hand and a gun in the other.

Suddenly, his foot slipped. He fell sideways, sprawling in the mud.

When I reached him, he was cursing, swearing. He was like a raging beast caught in a trap.

"Here, let me help you." I tried to speak calmly, but my eyes filled with tears at the sight of him lying covered with mire.

"No, damn it! No!" The fury in his face was frightening. "I'll get back myself if I have to crawl!"

He struggled, grimacing with pain, and tried to stand. His hands, face, clothes, tools, gun, and crutches were all coated with dark slimy mud.

I went inside to get Betsy, then rushed down to the doctor's house. By the time I returned with Dr. Allen, Josh had crawled into the house and was lying on the floor beside the door, his pallid face buried in his arms. At our approach he turned his head to look at us with dazed and empty eyes.

I stood for a moment, not knowing what to say to him. Collecting myself, I poured hot water from the kettle into the bowl, and began with trembling hands, to wash the mud from his face and arms.

Dr. Allen calmly observed the scene. "Let's get those muddy clothes off him and lift him into bed."

This time Josh had no complaints. As we undressed him, he leaned over and retched into the washbowl.

The doctor unwrapped the bandages and examined the leg. Shaking his head, he slowly raised his eyes to Josh's face. "You've broken it again."

"Josh, you have to be careful with this leg," Dr. Allen scolded as he replaced the splints and wrapped it with clean bandages. "Nature will heal a broken bone, if you just give her a chance. But you have to stay off of it."

"What am I supposed to do?" Weak as he was, Josh still sounded angry.

"Anything you can do *sitting down*. Maybe Carrie will teach you to knit."

Josh scowled and turned to the wall. "I don't think that's funny."

After Dr. Allen left, I sat down beside Josh and took his hand. "You could carve some powder horns. You're so good at carving. Just tell me what you need and I'll get it for you."

He stared morosely out the window.

"Please, Josh. Don't act like this. I'm sorry you're sick, but it's not my fault."

Slowly he turned to me and searched my eyes. "You don't know how I feel. I can't work. I can't even walk out in my own yard. I don't feel like a man anymore."

"Oh, Josh . . . Josh . . ." I bent down and embraced him. "You're the strongest, bravest man I've ever known. I love you."

I covered his face with kisses and held him close. We clung together for a long time. Finally, he began to relax.

After his mishap, Josh spent hours carving quietly on powder horns. When they were finished, I took them down to Hill's store to trade for supplies.

Carving gunstocks was his next project. Slowly, with painstaking accuracy, he cut scrolls and swirls into the curly maple stocks, then oiled and polished them to a satiny finish. I loved to watch him work, engrossed, his boundless energies focused on the piece of wood before him.

He was still testy, however. Even Betsy felt the sting. "Can't you keep her quiet?" he nagged.

"She's just singing to her dolls. Listen, she knows all the words to 'Fair Eleanor.' "

"Well, I have a headache and I can't stand the noise. The air in here is bad, too. Smells like smoke. I've got to get outside."

I looked out the window at snowflakes the size of chicken feathers, drifting slowly from the sky. "Just a little longer, Josh. It's almost Christmas. You'll be well soon."

Raw frustration creased his face as he scowled at his injured leg. "This doesn't feel right. I don't think it's healing straight." His stricken eyes met mine and held. "What if I'm left a cripple?"

# Chapter 17

Josh hobbled around on crutches for over two months, until the coldest, darkest day of winter, when Dr. Allen finally removed the bandages and splints. Josh glared angrily at his injured limb. It stretched out before him emaciated, pale— and no longer straight.

"Look at that," he spewed through clenched jaws, his face ashen. "What's wrong with it?"

Dr. Allen frowned, shaking his head. "That fall you took did a lot of damage. You're going to have to be especially careful now, with all the snow and ice outside. You could easily fall again and make it worse."

"I'll get around just fine, now that I don't have to use crutches. I can't stand to be cooped up in this house a minute longer. In fact, I'm going to saddle my horse and take a ride this afternoon."

He did not ride Lucky that day. Five minutes of limping around the house was enough to turn his face white with pain.

My heart went out to him. "Rest a little, dear. Then you

179

can walk some more and exercise your leg. It's bound to take a while to get your strength back.''

"There's no problem with my strength. My leg just isn't right. It hurts when I walk on it.''

"Don't worry, Josh.'' I tried to sound more optimistic than I felt. "Just keep exercising it a little bit at a time. Here, let me massage it. Maybe that will help.''

I gently pulled his leg up to my lap and kneaded it between my hands. The sight of the pasty flesh and withered muscles disheartened me.

With an angry snort, he scowled down at his leg. "Do you know how long I've waited for this day? For weeks I've been planning which jobs I'd do first. I'm so far behind.''

"It's going to take a while, that's all.'' The muscles in his leg felt slack and soft beneath my fingers.

Betsy, her face intense and sympathetic, laid her head against his arm. "I'll help you, Daddy. I can do lots of things.''

He winced, then slipped his arm around her tiny shoulders with a look of deepest melancholy.

"Just be patient, Josh,'' I told him. "In a month, you'll forget you ever had a broken leg.''

I was wrong. The accident left him with a limp, and pain that stabbed at every step. Worse, it left him with a bitter, underlying anger.

Life went on. In spring all New Salem celebrated Dr. Allen's marriage to Miss Mary Moore, a lovely belle from Lexington. Her stylish dresses, silks, laces, and kid gloves, made quite a contrast to our plain homespun clothes. She was young and eager to make friends, and soon she was a part of the community.

We freed Stilts, Betsy's fawn. He stayed nearby for two days, grazing in the woods behind the house. Then, with graceful loping bounds, he ran off into the hidden depths of the forest, searching for his own kind.

One day, when the spring floods had receded and the fields were dry again, Josh led the ox out to the farm to begin plowing. I fretted, knowing he couldn't walk behind a plow all day, with pain from his leg piercing him at every step. But I dared not try to stop him. Any interference from me reawakened his fury and frustration with his handicap.

As the morning crept by, I grew steadily tenser, thinking of the pain he must be suffering. I hurried through my baking and churning and set some rabbit stew to cook in the Dutch oven. Josh was still out plowing, hurting, pushing himself with inhuman drive.

My nerves were frayed; I felt as if ants were crawling on my skin. Needing a break, I took Betsy's hand and we walked down to the store, carrying a basketful of eggs to trade.

Sunlight filtered through the trees that spring day. Birds chirped merrily, flitting about and grabbing up loose twigs and grass to build their nests. Tiny wild phlox blanketed the ground with pink. Delighting in the gorgeous day, Betsy skipped along, bending now and then to pick flowers.

When we neared the store, I noticed a tired-looking horse out front, hitched to an ancient farm wagon. Two little boys and a girl sat high up on the piece of ragged canvas that covered the wagon's bulky load.

Betsy waved cheerily and called a greeting to them.

"Hi!" a freckled girl of ten or so responded. "Do you live here?"

Betsy nodded.

"Well, we're fixin' to move up here, too," the girl said eagerly. "My Daddy's goin' to get some land."

"You'll like it here," I told them, smiling.

Inside, a bull-necked man and his gangly wife were talking to Sam Hill. "I'm lookin' for a piece of land," the man said. "Just enough to keep my family. I ain't got a heap o' money."

Sam pondered, shaking his head dubiously. "Land around here's getting more and more expensive. Mostly big farms, too. But I'll keep my eye out for you. Where're you staying?"

"We're out to my brother's, out to Indian Point." The man twisted his hat between his fingers. "I'd sure like to find a place soon. Need to get some crops in."

My mind hummed as I finished my trading and hurried home.

When Josh returned at midafternoon, he looked grim. Fatigue weighed on him like a heavy pack, and lines of pain were etched into his face. "Don't ask me how I feel," he growled, throwing himself across the bed. "I don't want to talk about it."

I sighed and cleared my throat. Then I began cautiously, "There was a new family down at the store. They're looking for some land. . . ."

He sat up abruptly, eyes blazing. "Our farm is not for sale!"

"I know. Don't get upset. I was just thinking. . . . Maybe they could rent it from you. Just till your leg gets healed."

"Who wants to pay rent? They could use their money to buy their own land."

"Well . . . maybe they could pay you back in produce, give you half the crops they raise in place of rent. I've heard of people doing that."

He lay silent, staring at the ceiling, while I went out to feed and water the baby chicks. Betsy slipped outside to help me. We had both become overcautious in our efforts not to disturb him.

When I came in, he was sitting by the fire, staring at his steepled fingers. He looked up and spoke in a subdued tone. "Did you hear where those people are staying?"

My heart leapt. "Out with his brother at Indian Point."

"Well, I guess I could talk to them. It's a crime to have that house just sitting empty out there. If he would be willing to fix it up . . ."

The man, Dan Cooper, was more than willing. He was thrilled, in fact, to have a house already built, with good land to farm, without having to invest one penny. Josh even provided him with the ox and seed. Dan Cooper moved his family into the house within a few days and immediately began to work the fields.

After that our days were better. Josh could relax, relieved of heavy farm work and the sharp pains it caused in his bad leg. He built a tall stool, installed it in his gun shop, and resumed his gun work with fresh enthusiasm.

Busy as I was with the house and garden and chickens and churning, I still made time to walk down and see Sarah when I heard of the arrival of her new baby, Nancy.

Betsy looked down at the tiny baby lying in the cradle, and a puzzled frown creased her brow. "People babies sure are funny, Mama. They're not finished yet."

"Not finished?" I prompted.

"Yes . . . when chicks hatch and baby lambs are born, they can walk around and everything. Look at her. She doesn't even have any hair."

"You were like that once, too, honey. It just takes people babies a little longer to get started." Sarah and I stifled our laughter until Betsy had gone to play with the older girls.

"I'a like to take this baby home with me," I teased, as I cuddled tiny Nancy. "It seems that's the only way I'll ever get another one."

Sarah's face warmed with compassion. "Have you spoken to Granny Spears?"

"Yes, she gave me some squaw root. That's supposed to help, but it hasn't yet."

"And some women turn out a young'un every year, like milk cows. Feast or famine. Isn't that the way with life?"

"Well, I'm ready for some feasting." I kissed the baby's downy cheek. "Betsy's almost four now. She could use a playmate."

"Bring her here any time you like. My girls purely love to play with her." She pointed out the window. "Look at them now. They're all playin' with Abe's kittens."

"Those are Abe's?"

"They sure are. One's named Susan and the other's Jane. The other day he was studyin' them so seriouslike. Then he told me Jane has a better countenance than Susan."

I chuckled. "Guess Abe's pretty busy these days, with his surveying and running for legislature."

'He's seeing a lot of Ann, too."

'Good! That means she's given up waiting for that skunk, John what's-his-name. He probably has a wife in New York by now."

'She wrote a while back and asked John to release her from their engagement." Sarah snorted angrily. "He didn't even have the decency to answer her!"

"That poor girl," I said, slowly shaking my head. "Just think what she's been going through all this time. John always was a puzzle, even when he lived here. Abe may be poor and homely, but he's honest."

"You know, after you get to know Abe, you forget he's homely. He's such a good man, through and through. He lost his mama real young, and his only sister died in childbirth. I guess that's why he's so bashful around the girls. I get the feeling he thinks he's jinxed when it comes to women."

"Ann would be good for him," I said. "She has such a loving disposition. And she was always so happy and light-hearted before John. I'd like to see her that way again."

Sarah nodded, then tenderly lifted the sleeping baby from my arms and laid her in the cradle. "I think Ann really loves Abe," Sarah said, settling back into her chair. "He's been so kind to her through all her troubles. But, you know, John will have to come back some day. He still owns land here. Matter of fact, he owns the house Ann's family lives in."

" 'Oh what a tangled web we weave, when first we practice to deceive,' as Papa would say."

I thought of Ann as I walked home. Abe was poor. He was moody and given to losing himself for hours on end in books. But with Ann at his side . . . I laughed at myself. Just a born matchmaker, I thought.

Soon the summer was upon us, with its scorching days and humid, sleepless nights. Only the corn appreciated the steamy Illinois July; it seemed to grow an inch a day.

And in the wake of heat another cholera epidemic broke out. I heard that in Sangamon County seventeen people died in one day. Each night as I went to bed I prayed that we would still be well come morning.

Abe continued to read all the newspapers to the townspeople when the mail came in. We heard of the land boom in northern Illinois, now that the Indian scare was gone. People were moving in by droves from the eastern states, not just up from Tennessee and Kentucky, as before. Our state's population was steadily increasing.

On August fourth, Josh had his chance to vote for Abe again, and this time Abe won. It was a big step for a young man—he was only twenty-five. The night of the election all New Salem celebrated with him. The sounds of fiddle music and stamping, dancing feet rang from the crowded inn.

A man from Jacksonville bought the fancy carved gun Josh made when he was housebound. Later Josh received an order for six guns from a large store in that city. He was happier than I had seen him in a long time. He invited me and Betsy to go to Jacksonville with him when he delivered the guns.

The trip was hot and dusty. A hard blue sky stretched over us with clouds like puffs of cannon smoke. In my excitement over visiting the big city I scarcely noticed the fields and scattered farms along the way, the rich, ripe smell of summer in the air. I laughed and chattered like a schoolgirl. I was a country bumpkin come to town; my days in Cincinnati seemed as if from another life.

Finally our wagon pulled into Jacksonville. We rode down its sedate shaded streets, past large impressive homes, and I could see the town was flourishing. Some of the stores even rivaled Cincinnati's.

"Where will we stay?" I asked as we neared the city's center.

Josh spread his hands lavishly. "Take your choice. There are two fine hotels."

"Can we afford anything this nice?" I looked hesitantly at the fancy downtown buildings.

"I've been selling guns as fast as I can make them. And now this man wants some with carved stocks that will bring double the regular price. We're not going to scrimp on this trip, Carrie. You deserve a good time.''

So we indulged ourselves. While Josh talked guns, Betsy and I strolled the streets of downtown Jacksonville. There were sixteen stores—I counted them—and rows of offices for doctors and lawyers near the courthouse. The town had two newspaper buildings, too, and a book-printing company. It was a real metropolis.

Betsy's dark eyes grew round as pennies as we wandered from store to store. She was enchanted by the bolts of satin, brocade, and taffeta, and the lace, gauze, and rainbows of ribbons on the shelves. I was enchanted, too.

We stayed for two days, shopping, eating in the fancy restaurants, and sightseeing. We saw fine homes, big boarding houses, factories, and brickyards. One mile west of town, Illinois College lay in a shady grove of oak trees. Its spacious grounds and handsome brick buildings lent an air of dignity to the whole city.

When we set out for home, I glanced at the boxes in the wagon bed and smiled, thinking of the treasures they held: Betsy's new black slippers; my stylish bonnet with its satin ties and green rosette ribbons; and the patterned chintz dress goods for Betsy and me.

''This has been a trip I'll remember for a long time. Thank you,'' I said, reaching for Josh's hand.

His smile was wide and warm. ''We'll be back. I'll be coming over here pretty regular from now on. That man at the store wants all the guns I can make for him. He wants one for himself, too—inlaid with silver.''

Pursing my lips, I drew in a long whistling breath. ''How impressive! We should have enough money for a visit home pretty soon. I'm so happy to see you spending your time on gun work. That's your craft. Anyone can be a farmer.''

He turned and studied me with a slow, searching look. "I'm going to be a farmer, too," he said. "I thought you understood that. Do you know what land is worth these days? I want to buy some more before the price goes up again."

My stomach twisted in a cramp, but I tried to keep my voice light and cheerful. "As long as you can keep finding good tenants, like the Coopers . . ."

"I don't like to farm for halves," Josh said curtly, staring straight ahead. "When my leg gets better, we're moving to the country."

A wall sprang up between us. I wished I could just smile and say, "Yes, dear," as I should. I felt stubborn—"willful," my stepmother used to say.

But I thought Josh was being stubborn and willful, too.

# Chapter 18

The trip to Jacksonville fired Josh with new enthusiasm for building guns. He worked all day out in his shop, and rubbed and polished gunstocks by the fire at night.

"I need to hire an apprentice," he said one evening during supper. "Once I have one trained, I can get twice as much work done."

For a moment I sat silent, longing once again for our own sons to learn their father's trade. I swallowed hard and tried to hide the guilt and sorrow that swept over me. "That's a good idea, Josh," I said. "Do you know anyone you could hire?"

"I'll have to scout around. Gunsmithing is delicate work. It takes someone who's good with his hands."

After a few days of inquiry, Josh heard of a sixteen-year-old boy over by Sugar Grove. "They say he can carve birds and animals real as life," he told me. "Sounds like what I'm looking for. Guess I'll ride out that way and see if the boy is interested. I can fix him a bed out in the shop, and he can eat his meals here with us."

"Do you think his parents will let him come? These farmers usually need their sons to help in the fields."

"It's a good chance for a boy to learn a trade."

By the end of the week arrangements were made. Josh left with Lucky and the wagon at noon, and when he returned, a rangy, dark-haired youth accompanied him. "Carrie, I'd like you to meet Cole Nelson," Josh said as the two of them came inside. "He's going to be working with me."

"Welcome, Cole. I hope you like it here." I looked over the tall, shy boy who stood before me. He seemed all arms and legs. I noticed his big, rough hands with their knobby knuckles, and I wondered if he could do the delicate, skilled work required of a gunsmith.

"Say, Cole, this all happened pretty fast, didn't it?" Josh grinned. "Just bring your things along, and I'll show you the gun shop. I've got a corner screened off for you out there."

At supper, Josh began his long course of instruction. "Well, Cole, when I saw those ducks you carved, I figured you might have the makings of a gunsmith. You have to be a real craftsman, you know—a master at toolmaking and iron-working and blacksmithing. You have to be a kind of artist, too—able to do sculpture and inlay. There's men out there who crave a fancy gun, and they'll pay a big price for it. Then there's the plain poor-boy rifles most folks around here buy."

"I 'spect it'll take me a while to learn," Cole said. He swallowed hard and looked at Josh with solemn eyes.

"Yes, I expect so, Cole. It takes a lot of skill to make a good gun. The balance is real delicate, you know? You have to get just the right tension in the mainspring, so the cock won't strike the frizzen too hard or too soft."

Cole followed Josh's words silently, nodding, filling his mouth again and again with bites of roast venison.

Josh continued, "It has to be in balance with the flashpan spring, and that has to be just stiff enough to keep the pan cover closed, but not too stiff for the cock to be able to lift fast and smooth."

"Sounds complicated to me," I murmured, pouring coffee from the big iron pot.

"Well, if the metal in the frizzen is too hard, the flint knocks off such small sparks that they cool before the powder fires. If it's too soft, the flint cuts into it, and the particles are too big to spark."

Cole looked bewildered. "Will I be learning blacksmithing, too?"

"Yes, I do a lot of iron work. And brass. You'll learn to sand-cast brass. Tomorrow we'll start by freshing out the barrel of an old gun. We'll pour some lead down into three grooves and cut in new rifling."

"You'll show me how to do it?" the boy asked nervously.

Josh chuckled and patted Cole's shoulder. "Sure. You just turn the crank on the chuck, and I'll push in the barrel to bore it. Then we'll put it on the rifling guide. That's an iron rod with two steel teeth, mounted on a long piece of spiraled wood. I just turn that in the wooden frame to guide it. Five times to make the five grooves in the barrel. It takes a while. You'll see."

Cole slowly shook his head. "I sure do have a lot to learn."

"Sorry, boy. I didn't mean to give you indigestion, trying to tell you everything the first night. You'll learn it bit by bit, just like I did from my dad. I'll show you how to cut out stocks from patterns, how to make a whole gun from start to finish. There's lots of repair work around here, too. I'm snowed under most of the time.''

If he keeps busy with gun work, I thought, after Josh and Cole went out to the shop, maybe he'll forget about farming. He doesn't need to take on so much extra work, with his bad leg. And Betsy and I don't want to move out to the country.

I glanced at Betsy, who was drying dishes as I washed. ''You'll soon be big enough to go to school, young lady.''

''I can write my name already.'' Dropping the towel, she rummaged under the kettle for a piece of charred wood. Then, with painstaking care, she printed out her name on the fire shovel. ''See?''

''Very nice!'' I told her. ''Here, now write 'Mama.' ''

She copied my printing. ''And Cole. I can learn to write his name. Is he going to live with us?''

''Yes, he's going to help Daddy.''

''Is he going to be my brother? I always wanted a brother.''

I forced a painful laugh. Would Betsy ever have a baby brother? ''No, honey. He's not your brother. If you had one, he would be a little baby, like Nancy Graham. Let's hurry and finish here.''

I was silent for a long while, deep in thought. ''Come over here, Betsy,'' I said, finally. ''I want to show you something.''

She watched as I dug down to the bottom of the trunk and found my old blue lacquered jewelry box. With loving care I lifted my mother's cameo and held it out to Betsy. ''See this pretty lady? She's your grandma. Oh, Betsy, she would have loved you so. When you're older, I'm going to give this pin to you.''

Her dark eyes shone as she gazed at it.

* * *

Josh and Cole spent long days in the gun shop, trying to meet the demands of the thriving business. All the men in the community wanted their guns in top shape for fall hunting.

One day when I went to the store for supplies, I ran into Ann Rutledge. The bloom was back in her cheeks, and she seemed more like her old self; but I noticed subtle changes— the indelible scars of suffering.

"What are you doing these days, Ann?" I asked.

"I'm working for Uncle Jimmy Short now—helping his wife around the house. I'd like to go to school in Jacksonville next year."

"Say, what's this I hear about you and Abe Lincoln?" I teased.

She blushed at the mention of his name. "Oh, he comes over sometimes and talks to Uncle Jimmy. He likes to ride out and talk to Dad, too." Her eyes, sweet and blue as morning glories, told another tale.

"Now, tell the truth. He comes to visit you. He's a fine man, Ann."

"I know."

"Have you heard anything from John?"

She turned and looked into the distance as she slowly shook her head.

"That man!" I spouted, sorry to have brought up the subject. "I'd say it was high time you forgot him and got on with your life."

She looked back at me, the blue of her eyes bruised and injured. "That's what I'm doing, Carrie. It's just so hard to understand sometimes . . ."

I slipped my arm around her shoulder. "Everything will be all right. Abe is getting ready to go to the legislature, and

he's a young man. Who knows what the future holds for
him?''

Abe's future might have looked good, but his present was
still plagued with money troubles. Ann told me that in November there was a judgment against him, resulting in a levy
on Abe's personal possessions: his horse, saddle, bridle, and
surveying instruments—everything he owned.

"Uncle Jimmy outbid everybody, took possession, and
immediately returned the things to Abe. He said he wouldn't
see a man deprived of the means to make his living." Ann
was smiling with tears in her eyes.

Later that week I was happy to see Abe and Ann walking
hand-in-hand down the road at dusk, their heads thrown back
in laughter. Their cheeks were flushed and their eyes gleamed
with that glow I still remembered from my younger days.

The day Abe left for the legislature in Vandalia, the whole
town went to see him off. He stood beside the waiting stagecoach in a tailor-made suit, towering above the noisy crowd.
Friends and neighbors shouted words of encouragement and
advice.

With a final look at Ann, smiling and standing in the sunshine, Abe climbed aboard for that awesome trip to the state
capital. Congressman Lincoln. The driver slapped the reins,
and the creaking stage pulled down the muddy road. Abe
waved.

"Do right by us, Abe!" a voice from the crowd called
after him. No one doubted that he would. He was our boy,
part of our New Salem family.


The cold weather brought tormenting pain to Josh's leg,
and sleepless nights that left him tired and irritable. I watched

him limp cautiously across the yard to his shop each morning, and I could sense his pain with every step.

"Be careful, Josh. Don't slip," I called.

"Got to get these guns finished," he said, not turning back. "I'm selling them as fast as I can make them."

It was true. Our fortunes were improving rapidly. The half shares from the farm turned a good profit, and the gun shop flourished. From far and near men sought out Josh Strauman, master gunsmith.

The day before Christmas Betsy and I carried plates of cookies to our neighbors and lingered at each house to visit for a while. When we returned, Josh met us at the door, a broad grin creasing his face.

"Come in!" His eyes sparkled with suppressed excitement. "I have a surprise for you."

A Christmas present! A knot of anticipation gathered inside me. I beamed up at him, eager as a child. "What is it? Tell me."

"What have you been admiring down at Sam Hill's store?"

My eyes widened. I turned and looked up on the mantel. There sat the polished walnut Seth Thomas chiming clock with the little gold-leaf rosettes painted on the glass door.

The beauty of it took my breath away.

# Chapter 19

No one was happier than Josh to see the snows melt in the spring. The cold aggravated his injured leg, colored his every step with pain.

I tried to help him. Through the long winter nights I warmed the bed with hot bricks. And I kept small stones by the fire to wrap in flannel and pack against his sore joints when he sat in the rocker after supper. But the pain nagged at him without relief, draining him and aging him rapidly.

Then once again spring worked her yearly miracle, bringing new green life to the woods and fields. Once again wildflowers bloomed, and redbud trees lent the forest their vibrant color.

Although one by one, people were moving away from New Salem, this spring brought a flurry of hope and excitement with it, too. The New Salem area was going to get a railroad.

Almost everyone in town attended the big meeting in Springfield, where over a thousand people listened as the speaker proposed a railroad for our part of the state. If we couldn't have river transportation, a railroad could haul the produce and livestock to market and bring us needed supplies. It was the main topic of conversation for weeks.

One sunny afternoon Betsy and I ambled up the road to visit Sarah and her latest baby. A boy this time—little William.

My heart was heavy with envy as I lifted the tiny fellow from his cradle. He squirmed until he found the most comfortable position in my arms, then snuggled down and looked at me alertly. "What a precious baby, Sarah," I said. "But next time I think it should be my turn."

Sarah grunted. "I could use a rest, myself. So much work to do around here."

"I don't see how you keep this house so spotless. And with a big family to care for, too."

"It keeps me hoppin'. I lose track of everything else. What's new in town, anyway?"

I hugged the baby against me and began to rock. "Well, I'm sure you've heard about the carding mill Sam Hill is building. That's caused quite a stir among the women. You know what a chore it is to card the wool by hand. The mill's supposed to open by the first of May."

"I'm sure glad to see somethin' new goin' up. Seems like so many folks are leavin' town. I hear Sam's goin' to build a new house, too."

"A big two-story house, they say. He's getting married in July."

"Hallelujah! It's about time. Maybe that will mellow him a little."

"Could be. Do you think we'll have another wedding soon? What about Ann and Abe?"

Sarah's face softened in a smile. "Now, that would be nice, wouldn't it? But Abe has so many debts now that his old partner has died. Abe felt an obligation to shoulder all of Billy Berry's old debts, too."

"It's such a shame."

"Isn't it, though? Abe made some money at the legislature, and he's busy with surveyin', but problems just seem to hound him all the time."

"Poor Abe."

She brightened. "He's talkin' about studyin' the law. Some of the other congressmen at the capital told him he should try it. But he'll have to go clear to Springfield to borrow the books he needs."

"You know that won't slow Abe down. And then after he's licensed, he and Ann can get married." The baby was asleep now, so I tiptoed across the room to lay him gently in the cradle.

"Oh, Carrie, we're such romantics," Sarah said, laughing. "You'd think I'd have learned better by now, with this houseful of kids."

As I walked home, I hummed a happy tune, stopping along the way to help Betsy pick spring flowers. The meadow of greening grass was irresistible. I flung my arms out wide and ran with Betsy, laughing as the south winds swept our dresses out in billows. I felt lighthearted, born anew. Another harsh winter was behind us, and the spring and summer always brought us happy times.

But not this year of 1835; it was one of plague and famine. In early May the skies opened, and it rained for nearly forty days and forty nights, as in the Bible. Then the days turned hot and muggy. Swarms of flies and mosquitoes darkened the air. The stink of stagnant water and decaying vegetation filled the land, bringing with it sickness and death.

Crops fared poorly. The wheat was ruined. People brought food up from southern Illinois, where crops were spared, and we began to call that part of the state "Little Egypt," after the Bible story.

One morning in June I awoke with chills. The shaft of sunlight from the window brought no warmth to me. My teeth chattered. "Josh, I'm freezing," I said between shivers. "Could you bring me a blanket?"

"A blanket! You must be sick." He walked over and reached into the linen chest. "All this dampness in the air is causing a miasma. I'll bet you're coming down with ague."

I was too sick to answer. The chills gripped me harder until I shook, my teeth chattering. I had never felt so cold, not even in the winter of the big snow.

Josh piled blankets on me, but still I shivered. After an hour or so, the chills died down and were replaced by hot flashes. Soon I was burning hot, with cruel, stabbing pains in my head and back.

"I'll go get Dr. Allen," Josh said, his voice taut with concern.

"No," I protested weakly. "Wait and see if I get better on my own. You know what the doctor will do. Bleed me. Purge me with calomel and caster oil. Probably put blister plasters all over me. I'm too sick to go through all that."

In time my fever broke. Beads of moisture popped out on my brow, and soon sweat poured from me, drenching my sheets and pillow.

"I just thought of something." I tried to focus on Josh, but he seemed to be standing in a haze. "Becky Waddell bought some of those 'antifever' pills from a traveling salesman. Could you ask her if I can borrow some?''

"What's in them?" he asked skeptically. "Maybe you should let the doctor bleed you."

"No! Those pills are something new. Quinine, I think it's called. They say it really helps."

"I guess it's worth a try. The ague can keep coming back once you've had it."

Becky Waddell sent over some quinine pills, but the sickness hung on for three weeks. It left me weak and listless, and my strength was slow to return.

Illness struck many homes that summer. Fever stalked the land, and several families felt the icy touch of death.

One day Josh came in from the country with a somber face. His voice sounded tired and strained. "I just heard the whole Rutledge family is sick. Ann's real bad, they say."

The sickness and hardship of that year weighed upon me like lead. I stopped shelling peas and looked up at him. "Oh, no, not the Rutledges, too. If the whole family is sick, there's no one left to care for them. I'd better go out there."

Josh hung his straw hat on a peg beside the door. "Now, Carrie, you're still weak as a kitten," he said, as he lathered his hands in the washbowl. "You don't have the strength to take on any more chores."

He was right, I knew. The weeds growing freely in my garden proved it. "At least I can cook some extra food and take it out to them. Thank heavens the neighbors did that for us when I was sick. Why don't we drive out there tomorrow?"

The road to the Rutledge farm at Sand Ridge was a hot, dusty ribbon through the prairie. Overhead the sun blazed with pitiless intensity, and the air lay over us like a suffocating blanket. No breeze stirred the wide expanses of grassland or the fields of ripening cornstalks. The trip seemed endless.

"Do you know what's wrong with the Rutledges?" I asked. "Is it the ague, like I had?"

Josh frowned and shook his head, squinting against the sun's glare. "I don't think so. I heard it might be typhoid or brain fever. It's something bad."

"I'm glad I left Betsy with Sarah. She shouldn't be around all that sickness."

Josh pulled Lucky to a stop at the Rutledge farm. An eerie silence hung over the place. Wild grapevines grew up the walls of weathered logs. The garden was overgrown with weeds. Even the hound dogs looked sick, sprawled lethargically beneath a shade tree.

The silence was menacing. Josh and I gathered up the pans of pigeon pie, the cakes and biscuits, and walked up to the house. "Anybody home?" I called through the half-open door.

"Come on in, Carrie," a voice from inside called thinly.

I scarcely recognized the hollow-cheeked, doleful woman sitting by the table as Mrs. Rutledge. "Mary Ann! I'm so sorry to hear you've all been sick."

"Looks like you've been poorly, too," she said listlessly. "You're awful skinny."

"It's just the ague. Lots of people have that."

"We've been real bad around here. Ann's burnin' up with fever."

"Can I see her for a minute?"

Mrs. Rutledge pointed to a back room. "Go on in. It might perk her up to have some company."

As I stepped into her room, I gasped sharply at the sight of Ann. A painful thinness made her seem almost transparent. Her cheeks blazed bright red in her chalk-white face. Blue eyes, once sparkling and full of life, now held me in a glassy, feverish stare.

"Ann! Oh, Ann," I stammered, reaching for her hand. I found it difficult to speak.

"Carrie . . . it's Carrie come to see me." She seemed half-delirious, struggling for the words. A stale smell of sickness clung to her.

I tried to force some cheer into my voice. "I just brought some food out for your family. When I was sick, my neighbors cooked for us. Next month you'll be cooking for somebody else. We seem to be taking turns being sick this year."

"Abe's sick, too. . . ." She paused between each word.

"Yes, that's what I heard. But he's getting better now, and soon you'll be better, too."

An unutterable sadness seemed to envelop her. Slowly she shook her head, then turned to gaze out the window at the clouds that hung on the horizon. Her eyelids seemed heavy. They began to close.

"Rest, Ann," I said, gently patting her hand. "Just try to get lots of rest. You'll be well soon. Why, before you know it, you'll be riding your horse into town again." If I said it heartily enough, could I make it true?

I stood. She needed rest. She needed something—desperately. I took her hand. "Be sure to stop and see me when you come to town."

She turned and looked at me, her eyes suddenly clear and lucid. "Good-bye, Carrie."

Those two words carried a sense of finality that turned my blood to ice.

Tears crept into my eyes as I bent to kiss her cheek. A leaden weight lay where my heart should be. "Good-bye, my friend," I whispered.

# Chapter 20

A few days later a tornado struck. The day began like any ordinary August day—hot and sticky. In the early afternoon huge, threatening clouds appeared on the horizon. Thunder began to rumble in the distance. The clouds rushed across the sky, boiling up until they seemed like airborne mountains. An unnatural brightness illuminated the earth, a strange greenish light that made each leaf and blade of grass stand out.

The dark clouds rolled in closer, and torrential rain—then hail—poured down. We stood inside and stared up at the ceiling as the skies relentlessly pelted the house with chunks of ice. More rain followed, accompanied by winds that whipped tree limbs unmercifully. Thunder erupted like cannon fire and lightning burst in blinding flashes. Through it all, my heart pounded a deafening drumroll in my head.

I clung to Betsy, soothing her—or was she soothing me? Josh paced back and forth across the floor, peering out the window, jerking back as lightning cracked nearby.

In time it passed. I looked outside and saw our yard blanketed with hailstones big as birds' eggs, clear as glass. I heard the steady plopping as moisture dripped from heavy hanging branches. Broken tree limbs lay strewn everywhere, and a whole uprooted tree sprawled across our neighbor's garden.

Later we learned that a twister had touched down just outside town, leveling all the crops in its path. Trees in the woods snapped off like twigs, and fence rails scattered like broom straws. Miraculously no one was killed.

Sarah stopped by my house the next day and told of the devastation near their farm. "It's an omen," she said. "It means more death."

I bit my tongue, fighting back the urge to call her superstitious. "I hope you're wrong. There's already been too much sickness and death this year."

"You mark my words." Sarah claimed to know the signs for everything.

She was right. Within a week, Ann was dead. It was so hard to accept—that lovely girl cut down. Desolation engulfed me as I pondered the uncertainties of life. "She was so happy, so much in love—planning to marry Abe, after waiting all that time to hear from John. She was just beginning her life again. It seems so unfair," I told Josh.

His voice was low and husky. "Abe was with her right before she died. It's going to be hard on him."

I remembered, as if it were only yesterday, seeing the two of them together the previous spring, picking wildflowers in the woods at the edge of town. Their love had made them seem acutely alive, with Ann's merry laughter echoing through the greening trees and Abe's craggy face beaming with heartfelt joy.

At the funeral Abe's face was a raw wound. Each time I glanced at him, my tears began anew.

Ann was buried in Concord Cemetery. Beyond the clearing was a grove of oak and hickory trees. The grassy slope, peppered with old headstones, led to a little stream where willows grew. Shafts of filtered sunlight cut through the canopy of leaves, and in the branches birds chirped merrily, unmindful of the sorrow below. My heart tightened in a knot when I saw the fresh graves there. And now, Ann's.

Her mother, surrounded by her remaining sons and daughters, wept silently, her back bent with a loss too heavy to bear. Ann's father had been too sick to attend.

The grave, an ominous black hole, loomed before the crowd of grieving friends who listened to the preacher's final words. We sang a hymn, and Ann was gently laid to rest.

Abe's face was etched in grief. He stared at the grave, unconscious of his friends around him. As the last mourners began to leave, Abe stood alone beside the grave, unwilling to tear himself away from Ann.

After a time Dr. Allen gently took his arm. "Come on now, Abe. Let's go back to town."

Abe shook his head and stood unmoving as an oak.

Bowling Green wrapped a mammoth arm around Abe's shoulder. "Come stay with me and Nancy for a while, Abe. We'll look after you." Gentle hands led him away.

He stayed with the Greens for two weeks, but their kind ministrations did little to soften his loss. Day by day he grew more haggard, drowning in grief.

The whole town mourned the loss of Ann. A few weeks later her father followed her in death.

I was stunned when I heard the news. "Jim Rutledge gone?

I can't believe it. What will his wife do now? How can she manage the farm by herself?''

"Some of her boys are grown now," Josh said. "They can take care of things—at least to keep them in food. Jim had a lot of bad luck recently. He probably didn't leave them much."

"It would be so much easier for Mary Ann if she lived in town," I said. "All of us could help her. It's a long enough drive to visit her out in Sand Ridge."

Impatiently Josh brushed his hair off his brow. "I guess by now I know all the disadvantages of living on a farm. You never miss a chance to point them out to me."

"Oh, Josh. You've been so busy in the gun shop, I thought you'd given up the idea of farming."

"No, I haven't given it up," he said gruffly. "With all the people moving in and out, I thought I might be able to find a place near town. That wouldn't be so bad, would it?"

"I suppose not," I said, with a heavy sigh. "But your leg, Josh. It hurts you too much to do farm work."

He limped over to the door and turned to me. "By next year my leg should be all healed."

Cole rode in just then, back from delivering a gun to Concord. When he slowly trudged into the house, he looked pale and stricken.

"What's wrong?" Josh asked. "You look like you've seen a ghost."

"Abe Lincoln . . ." Cole said, dropping dejectedly into a chair. "He was sitting in the cemetery, talking to Ann's grave. He didn't even see me pass by. I've never seen anybody look so sad."

I thought of Abe, desolate, drowning in his grief. "He's torn up in little pieces, Cole. Ann's sweet disposition seemed to lighten up the serious side of him. Without her . . . I don't know. I don't suppose he'll ever be the same.''

Before returning to his workshop with Cole, Josh threw me a soulful, backward look.

# Chapter 21

Abe slowly resumed his life. His work as postmaster and surveyor occupied most of his time, while he prepared for the next legislative session. Still, a deep dolor hung over him, engulfing him like a shroud.

Two months after Ann's death we had another shock—this one bitter with irony. "You'll never guess who I just saw down at the inn," Josh said.

I looked up expectantly from my spinning. "Someone I know?"

"Oh yes, you know him. We all know him." He sat and stared moodily at the fire. For a long while the crackle of the blazing logs and the whir of my wheel were the only sounds in the room.

"Aren't you going to tell me who it is?" I asked, suddenly impatient.

"John McNamar!" he spat out. "Now, doesn't that beat all?"

My spinning stopped abruptly. "My God! It's been three years." I thought of Ann and how she had suffered waiting to hear from him. "Three years without a word to Ann. Just those two letters right after he left . . . And now she's gone."

"Her dad's gone, too. And poor Mrs. Rutledge and all those kids are living out on McNamar's farm."

"Well, did he say where he's been all this time? Three years! He must have some explanation."

'He's brought his widowed mother back with him. He said when he got back East, his dad was sick and he had to straighten out the business affairs."

"I'm sure he was much too busy to write." I sniffed. "When I think of Ann trudging to the store every week, looking for a letter . . . Oh, I don't even want to see the man!" Anger gave new energy to my spinning.

"You'll see him, all right. Looks like he's here to stay." Josh stood up. "Well, back to work. Just one more gun to finish, and then the load will be ready to take to Jacksonville. I have to make the trip before the roads get muddy."

Betsy breezed in at that moment, carrying the basket of eggs she had gathered. "That big hen pecked at me again! It's always the same one. I think you should stew her for Sunday dinner, Mama."

Her feisty spirit made me laugh. At five she was growing taller, her cheeks indented with deep dimples. That day her honey-colored curls were gathered into one long braid in the back and tied with a bit of red yarn.

"Will you teach me to spin?" she asked as she watched my movements with rapt attention.

"Let's see if you can reach the pedal."

I gave her my seat at the wheel, and guided her small fingers through the motions. After a few moments, she squirmed with frustration. "Ooh, it's hard," she said. "I can't reach up that high."

"You'll soon be big enough." I hugged her close to me. "You're always such a good helper. I don't know what I'd do without you."

"Almira and Minerva help their mama take care of the babies. I wish I could do that. That's lots more fun than playing with rag dolls."

Biting my lip, I concentrated on my spinning and tried to hide the hurt. Would the babies I had wanted for so long ever come? I could not understand the long delay. In the meantime I had Betsy, that golden child, to fill the house with life.

I could hardly believe my luck. My Betsy seemed immune to all the sicknesses that struck the other children of the village. When they were down with grippe or summer complaint, she positively bloomed with health.

"Chick, chick, chick," she would call out sweetly as she flung cracked corn and sunflower seeds to our hungry flock of chickens. She clucked to them in their own language; she cackled with them when they laid an egg. She mewed to the cats, baaed to the lambs, mooed to the cow, and neighed to Lucky. She was in love with life and the world around her.

Those days the thud and thump of my loom sounded often in our house. Having mastered the secrets of dyeing wool and linen to a rainbow of colors, I learned to weave all the fancy patterns. I had quite a repertoire: the star, rose, cross, diamond, wheel, and many others. Making pretty things was my delight.

More and more I traded woven goods for other things we needed. I made fancy tablecloths and runners, scarves, and baby blankets. Everyone in town seemed to want a bed coverlet, and my fingers flew at the loom as I turned them out in an array of colors and patterns. Because most of Josh's earnings went into our savings for the future, it was my weaving that kept us in ham and bacon the year around, as well as brooms, buckets, shoes and boots. I hoped we could even save up enough for a visit to Cincinnati and Betsy could meet the family she'd only heard about in stories.

In early December Abe Lincoln left for the legislative session in Vandalia. I took time out from weaving Christmas gifts to go down and see him off on the stage. He still looked sad, with dark hollows beneath his deep-set eyes, but he managed a smile for the townspeople when he waved goodbye. The driver slapped the reins across the horses' backs, and the heavy, rattling stage started down the road.

"Good luck, Abe!" I called after him. Turning, I searched the crowd, looking for a certain handsome, even-featured face, with eyes as cold as glass. But John McNamar was nowhere to be seen.

The next day Josh took a long ride in the country. When he returned, his face wore that intent expression I had come to know so well. I waited, dreading what was to come.

He came and stood behind my chair, his big frame throwing a giant shadow across my loom. "There's a farm for sale," he began, hesitantly. "Just seven miles outside town."

I treadled the loom, threw the shuttle, pulled the beater one more time, not even looking up at him.

"Those folks are moving out to Iowa," he continued. "I can't figure why. They've got the best of land right here. A good tight house, too."

"Itchy feet. Some men are never satisfied to stay where they are," I muttered, throwing my shuttle once again.

He cleared his throat and shifted nervously. "I was thinking I might buy that farm . . . We've been doing real well lately, with my gun work and the profit from the other farm.''

Strange spots of red began to blur my vision, and my muscles pulled into tight coils. "And my weaving. Don't forget that. I've been trading for everything we need around the house. I thought we were saving to go back home for a visit.''

"This man's real anxious to move on." Josh was speaking quickly now. "I made him an offer, told him what I could afford. I didn't think he'd even consider a price that low. . . . But he did. He said he'd take it.''

He sat down in his rocker by the fire and made an absorbed study of the ceiling. We sat in silence—the long deep silence of a snow-bound January midnight. My arm had turned to ice, frozen as I held the shuttle halfway raised. Finally, he spoke. "Well, what do you think?''

"You ask me that now? After you've already told him you would buy it?'' I began to weave again with clumsy, shaking hands.

"Well—'' he began cautiously, "we don't have to move till spring. No sense spending the winter out there.''

"Out there, trapped in by the snowdrifts. Out there, miles from a doctor if anyone gets sick or hurt. Out there, miles from school, and Betsy ready to start next year.''

"Carrie . . .''

"I'd think you'd rather move to Jacksonville. That's where most of your guns are selling.'' My throat choked up until I could hearly speak. "And to think you didn't even discuss it with me. You just went ahead and bought it.''

His mouth tightened to a thin, hard line. "I'm the man of the family. I have to make these decisions.''

I glared at him, anger and frustration smoldering inside

me. And yet I knew the die was cast. The course was set. There was nothing left for me to say.

I rushed about the house like a madwoman that day, driven by the vehemence of my silent rage.

That night, without a word, I climbed the ladder to the loft and slept with Betsy.

# Chapter 22

Josh and I argued bitterly for days over that farm.

"You're the most stubborn person I've ever seen!" he thundered, anger underscoring every word. "Why can't you see that land is everything? Illinois is growing fast. Whole new towns are springing up every day. Do you know what these new people want? Land! This good, rich land. That's why we came—remember?"

"I remember I married a gunsmith, not a farmer." Sullenly, I knitted one more row, then stopped to watch the orange tongues of flame darting up the black throat of the fireplace. Outside, a bitter January wind hurled itself against our cabin walls. I shivered.

"It's not that I don't understand the value of the land," I continued in a milder tone. "I just dread the loneliness of living on a farm. Seven miles from town. I'm used to seeing my neighbors every day. When I walk to the store, I run into at least a dozen people. I like that. I need human contact. Even in the country, you'll see people because of your gun work. But I need people, too . . . and Betsy needs her play-mates. It's hard to be an only child.''

The thought of this sore point silenced my outburst. I felt my spirits plunge from anger to emptiness.

Josh's frown softened as he glanced at me. "Don't you think there's still a chance we'll have another baby?''

"I don't know. I'm afraid there's something wrong inside me," I said dejectedly. ''Maybe it was that fever I had after Robbie was born. I've tried every recommended tea and po-tion. Nothing helps.''

"Don't worry about it, Carrie. We have Betsy.''

I hesitated, struggling to fight back the tears that threat-ened. "I know you want sons to learn your trade, to carry on your family tradition. I know I've failed you . . .''

Dismally I wiped my eyes so I could see my knitting. If I could not bear children, at least I could knit socks.

Josh, bless him, knew just what I needed. He stood and pulled me to him, enfolding me in an embrace. Gentle hands pushed back my hair and firm lips kissed my brow. "It's not your fault our babies died. I know how much you've suffered. Carrie, believe me, I couldn't ask for a better wife. And you're such a good mother to Betsy.''

"But you always wanted sons. I know that. And that's another bad thing about living on a farm. If we had a pack of boys to help you, like most of these farmers, it would be a lot easier. How can you do it all alone, with your bad leg? Don't you think I know how hard it is for you?''

"It's not so bad in summer, as long as I don't try to hurry. It's just in these cold months that it really hurts.''

I looked up at the strong lines of his face, which was still filled with youthful dreams and ambitions. "Well, I guess if you can stand to do the work with your bad leg, I can stand the loneliness," I said. "I'll try not to complain."

He held me close. "I'll bring you into town often, Carrie. I promise you that." After a long moment, he breathed deeply and said, "As soon as it starts warming up, I'll get us ready to move out to the farm."

On the first day of February, the winter sun glared down on the snow-covered prairie, blinding man and beast with its reflected rays. And with the sun came warmth, a brief respite from frigid winds.

"I think Cole and I will go hunting," Josh said at our noon meal. "The game should be out scratching for food on a day like this."

Betsy's eyes lit up. "More rabbits, Daddy? Maybe you'll get enough rabbit skins to make me a cape, like you promised."

"Could be, little lady. What do you say, Cole? Like to go hunting this afternoon?"

"Sure would," Cole said between voracious bites of chicken and dumplings. There seemed no limit to the food he could pack into his lanky body.

Watching them walk out the door, rifles in hand, I marveled at how quickly Cole had become a part of our family. He was fast learning the intricacies of cutting out the stocks and casting metal parts for guns. Between jobs he chopped the mountains of firewood for the gunshop and house that went up the chimneys to form part of the pungent haze hanging over town all winter.

While I cleared the table and washed the dishes, I made plans for moving to the farm. I thought about visiting my friends in town and bringing Betsy in to play with Sarah's girls. There would be quilting bees and socials. Maybe I'd even go to the week-long camp meeting up by Concord, where the people stayed in tents around the big prayer meeting shed. The women there got together and cooked in huge pots over an open fire. At least it would be a bit of social life.

These plans were still churning in my mind two hours later when I heard the clop of horses' hooves out back and heavy footsteps on the stoop. The door flew open. I saw the stare of shock on Cole's face and the look of naked anguish on Josh's as he hobbled in, leaning on Cole's bony shoulder.

"Josh!" A vise seemed to clamp around my chest. "Your leg! Did you fall on it?"

He eased stiffly into the rocker and leaned his head against the back. His whole body shook uncontrollably, racked by spasms of chill. His teeth chattered as he spoke. "The ice broke. . . . I stepped down off the creek bank and broke right through. Must have been by the mouth of a spring. I got water in my boot, and now the damn thing's frozen solid."

I reached down and tried to pull off his boot, but it was frozen to his foot. "Let's get my bucket, Cole. I'll put some warm water in it and thaw him out."

Cole brought in some snow to melt over the fire, and we poured the warmed water into Josh's boot. After a time the boot loosened. My fingers trembled as I eased off his soggy knitted sock.

His foot was dead white, completely bloodless, with a shriveled, helpless look. It was the leg that had been crushed and had never really healed. I stared at it in horror. "Does it hurt?"

"No . . ." His voice quavered from his chills. "No, I can't feel anything."

I filled and refilled the bucket with tepid water, soaking his foot, in an effort to bring it back to life. Josh sat motionless as granite, staring into space. The sight of his leg was almost more than I could bear. It was scarred and bent where the tree had crushed it, and now his foot was frostbitten.

As the hours passed, his foot reddened, then swelled, causing Josh excruciating pain. Low tormented moans escaped from deep inside him. Sinewy tendons stood out in his neck, and he clenched his jaw against the agony.

Cole and I helped him over to the bed. I swathed his foot with heavy blankets and laid a flannel-wrapped hot brick beside it.

"I'll get the doctor," I said, feeling that surge of energy that comes when strength is crucial.

"It's no use," he uttered, barely audible. "There's nothing can be done."

Josh was racked by pain for days, and walking was unbearable. His cheeks blazed with fever against the sickly pallor of his skin. Something was drastically wrong.

Dr. Allen came, but he could do nothing to undo the damage of the frostbite. Josh's foot stayed swollen. At first it was pale and shiny, but by the end of the week, the swelling had spread up his leg and darkened it to a dusky bronze. His foot began to turn a hideous greenish black. And it reeked.

Each day the nauseating smell grew worse. The sweetish stink of rotting meat permeated everything—sheets, blankets, clothes, furniture, even the water in the bucket and the food I cooked. Betsy and I were sick now, too, from the sight and smell of that grotesque foot.

The doctor examined Josh again. "The foot is gangrenous," he said, looking gravely into Josh's agonized eyes. "We have to take care of it. I guess you know what that means."

We froze into a silence stiff with tension. The steady ticking of the mantel clock lashed painfully upon my ears. Seconds ticked . . . ticked . . . ticked into minutes, and yet time suddenly stood still.

A sharp cry exploded from my throat. "Oh, Doctor, please! Please! Can't you do something for him?"

Dr. Allen took my hand and patted it; I saw the desperate hurt in his eyes. "Carrie, I can save his life. But only if I amputate his foot before the gangrene spreads."

I sank into a chair and clasped my hands over my face, wanting only to escape the monstrous words that echoed in my head. Amputate his foot. Amputate his foot. Amputate . . . The words whirled around me.

Josh was beyond speech now. He lay motionless, consumed with fever, breathing in shallow gasps. I prayed he was too sick to understand what was happening.

"We'll need some whiskey," Dr. Allen said. "You know I don't approve of drinking, but this time you can give him all the whiskey he will drink."

My hands shook as I grabbed the whiskey jug and poured out a mugful. I could not control my trembling. When I held it to Josh's fevered lips, I sloshed some of the fiery liquid onto his shirt. I gave him more, knowing it would be his only cushion against the pain.

Dr. Allen asked for a clean linen sheet and spread it over the table, laying his black leather bag on a chair beside it. From the bag he pulled forth his shiny instruments. Scalpels.

Needles. Saws. Oh, God! I looked from them to Josh and back again.

"Cole, run over to the blacksmith shop." Dr. Allen's voice was steady now. "Bring back some men to hold Josh down during the operation."

Ashen-faced, Cole grabbed his coat and hurried out, his big feet stumbling on the threshold of the door.

When he returned with four grim-looking men, I grabbed poor bewildered Betsy by the hand and stumbled across the snow-packed yard to the Johnstons' next door.

"What a shame! Oh, Lordy, what a crying shame!" Mrs. Johnston fussed, as she poured two cups of coffee and sat down opposite me with her sewing. A log in the fireplace hissed and flared as it broke apart.

I stared into my cup, studying the little curls of steam that rose from it. Wispy little twists of vapor rose languidly into the air. I could not bear to think beyond that cup of coffee. I tried to push aside thoughts of saws and blood and Josh's tortured screams. I knew I should be with him, holding his hand, trying to comfort him. The room was spinning around me. I had visions of Dr. Allen standing over Josh with that shiny saw with jagged dagger teeth.

I had to break the silence. "He just bought another farm, you know. He wants to move out to the country." I tried desperately to sound normal, but nothing was normal now. My voice quavered and seemed to come from far away.

Mrs. Johnston jabbed her needle nervously into the hem of some homespun jeans. "He'll have a hard time farming now."

My heart sank even lower, with a trembling kind of tightness. I need to be with him, I thought. They think I can't stand it, but he needs me now. Oh, God, the pain. The blood.

Was that a scream I heard? Was that the rasping sound of saw blade against bone?

I was getting dizzy. Everything was blurry. A roaring, whirlwind sound filled my head, then faded. Slowly, I sank into the beckoning blackness.

# Chapter 23

The amputation saved Josh's life, and for that we were thankful. Many died from gangrene; many lost far more than a foot. But still, it was hard to bear.

Josh improved slowly. As his fever cooled, his face regained its color and his strength gradually returned. Soon after the amputation he could sit on the side of the bed. A few days later, leaning on my shoulder, he hopped over to his rocker by the fire. The sight of him back in his chair renewed my hope.

On the first warm day of spring I opened wide the doors and windows and welcomed in the southern breeze, letting it waft away the last vestiges of gangrene smell. I helped Josh soak his stump in salt water, and bandaged it with bleached linen. When he was strong and steady enough, I brought down his old crutches from the loft, and he used them to hobble around the house.

His spirit was slower to heal than his leg. Never one to talk much, his silences now stretched into hours of brooding, broken by outbursts of temper.

"Look at me! A cripple!" he exploded. "I can't hunt, can't fish, can't do anything I like. I can't *farm*! What's going to happen to that farm?"

"It will get better for you, Josh. I remember a man in Cincinnati with a wooden leg. He got around just fine—limped a little, that's all. It takes time to heal." I tried to soothe him, but remembering his impatience when his leg was only broken, I knew we were in for a siege.

Josh suffered. He groaned with racking pains in a foot that was no more. He rolled and turned and cried out at night, reaching for his lost foot. By the dim light of the banked fire, I massaged his leg and tried to relax the cramping muscles.

How many nights did I stay up with him? And in the mornings I was up at dawn to stir the fire, start the mush for breakfast, feed the chickens, separate the milk that Cole brought in, churn the butter, wash the clothes, and spin and weave and sew—all the hundred chores that made the warp and weft of my life.

Cole milked the cow and fed the horses and chopped firewood. He brought in some tools from the gun shop, and he and Josh worked together in the house, rifling a barrel and replacing a damaged gunstock. Josh began to work on a carved stock for a gun to give to Dr. Allen in payment for his treatment. Most people paid the doctor in goods: hams or bushels of corn, shoes, wooden barrels, or buckskins.

I was pleased to see Josh so absorbed in carving the elaborate scroll design. "That gun is going to be a work of art," I told him. "It's much too beautiful to take hunting."

He laid his fine-honed carving knife on the table and looked up at me, his face pinched and grim. "Lucky for me I'm a gunsmith. Even a cripple can do that."

"It could be worse, Josh. At least you're alive."

Rage surged in his eyes. "You don't care, do you?" he snarled. "You never wanted to move out to the farm. Well, now I won't be able to farm, so we'll have to stay in town. That should make you very happy."

I felt as if he had slapped me. Exhaustion, after weeks of work and sleepless nights, had left me worn-out, but a spark of anger flared in me, too. "That's not fair! You know how bad I feel that you got hurt."

"Not as bad as I feel."

Sighing, I said, "Blaming me won't bring your foot back. It seems that all we can do is accept it and go on from there."

Without another word I wrapped shawls around Betsy and myself and led her outside. The chilly March wind nipped at us. The cold invigorated me. I embraced this moment, free from the stagnant smell of sickness in the house and Josh's accusing glance.

I decided to walk down the road and visit Parthena, Sam Hill's bride of last summer. Their new two-story home, with its sliding windows, covered front porch, and tasteful, expensive decorations was the talk of the town. Betsy was delighted.

Parthena looked surprised when she saw us standing on her porch, but welcomed us graciously. "Carrie! Betsy! Do come in! I was just hoping somebody might stop by."

Tea was served in fancy china cups, and Parthena lent Betsy an old lace scarf and feathered bonnet to play dress-up. Betsy looked quite the grown-up lady, sipping tea with us in her finery. The fire crackled cozily, bringing out the sparkle in the cut glass bowls and dishes on the shelves of Parthena's massive walnut china cupboard. Oblivious of the biting winds outside, we passed the afternoon in pleasant conversation.

For the first time in weeks, my mind was occupied by something other than Josh's foot.

When we returned to our cabin, Josh was sitting alone, huddled by the fire. "Where have you been?" he asked softly.

"Down at Parthena's. We had a nice visit."

"Carrie?" His voice was faint.

"Yes?"

The barest hint of tears glittered in his eyes. "I'm sorry."

I knelt before him and gently took his hand. After a moment's hesitation, I said softly, "Oh, Josh, I know how much you're suffering. If I could change things, I'd gladly trade places with you. But there's nothing I can do." My heart thudded painfully.

"Just be here, Carrie," he said, burying his head in my shoulder. "I've made up my mind not to let this thing destroy me."

My arms enfolded him and held him close to me. "I know you'll be all right. You're still the man who made the raft and navigated the Ohio, all the way to Illinois. You're just as brave and strong as you were then. And you're an artist, Josh. You can take a chunk of wood and create a thing of beauty."

"I can if you stick by me."

"I'm here beside you, Josh. You know I'm always here."

# Chapter 24

Somewhere deep inside me I discovered an unsuspected wealth of strength and independence.

Hitching Lucky to the wagon, I scoured the countryside looking for tenants for our new farm. Out past Athens, I found them—Willy Arnold, a husky farm boy, and Lucinda, his apple-cheeked bride. They thanked me heartily for this chance to move into the cabin and farm the land for halves.

"Just tell me what to do," I told Josh with newfound confidence. "I'll take care of all the details for the farms."

He broke into a rare laugh. "How my city girl has changed! Do you think your old Cincinnati friends would recognize you?"

"I'm a frontier woman now," I said, squaring my shoulders proudly. "I must be strong. Out here only the strong survive."

Survival was the ultimate challenge of the frontier, and there were those who could not meet it. Illness claimed the lives of many, including Dr. Allen's lovely Mary, his wife of only two years. We tried to comfort him as best we could.

That spring brought another blow to Widow Rutledge and her surviving family. When they couldn't pay the rent, their landlord, John McNamar, turned them out. The devastated Rutledge family packed their meager belongings into their old wagon and began the long hard trek to Iowa, where they had relatives. We saw them off, cursing John McNamar under our breaths.

Gunsmithing occupied most of Josh's time and energy. Every morning after breakfast he hobbled out to his shop on crutches. Sitting on his stool beside the workbench, he constructed new guns and repaired old ones, working longer hours as his strength returned.

"Remember that gun I made for Dr. Allen?" he asked me one sunny day in May. "The one with all the fancy carving?"

"How could I forget? It was a beauty."

"Well, he sold it to a gun dealer from Saint Louis, and now I have two orders for more guns like that. One of them's to be inlaid with silver."

I clasped his arm in delight. "Saint Louis! Josh, you're getting famous! I know I never saw a gun as beautiful as that. You're a real artist."

"Well, it's the one thing I can still do. Even with only one foot, I can sit and carve."

"You get around well on your crutches. I think you're doing fine, Josh."

"They say it's going to take six months or so for the stump to heal enough to fit it with a peg," he said dejectedly. "I'm sure going to be sick of these crutches by then."

"Well, think on the time when you'll no longer need them."

Those days I was busier than ever with the house and gar-

den, spinning and weaving, and now the trips out to the
farms. The tenants plowed the fields and planted the crops
and tended the spring birthings of calves, piglets, and lambs.
One of our ewes died in lambing, leaving a little orphaned
lamb.

"Mama, can I bring this lamb back to our house? Please?"
Betsy begged, stroking its curly fleece. "I can feed it with a
bottle. I haven't had my own pet since we gave the kittens
away."

"Now, honey, you still have the mama cat, and all those
baby chicks and guineas are like pets." But gazing into her
dark, imploring eyes, I weakened. *You were an orphaned
lamb yourself when you came to us,* I thought, bending down
to hug her. "Sure, you can have it."

The trembling lamb lay on a pallet of soft rags on the seat
between us as we drove home. Betsy cuddled him and talked
to him during the bumpy ride back to town.

Dan Cooper, one of our tenants, had sheared the sheep,
and the bulky bundles of fleece filled the wagon bed. Old
pieces of cloth, including an old petticoat, were wrapped
around the wool and held with large thorns.

Betsy and I hauled the sacks of wool to Sam Hill's carding
mill. I no longer had to card the wool by hand. A yoke of
oxen hitched to a forty-foot wooden wheel did the hard work;
all I had to do was collect the finished product later. Listening to the heavy clump of oxen hooves and to the creaky,
slowly-turning wheel, I thought of all the time this machine
saved for the women of our town. It had released us from the
endless job of rubbing those infernal cards together for sep-
arating and combing the wool for spinning.

The carding mill was a modern addition to New Salem.
Yet I knew our town was slowly dying. One by one the old

families moved away, most of them down the road to Petersburg. For some reason that new town was growing as fast as ours shrank. Oh, New Salem still had over a hundred citizens, more than twenty houses, but the course was set and undeniable.

The fatal blow struck our town in late May, when the post office was moved to Petersburg. Abe Lincoln was no longer our postmaster. By then, Abe was well established as a surveyor and, with all the new towns springing up, he kept busy with that trade. But his new love, the law, absorbed every free moment.

One day I saw him riding down the road in front of our house, his face buried in a leather-covered book. "Good morning, Abe! What are you reading today?" I called, leaving off sweeping the front stoop to walk toward him.

He looked up and waved at me. "Mornin', Carrie. I'm just back from Springfield. I borrowed another law book from John Stuart."

"How long do you think you'll have to study to get to be a lawyer, Abe?"

A rueful grin crossed his long, craggy face. "Well, I'm not sure about that. I'm runnin' for the legislature again this year, so I'll need to take time out to campaign."

"Now, Abe, there's no need to worry about that. You know you have the votes of all the men around here. If we women could vote, you would have twice as many."

"Well, thanks. That's good to hear. But Sangamon's a mighty big county. I've got to get around to all the towns."

"Good luck to you," I said. "And try not to work too hard on those books."

Glancing down at the page before him, he said, "You

know, I don't consider this work. Work is choppin' wood or cuttin' hay. This is what I do for pleasure.''

"I know just what you mean," I said, and waved as he rode away under the silky summer sky.

By late June Josh had a load of guns ready to take to Jacksonville. The two guns for Saint Louis, carved and polished with painstaking care, were nearly finished, too.

"That dealer from Saint Louis is coming by to get them. Around the first of July, his letter said.'' The summer heat clung moistly to the evening air as Josh rubbed more linseed oil into the maple gunstock. "He's paying me a big price.''

"Fine,'' I murmured, concentrating on the intricate threading of my loom.

"I can't believe what some men will pay for a fancy gun. It doesn't shoot one bit better than the plainest hunting rifle. But for some reason they crave that fancy inlay work.''

"It's more than a gun, Josh. It's a work of art.''

He shook his head. "To me the art is in the works of it. Getting all those little parts balanced just right—now, that's an art. Carving is a breeze.''

A few days later a handsome carriage pulled to a stop in front of our house. A portly, well-dressed man stepped out and strode up to our front door. Our guinea hens screamed out their customary alarm, fluffing up their gray-and-white feathers and scurrying in all directions.

The man greeted me with a slight bow. His fleshy face, neatly-trimmed beard, and modish clothes gave him the look of one who appreciated his position in the world. "I'm James MacAllister from Saint Louis. Perhaps your husband has spoken of me.''

My fingers fussed nervously with the button at the neckline of my faded housedress. I smoothed back a stray lock of hair and said, "Yes, let me show you to his shop out back."

As he followed me across the yard, the heavy dust settled on his highly polished boots. I glanced at them, and suddenly our little house and yard seemed painfully humble.

While Mr. MacAllister talked to Josh inside the shop, Betsy and I went out front. The sunlight filtering through the trees dappled his fancy carriage and sleek black horse with patches of gold.

Betsy's eyes were wide with wonder. "Is that the kind of wagon people have in Saint Louis?"

"Not everybody, dear. He must be very rich."

"Oh, Mama," she said eagerly. "That horse is beautiful!"

Mr. MacAllister overheard her words as he walked toward us carrying his flannel-wrapped guns. "You know, that's what my daughter named him—Beauty," he said, with a hearty laugh. "Would you like to take a little ride with me, young lady? Just down the street and back?"

"Oh, Mama, could I?" Betsy's face beamed.

"It's all right, dear. Just a little ways."

After lifting her to the high seat, Mr. MacAllister climbed up beside her and they rode off together jauntily. Betsy sat up tall and proud, a tiny princess surveying her realm. When they reached the store, they turned around and came back.

She jumped down into my arms with a squeal. "Oh, Mama! That was fun! You should have seen Eddie and Polly when I waved to them. They couldn't believe it was really me."

Josh and I were laughing as we bade the man good-bye. Then we stepped inside the house, and Josh said, "He's ordered six more inlaid guns. That's a lot of money, Carrie. I can't believe my luck.''

"You deserve it. It's time you had some good luck.''

His elation carried through to the town's big Fourth of July celebration. Old neighbors who had moved away came back to join in the festivities. The day before the holiday, the men dug long trenches and started fires in them. They hung huge sides of beef and pork on iron rods over the fires and stayed up all night to turn them, basting them with butter.

We housewives cooked all morning, then brought out our sumptuous dishes, loading down the long plank tables with the feast. A group of young girls waved dish towels to keep away the flies, as the mingled smells of ham and fried chicken, baked beans and garden vegetables, fruit pies and frosted cakes wafted over the banquet area.

During the afternoon candidates electioneered and speakers gave patriotic talks. Later someone read the Declaration of Independence. The young boys played bullpen, while the girls jumped rope and ran around the flying jenny. Best of all, the whole crowd joined together to sing the old songs.

The most exciting part of the day for us was the shooting match. A hush ran through the crowd as Josh clumped out on his crutches to the mark. Leaning on his left crutch, he lifted his long rifle to his shoulder and took careful aim. With three deafening blasts he shot out the flames of three distant candles. It looked easy, but no one else could do it. Josh had won the shooting match.

"Five dollars! What a grand prize, Josh!'' I said as we drove home.

Betsy tugged his sleeve. "Let me see it, Daddy. I've never seen five whole dollars."

His face radiated with pride. "Maybe I can't walk like other men, but I guess I'm still the best shot in this neck of the woods."

# Chapter 25

By late fall Josh's leg had healed enough to be fitted for a peg. With a flare of his old fiery spirit, he gritted his teeth, leaned on his new elaborately-carved cane, and began the painful process of learning to walk again. His armpits were calloused from months of using crutches and he joked that he felt half-dressed without them.

Josh did much better than I expected, all in all. He finally came to terms with his handicap, and stoically accepted it. When he realized he couldn't walk behind a plow, he contented himself with letting his tenants do the farming. A little laughter eased its way back into our home.

Another major milestone was reached when little Betsy was ready to start school. Mentor Graham was to be her teacher. One day in the fall, just before school started, we walked out to his home to visit Sarah and the girls and to catch up on the latest news.

Mentor, dressed for rough work, waved to us from the barnyard as Betsy and I neared the house. I couldn't help smiling at the contrast between the stained, worn clothes he had on and the formal black velvet vest and bleached linen shirt he wore to school. Yet, even as he labored at his stable chores or brick work, Mentor seemed preoccupied, his mind always on his books.

"Are you all ready for school, Betsy?" he called out to her that day. "We'll be starting soon, you know."

"Oh, I can't wait, Uncle Mentor! I already know my ABCs. Mama said you'd teach me how to read," she bubbled. Since her sixth birthday the past July, she had been counting the days until school would begin.

We walked past Sarah's flower garden, still a bright patchwork quilt of color, and she met us at the door. "Carrie! Betsy! Now, aren't you two a sight for sore eyes? Come in and sit a spell. I could use a rest myself."

Noticing the tired lines around her eyes, I said, "You work too hard, Sarah."

"Don't we all?" She brushed her hair back absently, as she dropped into a chair across from me. "Here I am with seven kids to take care of, and you're still waitin'. Isn't that the way of it?" She sighed.

"Let me help you with your work while Betsy plays with the girls. She gets so lonesome for children her own age."

"I'm just tryin' to catch up with mendin'. If you want to help with that, we can visit while we sew."

She reached into her sewing basket and handed me a threaded needle and some well-worn children's play clothes. "How's Josh these days?" she asked.

"Pretty well. It's amazing how a person learns to accept these things. You just go on with life the best you can."

Sarah walked over to the fire and got the coffee pot.

"That's what we've been tellin' Abe," she said, as she filled two ironstone cups. "Elizabeth Asbell's sister is up from Kentucky for a visit . . . Mary Owens, by name. She's a bright girl . . . got a good education, too. We're hopin' Abe might take to her. You know, he's been grievin' over Ann for more than a year now. It's been so hard on him."

"Does he like this Mary Owens?"

"Well, that's hard to say. You know how Abe is. He likes everybody. Mary's older than Ann was—and more outspoken. She's a big girl, tall and big boned. Abe's been squirin' her around a bit. Who knows what might happen?"

"Abe really needs a wife to make a home for him," I said. "He's been boarding around in other people's houses ever since he came to town."

I thought of Abe in his habitual pose, nose buried in a book. He always seemed alone these days, even when surrounded by other people. He had become a gaunt and sad-faced, solitary man.

Sarah bit off a length from her spool of thread. "He has his license to practice law now."

"Good for him! That's a big step."

"Yes, and he's off to the legislature again the first of December. That election sure was a boost to his confidence."

"I'm glad for him." I picked up a shirt and chose a button from the basket to replace a lost one.

"I suppose now that Abe is licensed, he'll want to move to Petersburg, like everybody else." Sarah jabbed a needle through a torn hem. "Now, there's a town that's boomin'. Already has seven stores. Poor New Salem just keeps goin' downhill.''

''Somebody said that in the last three years more than five hundred new towns have been laid out in Illinois. I just can't understand what's happening to New Salem.''

''Folks are so blamed anxious to move on,'' she said with an angry sniff. ''They just yank down the logs and carry off their houses to some new place. Not us Grahams. These bricks are here to stay. We've got our house and farm and brickyard, and Mentor's got his school down the way.''

The baby began to cry in the bedroom. Sarah brought the chubby little fellow out and nursed him by the fire as I watched with envy.

She then handed him over to my waiting arms. I rocked him, snuggling the flannel blanket around his contented face. ''Oh, Sarah, how I wish I'd have another baby,'' I moaned. ''Betsy can't wait to start school, but I don't know what I'll do without her. My house will seem like a tomb without her bustling around all day.''

How right I was. When I walked Betsy down to school the first day of the session, my throat choked up so that I could hardly swallow.

My little girl seemed just a baby to me as I watched her talking with the other children. Then the students formed into groups. Some of them looked nearly grown, taller even than me. I glanced down at Betsy's wide eyes and eager face, and I thought my heart would break. I longed to keep her home with me forever.

When Mentor showed her to her place on the log bench,

down in front with the youngest children, I knew the time had come for me to leave.

The lonely walk back home seemed endless, with silence my new companion on the wooded path. Where were the chattering squirrels and cheery robins that had greeted us on our way to school? I trudged along, dreading to face the empty house that awaited me.

After school Betsy ran all the way home, filled with news of her exciting day. "I have my own slate, and I'm going to learn to write real pretty," she bubbled at suppertime. "Uncle Mentor's going to teach me to read and spell and do my numbers. We get to play outside sometimes, too."

"That's nice, honey." I knew my baby girl was truly gone now.

"One girl brought a jump rope and I learned some new songs to sing while I jump."

Josh laughed, ruffling her curls playfully. "You learned all that the first day? Just think how smart you'll be when you've gone to school a week."

Josh was busier than ever in his shop. Cole had learned the trade well, and the two of them worked all day making guns. Josh made the fancy rifles for Saint Louis, while Cole concentrated on the solid utilitarian guns used around New Salem. A steady stream of customers crossed our yard for the shop out back, each one setting off a wave of alarm among my guinea hens.

When Betsy was at school and the silence became unbearable, I went out to the gun shop. I loved to watch Josh work, each movement of his hands meticulous and exact. The shop smelled of the linseed oil the men used to polish the gunstocks.

The place was always hot and noisy, and crackling with activity. Josh would limp over to the forge, plunge a piece of metal into its fiery belly, heat it red-hot, and hammer it to new shapes on the anvil. The steady clanging of his hammer sent tangible vibrations through the air. Sometimes Josh greased the rifling guide with lard, and he and Cole cut rifling into the long iron barrels. Behind the workbench, a hundred tools lined the wall, each for a different job.

My husband was an artist at his work, a master craftsman, and I was proud of him. And now, more than ever, I respected the manner in which he dealt with his handicap. He was a better man on one leg than many were on two.

That year we had another dismally hard winter. It started early. On December twentieth a cold, hard rain fell for hours. Then the wind shifted, bringing with it a sudden freeze, a drop of over forty degrees within a few minutes. The slush turned instantly to ice.

Behind our house the chickens' feet froze to the henhouse yard. Cole threw on his heavy coat and gloves and ran out with the ax to free them. If he hadn't rescued them in time, they would have died.

The instant freeze killed several travelers caught out on the prairie and many head of livestock in the fields. Later Josh came in from his shop with yet another horror tale. "I heard about a man who was riding to Springfield when the freeze struck. By the time he got there, his coat was frozen solid to the saddle."

I shook my head and pulled my shawl tighter around my shoulders.

"His friends in town had to ungirth the saddle and carry

it inside, with the fellow still attached. I guess they finally thawed him out by the fire.''

"It's a wonder any of us survive these cruel winters," I said grimly. "What a bitter price we pay to live in Illinois."

A bitter price indeed. Yet, we knew that after winter came spring. We knew the fields and woods would bloom again with wildflowers as they did nowhere else. Once again the gentle southern breeze would waft its sweet perfume across the fertile, waiting soil of our vast prairie.

# Chapter 26

That year, 1837, our nation inaugurated its new president, Martin Van Buren, in Washington, D.C. How far away that seemed. It might as well have been on the moon. Far more important to us in New Salem was the fact that our state legislature had voted to move the capital to Springfield. The crowd in front of Sam Hill's store was caught up in a fever of excitement.

"Reckon we know who we got to thank for this move."

"Yep. Old Abe's done some mighty fancy logrollin' for us this time around."

Abe Lincoln had a busy spring. The first of March, before the legislative session ended, he was admitted to the bar. He had made quite a name for himself at the capital, with his keen mind and his gift for clear commonsense expression. When he returned to New Salem a full-fledged lawyer, we knew his days in our little village were numbered.

John Stuart, one of the state's leading political and legal figures, had offered him a partnership. So, early in April, after a series of long farewells, Abe packed his saddlebags with his few clothes, books, and surveying tools, and moved to Springfield.

We had watched so many people move away from New Salem, but Abe was special to us all. He came to our town as a boy, and we took him in. He ate at our tables, slept under our roofs, read our books and newspapers. We watched him grow in knowledge and experience, until our town was too small for him. Springfield, our new capital, was the best place for an up-and-coming lawyer.

Yet, Abe would always be a part of us. He was family—and we wished him well.

We had a cool, rainy spring. The river ran high and fast, relentless in its quest to drain the land. The roads were spongy with mire.

I worried about Josh, with his wooden peg. "Be careful when you walk out to the shop. It's so muddy in the yard," I cautioned him.

He grinned and patted my shoulder indulgently. "Don't you worry about me. I stay right on the boardwalk Cole laid down."

"What would we do without that boy?"

"I don't know. He's turning into quite a gunsmith, too." Josh shook his head pensively. "I suppose one day he'll want to move out on his own."

"Before long we'll be the only people left in this town. I can't believe how many families have moved away."

"Well, it hasn't hurt my gun business. I'm swamped with orders from Springfield, and there's always Jacksonville, and MacAllister in Saint Louis. We're doing real well, Carrie."

I smiled as I caught the gleam of pride in his eyes. "I always knew you would."

"Maybe when I get more money saved, we can think of

moving, too. We could get a bigger house somewhere. Build a bigger shop, with a better room for Cole.''

"Uh-huh," I murmured absently. Betsy came running through the doorway then, and I reached out to take the basket of potatoes she had brought up from the root cellar.

I didn't want to argue with Josh, but I was in no hurry to leave New Salem. My friends were there. They were more family to Betsy than her own grandparents, aunts, uncles, and cousins in Ohio, whom she had never seen.

A few days of warm spring sunshine had brought out masses of wildflowers. The bees found the phlox and burrowed into the pink blossoms. Soon they would find the violets and Dutchman's breeches, the lady slippers, sweet Williams, and bluebells. I opened the doors and windows wide, and the fragrance of the flowers wafted through the house, carrying away the last traces of winter's mustiness.

That morning I was driven by an urge to start anew. I began to clean the house. I polished furniture with linseed oil and pulled apart the beds to wash the sheets and quilts, and put the feather mattresses out to air in the sunlight.

"Can I go with Lucy to pick wildflowers?" Betsy asked me, as I hung my laundry on the fence.

I stopped my work and gazed down at her. She seemed to glow with vibrant life and health, her dark eyes gleaming, soft hair glistening in the sunshine. "Just be careful, dear. It's muddy yet. Don't fall and stain your dress," I said, smoothing back her hair and retying her blue yarn bow.

Impulsively she reached out to me and kissed my cheek. Her sweet fragrance lingered in the air as she and Lucy skipped on down the road, long skirts bouncing.

Those little girls don't have a care in the world, I thought.

Oh, to be a child again, to find that same delight in picking wildflowers.

After I had finished hanging up the wash, I went inside, skimmed the cream from the pail of milk, and began to churn butter. I was still churning when I heard agitated shouts from down the road.

"A little girl fell in the river!" someone yelled.

My hands froze on the churn. My head spun. All the blood drained from it. With a frenzied burst, I flew out the door and down the street, oblivious of the people running alongside me. Betsy. Betsy. Betsy. Her name echoed through my mind with every panting breath I took.

When I reached the bluff that overlooked the swollen river, I saw Lucy, Betsy's friend, sobbing against her mother's skirt.

"Where's Betsy?" I demanded.

Lucy's sobs became hysterical.

I shook the child insanely. "Where is she? Tell me!"

Someone took my arm. "They're looking for her now. She slipped. . . ."

"Don't be silly! Betsy knows better than to go down by the river," I insisted angrily. "She would never . . ."

Lucy lifted her tearstained face and twisted her hands together nervously. "It was the white violets. She wanted to pick some for you." The child sniffed convulsively. "They were growing on the side of the bluff."

White violets. My favorite.

Slowly all the life drained from me. My legs could no longer hold me. I sank down to the ground, burying my head in my hands. I knew I must shut out the world, escape the madness of this day.

A grim-faced band of men searched for her. Josh helped, hobbling through the mud along the river. Someone found her lifeless little body washed up downstream, in a grove of willows at the water's edge.

Drowned. Dead. The words held no meaning for me. I felt a coldness passing over me. Numbness enveloped me. I could feel no sorrow, only cold and emptiness.

It was not possible that Betsy was gone. Why, any minute now she'd come running through the door, laughing, spilling over with excitement as she handed me a big bouquet of wildflowers. White violets.

I don't remember how I got back home. I only know they brought my Betsy back and laid her out there. I remember that our neighbors came and sat up the night with us. They spoke softly, their conversation touching a hundred inane subjects. Politics and weather. Sicknesses and family histories. Everything but Betsy.

Josh sat in silence, staring at the floor. He looked like an old man, his face drawn and ashen.

My thoughts were all with Betsy. Little Betsy, when she came to us, borne in Bowling Green's massive arms. An angel sent to take the place of my lost babies.

That still, pale figure in the coffin was not my Betsy. Betsy could never stay silent for a minute. Even in her sleep she smiled.

I could see her running across the meadow toward me, arms outstretched, her curls and long skirt flying out behind her, her face a picture of delight. Then, giggling, she caught me and threw her arms around my waist. Laughing, too, I bent down and kissed her little nose.

I thought of her lovely angel face. Not cold and white, like that poor child's in the coffin. Betsy's face was a pale peach, set with huge dark eyes and framed by soft, silky hair that glimmered like spun sunlight. She was a big schoolgirl now, learning to read and write and cipher.

An icy hand gripped my heart. Betsy was gone. With stark clarity, I knew it was true. She would never see her second year of school. Never see her seventh birthday. I retched, ran outside, and retched again. I beat my fists against the doorframe, battling the flood of memories.

I stumbled back inside and threw myself across the bed. Still silent, Josh came and sat beside me. His sweaty hand and my trembling one joined and held. Listening to the muted voices of our neighbors, I tried to take some comfort in their presence. All of them had felt the cruel scythe of death in their lives, too. I knew I was not alone.

But the hurt was overwhelming. Little Betsy. Angel child. She had filled our home with song, with smiles, with sunlight, since the day she came. How could I go on without her?

Survival. Endurance. That was all that mattered now. Life must go on. I could not remember why.

I pinned my mother's cameo to Betsy's dress before we buried her.

# Chapter 27

I cooked, I cleaned, I worked the garden. I fed the chickens and envied them their senseless scurrying for grain. Never did they mourn a lost child. Never did they ache to see a father and sister far away.

I could not bear to write my family that Betsy had died. A dozen times I began the letter; a dozen times I threw down the pen in frustration. Where could I find words to tell of my grief?

My sister still wrote to me. Eliza's letters seemed written in some strange foreign language, from a long-forgotten world where fashion was the all-consuming interest. She told me that leg-of-mutton sleeves were going out of style. The newest dresses featured sleeves narrow at the top, with full-ness below the elbows. She said she bought an elegant white satin bonnet with a high crown, a wide brim, and an attached lace veil.

When I read her letters, I could only shake my head and wonder. Had Eliza always been so frivolous and shallow?

The trappings had long ago been stripped from me. I was down to the essentials now: birth and life and death.

All summer my loss was like a leech, sucking my life's blood. Every night Josh and Cole and I sat around the supper table, eating silently, always conscious of the empty fourth place. How I missed the eager little voice that never stopped its questioning.

After meals I washed and dried the dishes all alone, longing for my helper, longing for the sound of her sweet songs that made work seem like play.

I knew work was a blessing, a pretense at normalcy. I had my work to do, and Josh had his. Every morning after breakfast he leaned on his cane and limped out to his shop, where he worked all day to fill the growing stack of orders for his guns. He was totally absorbed in his work, grim and silent.

Our private grief became a dark secret we tried to hide from one another, as if in sharing it, it might somehow magnify. We did not speak of Betsy, not even to say her name. There was a bottomless black pit where she had once been, one we cautiously sidestepped as we tried to carry on our lives.

One early-August morning Josh said, "MacAllister in Saint Louis says he needs three more inlaid guns. I'll have to start them right away."

"It's going to be another hot day." I sighed and pointed out the window. "Just look out there. You can almost see the moisture in the air. It's like steam from the teakettle."

"Yeah. I'll have to get the forge work done early, while it's still fairly cool."

"Will you be doing more iron work, now that the blacksmith has moved away?"

"I can't say. I'm swamped with gun orders." His wooden

peg clumped heavily on the floorboards as he limped over to the door. He stopped and glanced at me with sad eyes. "God, I hate to see all these people move away."

The air in the house felt heavy and oppressive. "I can't understand why they all want to leave New Salem," I said. "What's so special about Petersburg?"

"They're not all moving there. Some are going farther west. Jack Kelso, Waddell, Morris, and Burner, too."

Jack Kelso. I thought of that whimsical gypsylike man and his guitar. He would be sorely missed at future celebrations.

I wiped the table with nervous vigor. "I hear Jacob Bale is buying all the land when people move away."

"He's buying out the carding mill and wool house, too. His son Hardin's going to run it. With that and the grist mill and the tavern to operate, Jake should have enough work to keep all seven of his kids occupied."

"Well, I'm glad they're staying here," I said. "There are still a few of us."

Josh hesitated for a moment, chewing on a broom straw. "Who would have thought it?" he asked. "When we came here seven years ago, everybody thought New Salem was the great city of the future."

"Seven years . . . Has it been seven years?" I blinked away the mist that filmed my eyes.

"Hard to believe, isn't it?"

"I haven't seen my family in seven years. Papa is getting old . . ."

"Yes, so are my folks." He gazed down at the floor for a long while, pondering. Then, in a low voice, he said, "Maybe this fall, if things go right and the guns keep selling . . . we can make a trip back home."

My pulse quickened as I caught my breath. Instantly the lump of hurt inside me lightened.

Josh wrapped his arm around my shoulder. "Would you like that, Carrie? Would that make you happy?" From beneath his furrowed brow, his eyes searched mine.

I nodded and tried to smile. I suddenly realized how long it had been since my mouth had formed a smile. "Yes, Josh. We should go."

All that day my thoughts lingered on the trip to Cincinnati. I longed to see our families, meet the little nieces and nephews who had been born since we came to Illinois.

There would be pain, I knew. I would have to tell them about Betsy. How many times had I promised her that trip, described to her the city and her grandparents' homes. It would be painful to go without her, but Josh and I both needed to be with our families for a while.

The next day Sarah stopped by to see me, never asking why I hadn't been to her house lately. She must have sensed I couldn't bear to see her children playing without my Betsy there among them.

"Carrie, I haven't seen you in a coon's age. Come walk with me up to the store," she said. "Sam just got in some new goods from Saint Louis."

"Oh, Sarah, I need to work in the garden."

"Now, you know good and well you can always do that later. Come with me. There's some new dress goods I want to show you. I think I might just make me a new Sunday dress."

"Well . . . all right." I reached back to untie my apron. "To tell the truth, I haven't been anywhere for weeks."

"That's just what I figured. Carrie, you've got to get hold of yourself. No use givin' way and broodin' over things."

"I know."

"Remember what we talked about when you first came out here? Frontier women have to be strong. That's just a simple fact. It's the only way any of us can survive."

"I know, Sarah. I know you're right." I choked back a sob. "But it hurts so bad."

Her strong, wiry arms wrapped around me and her voice crooned soothingly against my ear. "Oh, don't I know it, honey. Don't I know how bad it hurts."

I could no longer hold back the flood of tears I had bottled up inside me for so long.

Later, when we walked down to the store, I sensed an eerie quiet in the town. Uncurtained windows in empty houses stared at me, as if to ask why I was still there. "It seems almost funny now," I said. "I was dead set against moving to the farm because I thought I would be lonely. Pretty soon I'll be alone right here in the middle of New Salem."

But the porch outside Hill's store still held its lively group of people from the area, discussing all the weighty matters of the day. The air was filled with talk of slavery.

"It's a sin. Just flat out simple," stated one.

"Plain as the noonday sun."

Another shook his head. "Things are a durn sight different down in cotton country. I seen it with my own eyes. Some of them fields is big as whole farms in these parts. A man's got to have a powerful heap o' help to farm that."

"Help, maybe. But not slaves. They're gonna have to free the slaves, for a fact. It just ain't Christian. You can't own another man."

"You claim it's Christian to take a man's rightful property away from him? Them slaves have been bought and paid for legal."

"You're a damn fool! You can't buy people! It just ain't right!"

"Here, boys, now settle down," a calmer voice interjected. "We don't want no riots here. Bad enough to have that stuff goin' on down in Alton. I don't reckon our jawin' 'bout it's gonna make no difference one way or tother."

Sarah and I stepped into the store, glad to escape the dissension on the porch. Inside, the tang of fresh spices mingled with the smell of new things: cloth and crockery, wooden bowls and iron tools, leather saddle bags and candy in glass jars, lead and gunpowder, scrub brushes, mats, and hats woven from corn shucks. Two of Josh's guns hung on the wall above the whiskey barrel.

"What can I do for you ladies this fine day?" Sam asked.

Pointing to the shelf behind him, Sarah said, "That new dress goods from Saint Louis. I'd like to feel of it."

His no-nonsense Yankee face was inscrutable as he laid six thick bolts down on the counter and unrolled each one a half a yard.

"Sam, you won't be moving away, too, will you?" I asked. "So many people have left this town."

He rubbed his chin thoughtfully. "Well, I can't say. To be honest with you, business hasn't been too good lately. I guess everybody feels the pinch of the Panic."

On the way home, I asked Sarah, "Do you know what caused the Panic?"

"Too much borrowin', I think," she said, shifting her bundle of dress goods to her other arm. "Folks borrowed to buy land. Then the price of produce fell, and now they can't pay back the loans. Mentor reads all the newspapers, and he says banks have failed all around the country. Lots of folks are out of work in the cities."

I felt a sinking feeling in my chest. "Do you think the price of grain will go back up this fall?"

"If it don't, we're all gonna end up farmin' for our health," she said glumly.

Just then I noticed three little girls playing in the side yard by the Johnstons' house. Checked gingham dresses and long braids fluttered in the breeze, as the girls reached up to pick the bright blossoms from the towering hollyhocks.

"My mama knows how to make dolls from these," one young voice called out gleefully.

Hollyhock dolls. The blossoms forming wide ruffled skirts. How Betsy loved them, standing them in rows, pretty ladies filling an imaginary dance floor.

Betsy. Darling Betsy. My hands began to tremble. The knot in the pit of my stomach tightened. Everywhere I looked my world was filled with agonizing reminders.

Why had I let her go pick flowers that day? I should have kept her home with me. I should have watched her closer, should have . . .

Sarah pointed to the children. "Those girls are fixin' to have themselves a good time."

My step accelerated, as I tried to escape the sounds of their laughter.

"Carrie, look at them," Sarah said.

"No. Don't ask me to." I turned and pleaded with my eyes. "What are you doing to me? They're alive, and Betsy's dead."

"The way I see it, there's only one way you can hold on to someone even after they're gone. In your memories. In your mind you can always have them with you. You can remember all the good times you had together."

"She's gone. I can't bear to think about her."

''If you push her from your mind, then she really is gone. If you won't let yourself see her and hear her voice in all these other young ones.'' Sarah's voice was soothing as warmed oil. She gently laid her hand on my arm. ''I don't mean to preach to you, but if I was in your place, I'd try to remember every single minute I spent with Betsy. I believe I'd try to be thankful for the time we had. Life is mighty fragile, you know, and death is just a breath away from all of us. Oh, Carrie, please don't let your grief keep eatin' at you. Life's too short for that.''

I nodded, feeling weak and childish as I thought of all the others who had borne their sorrows so courageously—Abe and Dr. Allen and Mrs. Rutledge. From now on I would be braver, too. If I could just reach out to Josh . . . if we could share our grief . . . maybe that would lighten it.

But we had each built up hard, protective shells until we were like two polite strangers. The warm intimacy of our early years was only a memory. Like Betsy.

At night we lay separate and distant. Long after I had crawled between the sheets, Josh sat rocking silently beside the hearth. When he finally came to bed, reeking of the whiskey he downed during his solitary vigils, I feigned the sleep that eluded me.

I was certain Josh no longer loved me. I had failed him in so many ways. Where were the sons to carry on his family trade? The daughters to brighten our silent home? Where was the strong wife who could comfort him and ease his burdens, instead of always needing comforting herself?

By September, the Panic had grown worse. Prices for farm crops would not repay the cost of seed. Men who had ordered guns from Josh saw they would not have the cash to pay for them. Sudden cancellations from Springfield and Saint Louis left Josh with a shop full of guns he could not sell.

"Carrie . . ." he said hesitantly, "I hate to tell you this . . ."

I knew what was coming.

He cleared his throat. "Maybe next year."

"Yes. Of course." I looked away, trying to hide my bitter disappointment.

"I'm real sorry, Carrie, but we just don't have the money to go back home this fall."

# Chapter 28

In the middle of my own painful struggle, I had to watch the slow death of our little town. Dr. Regnier moved to Clary's Grove. Alex Ferguson, the shoemaker, moved out to a farm. The Wharys, Burners, all the new neighbors were gone now.

That fall I peered from my window at the handful of children gathering walnuts in the woods behind our house. Two years earlier there had been an army of them, their boisterous laughter clamoring through the trees.

Betsy had gone out with them. I remembered how we giggled at her little hands, blackened with walnut stain.

I busied myself with weaving things for Christmas, trying to drown my memories in mind-numbing activity. The hands that threw the shuttle looked like a stranger's hands to me. Strong, bony hands they were, brown and freckled from long hours of gardening.

I glanced down at my gaunt body and suddenly recalled the soft, warm curves of the bride from Cincinnati. Where was that girl now? My rare glimpses in the little mirror on the wall showed me a woman with sad, dark-rimmed eyes, old at twenty-seven—a woman who had forgotten how to smile.

"What are you making?" Josh asked, as I sat weaving one chilly autumn day.

I looked up from my loom, surprised at his sudden interest. "Oh, just a blanket for Willy and Lucinda's new baby. They're good tenants, aren't they?"

"Sure are. It's a shame the market is so bad. Those kids have worked hard. I'm just afraid they won't have much to show for it this year." Josh seemed in a rare talkative mood.

"At least they have a place to live and enough to eat," I said, exhaling a long sigh. "Maybe next year will be better for all of us."

"The Coopers probably would have bought their own land by now if it hadn't been for the Panic. They've been farming our place for four years now. The price of land is still high, though, even with the Panic. I guess people know that land is real . . . something you can hold to. Not like this damned paper money. The value of it jumps up and down like a jack-in-the-box."

After a long hesitation, I murmured softly, "You were right to buy the farms, Josh. I'm sorry I fought against you about it. It seems ironic now. I didn't want to move away from town, and now the town is moving away from me."

He walked up behind my chair and began to knead my shoulders with his strong fingers. I quivered with the rush of feeling his touch brought to me. It was months since he had touched me.

"No, I think you were the smart one," he said. "Maybe you had a premonition something would happen to me. Look at me. Farm work is beyond me now." His fingers stopped abruptly, then resumed their kneading with a lighter touch.

"Anyway, I have my hands full making guns. Thank God Cole is here to help me."

"He left right after supper again last night. Where did he go?"

Josh shrugged. "He's out courting Mary Martha. Well, he's nineteen now. One of these days he'll be wanting to start a family of his own."

Josh limped over to stir the fire, and I thought of the big families that were standard for those parts. Eight, ten, even twelve children. And here we sat with none. Not one. Only graves down the hill, resting silently beneath the giant oaks.

I felt I could not bear the gloom of another winter. Desolate gray days, without my Betsy's songs to bring some cheer. Christmas, without her squeals of surprise and delight. January blizzards. Snowbound days. Empty, silent days, without a ray of sunshine to relieve the dreariness.

One such gloomy day in November I felt the first fateful sign of illness—a shiver, then an icy chill. I changed into my gown and crawled beneath the blankets, shaking after a while with violent chills.

When Josh walked in and saw me lying in bed, he stopped, a startled look on his face. "What is it?"

"I guess it's the fever, like I had before." My teeth chattered noisily as I tried to talk. "Can you find me another blanket?"

"Sure. Then I'm going to get the doctor. You haven't looked well for a long time. You're so thin and pale."

I was shaking too hard to reply.

Dr. Allen was out at a birthing. When he finally came hours later, my body was burning with fever, like a chunk of meat being braised over a fire.

"Open wide, Carrie. Let me check your tongue," he said.

"I'll take your pulse. All right. Now you'll have to sit up in a chair."

Shakily I eased my achy burning body from the bed. My head felt huge and full, and spun as Josh helped me to the rocker. They made me extend one arm, and Josh handed me a stick to hold while the doctor tied a cord halfway between my elbow and my shoulder. Then he stabbed me in a blood vessel with a thumb lance, and he bled me.

The room whirled around me. An eerie humming filled my head as I watched my thick red blood slowly, slowly flow out into a glass jar.

Dr. Allen then gave me an emetic, and I gagged and vomitted into a bowl. I was weak. Weak and sick. All I wanted was to lie down.

But the doctor wasn't finished yet. He still had his final purging. Calomel and jalop, then a dose of castor oil, to completely cleanse my bowels. I was drained, an empty shell.

Dizzily I sank back against the pillow and heard the doctor say, "Just chicken broth for her. Nothing more than that. I'll send down some pills in a day or two."

My eyes closed. I felt as if a black cloth had been pulled over me, shutting out the world.

I lay for days and weeks, too weak to raise my head. The fever never left me. My blood felt like liquid fire in my veins. My eyes could not focus through the misty haze that seemed to fill the room.

I woke and slept, and when I slept, I dreamt of Betsy. I dreamt that she was playing in our yard beneath the maple trees. She was pulling a tiny baby in a wagon. My lost little Robbie.

When I woke, my fever raged again. I had been sick so long; I could not recall that I had ever been young, full of health and hope. I could not recall that I had ever known love. Now there was only sickness and the black cave of despair.

"Josh, will you bring me some paper and a pen?" My voice quavered weakly as I spoke.

He rummaged through our wooden letter box, then handed them to me with a dubious frown. "You're too sick to write."

"Just a few lines . . ." I knew what I must write. The fog inside my head cleared just enough to let me give words to my feelings. My shaking hand scratched out the barely legible words on the sheet. When I finished, I handed it to Josh.

"What's this?" he asked.

I could hardly speak. "I'm so sick, Josh. I know I'm going to die. I want you to carve this on my grave for me. You carve so well. . . ."

He was aghast, eyes round with shock. Slowly he lowered his eyes and read the simple verse I had written:

> *Come and get me, Betsy darling,*
> *Come and take me by the hand,*
> *Take me from this vale of sorrow,*
> *Take me to the promised land.*

The steady ticking of the mantel clock seemed to fill the whole room. Josh looked up from the paper and stared at me.

Voice croaking hoarsely, he demanded, "Is this what you want? You want to die?"

"I'm sick. I get sicker every day," I said shakily. "I miss Betsy so much . . . and my babies, and Ann, and all the others who are gone. I'm so weak, Josh. What's the use of struggling?"

He grabbed my frail shoulders and searched my face. Finally he spoke in an anguished tone. "What about *me*, Carrie? Don't I mean anything to you?"

I could not bear to face the raw pain in his eyes. "Of course you do. But you're strong. You can stand all these hardships. I can't."

He drew in a long, jagged breath. "Carrie, I'm sorry," he moaned. "I'm so sorry I dragged you out here. I've been so selfish. I could have made a living in Cincinnati . . . but, no, I had to be a big land owner."

"It's not you, Josh. It's me. I'm just not strong like you."

"Oh, Carrie, don't you know? I'm only strong when you're beside me. I could never have come out here without you."

I wanted to believe he still loved me, still needed me, but yet . . . "You'll find someone else. . . ." I said. "Someone who can give you children."

His voice broke as he embraced me. "If you go, you'll have to take me with you. I don't want to live without you."

Tears streamed down my face. "I'm just so tired. It's been such a long road. . . ."

"Stay with me, Carrie!" he cried, holding me close. I could feel the quickened beating of his heart against mine. "You can make it if you try! You and me together. That's all we had when we started down the Ohio. Remember those nights on the raft? Just you and me together in the moonlight?"

A flood of warm and happy memories washed over me. The river's gentle lapping as I lay within his arms. The wonder and the magic of our love. Josh, young and strong and handsome, leading me into a bright new world. Had anyone ever known such joy?

I sobbed and clung to him. "It was beautiful. We were so young and full of dreams."

"We haven't changed so much. We still have each other." His voice, choked with emotion, touched my soul. "Oh, Carrie, I love you. You're my whole life. Stay with me."

"Don't overdo it. You've been sick. Here, let me help you move this. Where do you want it in the sun—

"Thanks,"

# Chapter 29

How strange, how strong, the power of love. I began to heal that day, though my illness lingered on for weeks. Gradually my strength returned. I was still bone thin and weak, but I survived.

Josh and I survived together. There was a stronger bond between us now, woven thick with shared sorrows. We had lost so much, yet we had a closeness I could not have imagined on my wedding day.

One day in late spring I felt a burst of my old energy. Josh walked in to see the house completely torn apart. "What in God's name are you doing, girl?" he asked, a bewildered expression on his face as he looked from the pulled-out furniture to the stripped bed to the pail of steaming scrub water.

"Spring cleaning," I answered, smiling. "I want to have everything cleaned and aired by lilac time, so I can bring in bouquets and fill the house with their perfume."

"Don't overdo it. You've been sick. Here, let me help you move the mattress outside to the sun."

"Thanks. We may be the last people left in town, but at least our house will be clean."

When we had laid the feather mattress across the weathered split rail fence, he said, "I have to make a trip to Springfield next week. Would you like to come with me? We could stay over for a day or so and look around."

Blood rushed to my cheeks. "Yes, I'd like that. I suppose the town has changed a lot since it's become the state capital."

A drenching spring shower fell the night before we left for Springfield, and the road oozed mud. Josh had to pull the reins from side to side as he drove, to guide old Lucky around the deep ruts and puddles. Our wagon, heavy with a load of guns for the Springfield store, grumbled along.

"Maybe we can stop and see Abe Lincoln while we're in town," Josh said. "He's making quite a name for himself as a lawyer there."

"I wish he'd find a wife. He needs a real home. Sarah told me Mary Owens went back to Kentucky. I guess she and Abe just didn't take to each other."

"Abe will be all right. Everybody says he has a good future in politics. Think how far he's come in these few years, and he's still a young man. Abe's an original," Josh said, smiling.

As Josh drove, I mused, gazing at a cluster of blossom-laden apple trees beside an isolated farmhouse in the distance. "There's something deep about him. . . . I think it's the fear of loss. He lost his mother and his sister . . .

and then Ann. When you've lost the ones you love, it makes you afraid to love again.''

Josh took my hand. His voice sounded strangely old to me. "We all have to learn to live with loss, Carrie. It's the hardest lesson I know."

Our thoughts touched, and we drove on in silence.

I looked out to the azure line of the horizon, across the greening miles of prairie land. These days there were patchwork blocks of plowed fields, with a sprinkling of farm houses to relieve the sameness of the scene. The prairie was unique—beautiful when bright flowers and tall grasses nodded in the sunlight and melancholy when rain fell from darkened skies.

The sight of the prairie stirred conflicting emotions in me: a sense of awe at its majestic grandeur, and a sense of loneliness and isolation in its boundless sweep. After all these years the prairie had become a part of me.

When we reached Springfield, I could feel the vitality of the city in the air. There was so much to see. Workmen were constructing the new capitol building in the big grass-covered square, laying the pink dolomite stones that were quarried right in Illinois. The bank and courthouse and governmental buildings lined the streets around the square. Businesses of all kinds flourished: dry goods, drug stores, tailors, hatters, watchmakers, and barbers. There were hotels and offices for the many lawyers and doctors. Beyond the business district stood rows of houses, some of them immense and grand. In the streets handsome carriages and proud steeds mingled with farm wagons and old nags.

Josh and I strolled around downtown, looking in the store windows. "Eliza would be mortally ashamed of me," I said, glancing down at my old Sunday dress. "I don't even know what the styles are anymore."

"Go ahead and look around. Do some shopping. I'll have plenty of money after I deliver this load of guns."

I stepped inside a ladies' shop, enthralled. Bolts of gorgeous cloth filled the long white shelves. I was surrounded by silks, velvets, satins, laces, crepes, taffetas, and failles. Their poor relations, organdy and cambric, muslin and cotton, were there, too. Shelves overflowed with silk stockings and ribbon-covered corsets and pretty flaring bonnets abloom with flowers and feathers.

"Everything is so beautiful," I murmured breathlessly to the chic-looking clerk.

The woman smiled at my delight. "We have the finest merchandise here. Even things all the way from New York and Philadelphia and New Orleans. And these plates here show the latest styles."

I studied the illustrations of dresses with the new sleeves Eliza had described, and of those with puffed sleeves and deep-draping necklines and fluted bodices, and the new square-toed evening slippers. Then I indulged myself in the almost-sinful pleasure of fingering the rich textures of the varied cloths. It was so hard to decide. "I think I'll take some of this pale green silk. And let me try on that big bonnet with the yellow roses."

When Josh returned, he paid for my purchases and we strolled on down the street, peering into all the shop windows. We saw furniture that took my breath away, fashioned of rosewood and maghogany, cushioned with silk brocade. There were velvet carpets and lace and damask curtains, too. I had almost forgotten such lovely things existed.

That evening I wore my new bonnet when we dined in a fancy restaurant with snow-white linen and gleaming silverware. I savored the serenity of the genteel atmosphere, far from the kitchen heat and the clang of pots and ladles. It was another world, although we were only twenty miles from home.

"We can look the town over tomorrow and drop by Abe's office on Hoffman's Row. In the evening we can go to the theater," Josh said as we retired to our hotel.

"The theater! Oh, Josh, how grand!"

"We might as well enjoy ourselves. I have orders for another load of guns, as soon as Cole and I can make them."

The next morning we drove our wagon slowly around the city, through streets with huge, pretentious houses and past the humble homes of working men. We saw the schools and churches, mills and brickyards.

"What do you think of Springfield these days?" he asked.

"It's growing so fast! Having the state capital here will make a big difference."

"Would you like to live here?"

With my heart in my throat, I turned and studied his face. "Are you serious?"

"I sure am," he said, nodding slowly. "You know New Salem's dying on the vine. I have lots of business here, and there's good transportation to Saint Louis and Jacksonville."

I stared at the ground alongside us, trying to collect my

thoughts. I had helped build our little house in New Salem, and I felt a strong tie to it. It was our first home, and our only home for nearly eight years. That house had seen us grow and change.

And yet, the house was haunted by sad memories. Every log and floorboard was a part of our history. Two longed-for babies were lost there. Betsy was laid out there in her little casket. Josh's foot had been amputated there, in the same room where he had danced on the fresh planks for our housewarming. And lately we had watched our neighbors, one by one, pack up and move away.

Finally I answered softly, "Yes. I'd like to move to Springfield. It's time to put aside the past."

That afternoon we climbed the narrow stairs to Abe Lincoln's law office. Sunlight streamed through the uncurtained windows onto his dark hair and lanky frame as he bent over the clutter of papers and thick law books laid before him on an old dilapidated desk. He glanced up and greeted us enthusiastically, "Josh and Carrie! What a sight for sore eyes! Come in and sit a spell. Fill me in on all the folks in New Salem."

We sat in the worn chairs across from him. Then Josh frowned and slowly shook his head. "Not many people left there anymore. Even Sam Hill's talking about moving to Petersburg. Carrie and I are thinking we might do what you did—and move to Springfield."

"Well, I don't think you'd regret it," Abe said, his deep-set eyes crinkling as he grinned. "This is an up-and-coming town. There'd be plenty of business for you here."

"What about our farms?" I asked, feeling suddenly insecure. "Could we oversee them if we lived in Spring-field?"

"Sure you could, if you have good tenants," Abe said. "Or you might want to sell out. You know, land out there is bringing ten dollars an acre these days."

Josh and I stared at each other for a moment. Then I blurted out, "Ten dollars an acre! Why, that's a fortune!"

# Chapter 30

The next six weeks passed in a flurry of activity. The evening before we moved to Springfield, Josh found a moment to sit down and rest in his old rocker by the fireplace, while I wrote in my journal. His eyes moved around our little cabin, taking in each detail of the log walls, the floorboards, the furniture he had made with his own hands. He sounded nostalgic as he said, "You know, Carrie, it just doesn't seem possible— our last night in this old house."

Our last night. The words hung heavy on me. "I wonder how many meals I've cooked at this fireplace in the last eight years," I said, as I bent low to lift the Dutch oven from the hearth. "I feel like I've spent half my life stooped here."

"But no more."

"No more. Oh, Josh, I can't believe you're buying me a stove! It's such a luxury. I'll feel positively grand in our new house, standing up to do my cooking."

"Lots of things will be better for us in Springfield," he said, grinning broadly. "There's traveling theater companies and musical programs. There's always something new to see."

While eating our roast pork and yams, I thought back on the years we had spent in this little cabin. I remembered the day we came into town, young and eager strangers, filled with dreams of adventure—and how all the people had pitched in to help us build our house.

"Do you think we'll ever have friends and neighbors as good as the ones we've had here?" I asked, with a catch in my voice.

Josh pondered solemnly for a moment. "No, we probably won't, to tell the truth. This was the frontier when we came. People just naturally help each other more on the frontier."

"Springfield is a big city now—the state capital. Everybody will probably be more concerned with styles and social life. They won't have time to worry about whether a neighbor is sick or needs some help."

I ate silently, remembering the many times New Salem neighbors had come to help us in the last eight years. How many pots of stew, how many strong arms wielding axes, how many words of comfort and understanding handclasps had they given us? I missed everyone already.

Josh took a long sip of coffee, then slapped his hand firmly on the table. "We'll get up early and load the wagon," he said. "When all the furniture and things are in the new house, Cole will come back with me and move everything from the gun shop."

"That will be different, too—Cole boarding with his aunt in Springfield instead of living with us. I'll miss that boy. I'll miss his bashful grin and his big feet stumbling on the rag rug and the way he cleans up every last morsel of a meal. He's a part of our family."

"Well, he'll still be working with me in the shop. I suppose before long he'll be wanting to get married. He's sure stuck on Mary Martha." Josh chuckled. "Reminds me of myself when I was courting you."

My cheeks flushed as I slowly raised my eyes to meet his. "That was so long ago, Josh. Remember when we walked up to Mount Auburn?"

"I remember how I rattled on and on for hours about going to Illinois. About making a fortune way out west." He smiled and reached across the table to take my hand. "Well, I guess we made our fortune. We've got a good business now, and we sold that farm for ten times what we paid for it. Dan Cooper found a nice place of his own, too, after all these years."

"And we still have the other farm, with good tenants on it. We couldn't ask for better than Willy and Lucinda. We really have been lucky in some ways."

"Yes, we've done all right, Carrie. We'll be lost in that big new house in Springfield. Five rooms!"

"And a stove! I still can't believe it."

I slept fitfully that last night in our little cabin. The new house would be nice, but there were memories here engraved in every log. The floorboards had been smoothed by our daily steps and dancing feet at parties, by visiting friends, and by Betsy's little slippers.

Early the next morning we loaded the wagon with our furniture and the barrels of pots, books, and dishes I had wrapped so carefully in towels and linens. New Salem's few remaining families, the Bales, Hills, and Onstots, came to see us off. Mentor came with a tearful Sarah.

"Be sure to come and visit us in Springfield," I told all

of them. "We'll have an extra room with nothing in it but my loom, and I'll be glad to fix it up for company."

Sarah grabbed my hand and held it tightly. "It just won't be the same without you."

Dear Sarah. Would I ever find another friend like her? For eight years I had leaned on her, depending on her warmth, wisdom, and compassion. She had seen me through my darkest times.

"It's hard to leave," I murmured, hugging her. "But then, it's been hard to stay, now that Betsy's gone."

"Come back and see us, Carrie."

I blinked back my tears. "I will. I promise. When Josh delivers guns out here, I'll ride along with him."

Our departure from New Salem seemed as final as the one from Cincinnati, although we were moving only twenty miles. I was not the naive, shallow girl I had been eight years ago. A big house and new furniture could never take the place of my true friends, nor of little Betsy.

I arrived at our new house in a somber mood, but when we finished setting up our furniture, I had to laugh at the pitifully bare look of the place. Our few belongings were spread throughout a dining room, a separate kitchen (with a stove), two bedrooms, and a formal sitting room. It seemed a mansion to me.

Josh paced about, surveying everything, the thud of his wooden peg echoing through the nearly empty rooms. "We'll buy a settee, like the one in that store window downtown. And I'll build a bookcase, instead of putting up shelves like we had before. I'll make a big cupboard for the kitchen, too. We might even get a desk."

"I'll be busy for a month, just making curtains for all

these windows. It'll take a while to get used to this big house.'' I laughed.

"Well, I can sure use the extra space I'll have in my shop. Things were getting pretty crowded. I might even take on another apprentice.'' Josh relished new plans and challenges.

His optimism was contagious. I would finally accept the fact that I was childless. In a city like Springfield I would find other outlets for my energies. I could weave beautiful things. Someday I might even open my own little shop and sell my woven goods. Why not?

The first night in our new home Josh's arms reached out for me. Our love, so old and yet so fresh and eager, warmed to passion in the strangeness of this unfamiliar place. It was the beginning of a whole new life for us.

The next morning, after Josh left to pick up his tools and gun supplies, I stood in the middle of the sitting room and stared about me in confusion. The house was filled with barrels and boxes. I couldn't decide where to begin unpacking. Somewhere in all these things, I knew, was my old blue-lacquered jewelry box. Somewhere was the trunk I'd kept of Betsy's clothes and toys. The smells of fresh plaster, paint, and varnish seemed cold and sterile. The silence hung around me heavy as a shroud.

Keeping busy is the best remedy for ailments of the spirit, I reminded myself. I lifted a quilt from one of the barrels and carefully unwrapped it. There was my pride and joy—my beautiful Seth Thomas clock.

Cautiously I set it on the walnut mantel and stepped back to admire its polished wood and gilt-trimmed glass door. The clock obligingly began to strike the hour, in deep, commanding tones. I felt enormously uplifted, as if this familiar old sound were welcoming me to my new home.

Suddenly from outside a child's sharp cry cut through the air. I recognized that kind of cry—someone had been hurt. I rushed out to the porch and saw a tiny, dark-haired girl in the yard next door, sitting on the grass holding her foot and bawling in deep, gasping sobs.

"What happened, dear?" I called, instinctively running over to her.

She cried inconsolably. "I 'tubbed my toe." She tried to rub away the flood of tears with a clenched fist.

Another dark-haired girl, no more than fourteen years old herself, ran out of the house and down the steps. "Don't cry, Nancy," she called. "It'll be all right."

I patted the wailing child's bent shoulders, trying to comfort her as I spoke to the older girl. "I'm Carrie Strauman, your new neighbor. I heard a cry, and I thought I could help. I . . . I used to have a little girl."

"Well, thank you, ma'am," the older girl said shyly. "I'm real pleased to meet you. My name's Sally Wilson, and this is my little sister, Nancy."

"Is your mother home? I'd like to meet her, too."

A stricken expression crossed the girl's thin face; she blinked and lowered her head, staring at the ground. "Mama died last winter . . . Pneumonia." Her voice sounded aged and desolate. "There's just me here to take care of the house and watch out for the other kids. My daddy has a tailor shop downtown."

"How old is Nancy?" I picked up the little girl and wiped the tears that stained her sun-kissed cheeks.

"She just turned three. Bobby's ten, and Eddie's six today." She shook her head and breathed a deep sigh. "I'm trying to make a birthday cake for him, but I can't get it right. I never made frosting before.''

My eyes scanned Sally slowly. She was a frail thing, with a sad and harried look. The story of her life was written on her thin face.

"I'll take Nancy inside now," she murmured, reaching for her little sister.

Impulsively I slipped my arm around Sally's thin shoulder and walked with her up the wooden steps. The barrels waiting to be unpacked at my house had been forgotten.

"Let me show you how to make frosting, dear," I told her, with a smile. "I'll be glad to help you, anytime."

## Author's Note

New Salem did indeed die away. By 1840 the village had ceased to exist. Over ninety years later, the state of Illinois began its reconstruction of the cabins on their original sites, and today the village lives again, complete with authentic furnishings, thriving gardens, and chickens in the backyards. Carrie would feel right at home.

Carrie and Josh are fictitious characters, representing the thousands of courageous pioneers who settled America's heartland. All the other characters in this book actually existed and lived in the New Salem area, with the exception of Betsy and her family; Josh's apprentice, Cole Nelson; the tenants Dan Cooper, and Willie and Lucinda Arnold; the gun dealer, James MacAllister; and Old Joe, the fiddler.

A historical work such as this draws from many sources. Months were spent researching Illinois history, Lincoln biography, and all facets of pioneer life. I am especially indebted to Benjamin P. Thomas for his book LINCOLN'S NEW SALEM, and to Duncan and Nichols for their MENTOR GRAHAM, THE MAN WHO TAUGHT

LINCOLN, which introduced me to Sarah and gave Carrie her dearest friend.

To all who helped in any way, if only by encouragement, my heartfelt thanks.

## About the Author

*SUSAN HATTON MCCOY* grew up in a small town near New Salem. She traces her roots in America back to the years before the Revolution, and she has enjoyed a lifelong interest in history. A former teacher, a mother, and grandmother, she lives with her husband beside a lake in Pekin, Illinois.